FOLLOWING THE FOLLOWERS

Milo revved his engine, a dragon's roar, and popped on the headlights. The beams carved a path for the Roadmaster, straight through the lot, across the street, and into the alley, where a human kid gaped and an elf looked very grim.

The Roadmaster leaped like a panther after prey. Trapped in its headlights, the human kid started to rise, as if he was going to abandon the sidecar and run. Then the elf stood and kicked the bike's starter. The human dropped back into the sidecar. He had more faith in his partner than I would've.

As the Roadmaster's engine crossed the edge of Milo's lot, it coughed and died. The headlights went blind. But nothing altered the Roadmaster's direction or momentum: It was crossing First Avenue at something like seventy kilometers an hour, aimed at the mouth of the alley. The watchers' choices were to drive forward to meet it or race backward to escape it—but Milo had said the alley dead-ended in less than thirty meters.

Just as I began to imagine the Roadmaster rolling into the alley while people screamed and metal crashed, the watchers' bike whipped into the street. The shriek of its spellbox filled a vacuum of sound. The elf and the human leaned into a tight turn within inches of the Roadmaster's front bumper. I wanted to close my eyes but couldn't.

Maybe Milo used magic to slow the car at the last moment. Maybe the elf was as fast as we'd hoped she'd be. The Roadmaster's bumper kissed the elf's back tire, making her slew sideways. Then her wheels gripped the road, and she shot toward Soho.

Will Shetterly's books,
and the Borderland Series

The Liavek Series,
edited by Will Shetterly and Emma Bull

The Borderland Series

NEVERNEVER

WILL SHETTERLY
P.J.F.

TOR
fantasy

A TOM DOHERTY ASSOCIATES BOOK
NEW YORK

This is a work of fiction. All the characters and events portrayed in this book are fictitious, and any resemblance to real people or events is purely coincidental.

NEVERNEVER

Portions of this book, in substantially different form, originally appeared as the novella "Danceland" by Emma Bull and Will Shetterly, in *Bordertown*, edited by Terri Windling and Mark Alan Arnold, New York: Signet Books, 1986. *Bordertown* copyright © 1986 by Terri Windling. "Danceland" copyright © 1986 by Emma Bull and Will Shetterly. Other portions of this book, in substantially different form, originally appeared as the story "Nevernever" by Will Shetterly, in *Life on the Border*, edited by Terri Windling, New York: Tor Books, 1991. Life on the Border copyright © 1991 by Terri Windling, The Endicott Studio. "Nevernever" copyright © 1991 by Will Shetterly.

Bordertown and the Borderlands were created by Terri Windling, with creative input from Mark Alan Arnold and the authors of the stories in the anthologies *Borderland* (NAL 1986), *Bordertown* (NAL 1986), and *Life on the Border* (Tor Books 1991): Bellamy Bach, Steven R. Boyett, Emma Bull, Kara Dalkey, Charles de Lint, Craig Shaw Gardner, Michael Korolenko, Ellen Kushner, Will Shetterly, and Midori Snyder. Borderland is used by permission of Terri Windling, The Endicott Studio.

Cover art by Dennis Nolan

A Tor Book
Published by Tom Doherty Associates, Inc.
175 Fifth Avenue
New York, N.Y. 10010

Tor® is a registered trademark of Tom Doherty Associates, Inc.

ISBN: 0-812-55151-6

First Tor edition: October 1995

Printed in the United States of America

0 9 8 7 6 5 4 3 2 1

For Beth Davis and Barbara Friedman

An acknowledgment:

When Jane Yolen requested an encore,
Terri Windling permitted my players
to use her stage again.
If I can be more than eternally grateful, I am.

CONTENTS

CHAPTER ONE

Dating Outside of Your Species

You expect people to get quiet when a werewolf walks into a restaurant. You only expect them to scream when a werewolf *runs* in. I walked in as if the only thing on my mind was finding a seat, a waiter, and a plate of spaghetti, in that order. Everyone in the room—about fifty kids—got quiet. No one screamed. I was learning the rules. That amused me, so I smiled.

My smile widened when I spotted Sparks's blue-black hair at the back of the room. Engrossed in a paperback, she was the only person who hadn't seen me enter. I wanted to yell and wave. I contented myself with a flash of white, sharp teeth—

A definite mistake, even in a place like Godmom's, where anything might wander in from Bordertown's streets.

Someone gasped. A waiter dropped a tray, splashing spaghetti, calzones, and tomato sauce onto the black-and-white tile floor. A human in Pack black, from biker boots to dyed hair, and a silverlocked elf in True Blood red leather stood side by side, faces grim, right hands deep in their jacket pockets. I doubted they were fingering good-luck charms.

I couldn't smile to say I was harmless; my fangs had created this predicament. I couldn't turn and run; the fifty or so kids in Godmom's would have been after me like the village mob in every Frankenstein movie ever made.

Most of the humans were triple-checking the location of the back door. A few touched their knives and forks as if hoping werewolf legends were true and Godmom used real silverware. Who knows what the elves were thinking? Clearly, they were feeling something profound, maybe fear, maybe amusement, because they weren't showing any emotion at all.

The song on the juke—Oyster Band's "Angels of the River"—ended then. Silence is the scariest thing I've ever heard.

My greatest danger came from the unlikely allies, the Packer and the True Blood. Each had a few gang members sitting nearby, ready to follow their leader's move. In Godmom's, it wasn't supposed to matter whether you were Bordertown born or you came from the World or from Faerie, whether you were a member of any of Soho's many gangs or no gang at all. If you wanted the best pizza in town, you ignored anyone you couldn't treat civilly. But the Packer and the True didn't know *I* knew that. And no one knew if Godmom's truce included creatures no one had seen before.

I looked for a friendly face, someone whose smile would say I belonged here. I couldn't think of any way to interrupt Sparks's reading that wouldn't seem threatening.

I looked over one shoulder and out the window. Something small might've moved on the street in the shadows, but I didn't have time to wonder about that. I looked back at the crowd, then over my other shoulder.

Then I bent my head down, sniffed each of my armpits, raised my head, and lifted both hands in a gesture of complete bafflement.

Someone snickered. A few people smiled cautiously. The True and the Packer did not.

Before anything could happen, a large woman in a flowered dress and a hat like a bowl of fruit came flying out of the kitchen. Maybe literally: I can't swear that her feet touched the ground. She stopped before me, blocking my way and shielding me from the diners, and said, "May I help you?" I couldn't tell whether she meant, "May I help you out the door?" or "May I help you change your life?"

I nodded toward the back of the room. Sparks still hadn't looked up from her book. Godmom followed my gaze, then winked at me.

"Ah!" She saw two kids meeting for dinner and looking their best, Sparks in a fringed motorcycle jacket, a green-and-yellow sundress, and blue cowboy boots, me in a long-sleeved black T-shirt, baggy purple trousers, and red sneakers. She assumed romance was on someone's mind, even though Sparks was obviously human and I looked like I'd escaped from the wildest lands of the Nevernever.

Godmom couldn't be more wrong, I thought as she stepped aside and flipped a coin across the room. Almost every eye in the house tracked it.

The waiter who'd dropped the tray laughed, caught the coin, spun smoothly about, and slapped it into the jukebox. The tension in the room disappeared with the coin. Cats Laughing's cover of "Stomping at the Savoy" filled the air. People began to talk as if they'd never paused. I was the subject of a few whispers: "Born that way?" and "Must be a spell," and "Saw 'im at Danceland the other night," and "Man, some people will do *anything* to be noticed."

The Packer and the True looked at me, then at each

other. The elf curled his lip in a fine sneer. The Packer managed to bump him hard as she moved to let me pass. He didn't say anything, so the truce held a little longer in Godmom's.

When my shadow fell on Sparks's table, she glanced up with an Is-that-the-person-I-was-expecting-oh-it's-a-monster-from-the-darkest-pits-my-date-must-be-late look. She turned back to her paperback, an Oscar Wilde collection. When I put my hand on the chair across from her, she gave me her best Why-are-you-stopping-here-when-you-must-be-planning-to-maul-someone-at-another-table?

I pointed a claw at myself and tried to smile without showing my teeth. Sparks frowned. I began to sit. She said, "Sorry, I'm—"

I held up a hand, pulled a pencil stub and a notepad from my pants pocket, then leaned over the table to write, IT'S ME.

She blinked at that, squinted at me, then squinted at my writing again, undoubtedly comparing it with the invitation I had sent her.

I added, I SHOULD'VE WARNED YOU.

She said, "R—"

I raised a finger to stop her. WOLFBOY. I tapped my chest.

She said softly, "Oh, Ron."

I smiled, shook my head, and wrote, IT'S OK. BETTER THAN: IT'S GREAT.

She said, not quite a question, "You can't talk."

I wrote, DIDN'T SAY IT WAS PERFECT.

"What—" She noticed that a lot of people were trying very hard to ignore us. "Sit down."

I smirked and sat. When there's nothing else to do, be amused or be amusing—it was a new philosophy for me, but it seemed to work.

Sparks stared at my face. I thought I knew what she was seeing: golden eyes, reddish fur, extended jaw, gleaming fangs. She looked at my furry, black-clawed hands. When she glanced up, I had a grin ready to show her everything really was fine.

Two tears rolled down either side of her nose.

We stared at each other until she jabbed her napkin at the corners of her eyes. "I hate it when I cry."

I pointed a finger tentatively at the penultimate line I'd written.

"Okay?" she read.

I nodded.

"Why?"

I shrugged, then wrote, I WAS A GEEK.

"No way. You were cute."

I wrote, TOO LATE TO DO ANYTHING ABOUT IT NOW.

"Maybe."

I glanced at her. She laughed self-consciously and said, "What's it like?"

I was grateful for the chance to look away. It hadn't occured to me that she might still have a crush on me.

I wrote, BEING KID COYOTE?

She nodded.

I wrote, I HEAR BETTER. NOT EVERYTHING AT ONCE, THO. HAVE TO SORT THINGS OUT. SMELLS, DITTO. I sniffed to illustrate. SOMEONE BURNED SAUSAGE IN THE KITCHEN. THERE'S LOTS OF ROSEMARY IN THE TOMATO SAUCE. GUY OVER THERE—I lifted my chin toward a distant table—HAS A COLOGNE, SMELLS LIKE JASMINE. YOU— I'd already started, so I wrote quickly, hoping she wouldn't notice that I'd paused—SMELL LIKE AUTUMN: PINE NEEDLES AND WOOD SMOKE.

She smiled. "That's nice."

I smiled back. I'd been about to write that I could smell something pleasantly tart and specifically Sparks. But that might've embarrassed her. It certainly embarrassed me. Maybe the best thing about being the Wolf was having fur to hide my blushes.

Then I decided that was silly. I wasn't attracted to

Sparks. She had acne scars, a small chin, an overbite that made her look like a gerbil, and posture at least as bad as mine. And I was the Amazing Mutt-Man now. Those were all good reasons to keep thinking of her as just a friend.

Our waiter appeared then. "Tonight's special is Pizza Florentine. That's spinach and mushrooms in a cream sauce on a thick whole-wheat crust. For the carnivores"— she glanced at me and plunged bravely onward—"we add shredded beef, smoked ham, or pepperoni. We didn't get seafood today, but we have everything else that's on the menu."

I looked at Sparks. She said, "Florentine sounds good. Vegetarian?"

I suddenly realized I didn't like the idea of eating animals now that I was at least partly one. I nodded.

"To drink, there's wine, beer, cider hot or cold, root beer, milk, iced Lemon Zinger tea—"

"Milk sounds good."

I nodded again. The Wolf undoubtedly needed all the calcium and protein it could get.

The waiter gave me a nervous smile, said, "One Pizza Florentine, two milks, right away." I watched her flee.

"That bother you?"

I shrugged, wrote, MICKEY SAYS IF I'M PATIENT, PEOPLE WILL LEARN I'M A PUPPY DOG INSIDE.

Sparks covered my writing hand with her palm and smiled. "A sheepdog. All shaggy and kind and dependable."

I wrote, OH. Part of me thought that was the corniest thing I'd ever heard. Part of me was blushing again. I wrote, WHO DO I SEE TO BE SLEEK, DANGEROUS, & UNPREDICTABLE?

She laughed, squeezed my hand, said, "Hey, I like sheepdogs. I had one when I was a kid. I fell in the

6

Mad River, and she pulled me out. I could swim; I wasn't really in danger. But she didn't know that."

OK, I wrote. I'M A SHEEPDOG. Sparks's expression was so funny that I leaned over and licked the back of her hand.

She swatted my head and whispered loudly, "Down, boy! Down!"

I started to growl an answer. Something snagged a leg of my chair, twisting it from under me, dumping me onto the floor. I caught myself on one hand. Before I could spring up, a black motorcycle boot pressed my fingers against the tiles. I looked up. The Packer stood there, backed by a thin black guy and a stocky white guy, both dressed like her, in black denim and leather.

Not having to decide what to put on in the morning must give you more time to solve world hunger and plan great works of art. Or maybe the Packers were just sartorially challenged.

"Sorry." The leader didn't sound very. "Gets crowded in here." She smiled as she stepped off my hand. Under other circumstances, it would've been a nice smile. Her dark brown eyes and strong jaw reminded me of someone.

I didn't have time to think about who. Sparks said, "Gorty!"

I recognized the white guy then. It shouldn't have been a surprise. Gorty had brought me to Godmom's back when he, Sparks, and I had all lived at Castle Pup, and Sparks had told me that he'd joined the Pack since then.

He gave us an arrogantly dim grin. He'd lost twenty pounds, grown his hair out and dyed it black, and joined the biggest and most boring of Bordertown's human gangs, but he was still Gorty.

My little rush of fondness went away as soon as he said, " 'Ey, Sparks! Plannin' to do the wild thing with a real wild thing?"

The leader said, "You know her?"

Gorty said, "Oh, sure. Sparks there likes a bit of the other with the *other*." He guffawed and poked a thumb toward me. "That's about as other as you can get."

Sparks said, "Oh, Gorty."

The Pack leader looked from me to Sparks, narrowed her eyes, then turned away, saying, "C'mon."

Gorty put his hands on his hips and said, "Sparks, you want a real man, you need a real *man*, know what I mean?"

The black Packer grabbed Gorty's shoulder. "Gort, no need to give her my address. Word gets around."

Gorty said, "Heh, right," to him, then, "Be seeing you, Sparks," to her, and, "Bye, Bowser," to me. He tossed something small and foil wrapped onto our table and told Sparks, "You don't know where Bowser's been. And you're too young for a litter, anyway." He left chuckling to himself.

Sparks glared at a Grail brand condom. "I liked Gorty. I really did. He was always a jerk, but not like that."

I picked up the condom. The Packers were watching from their table, so I dropped it into a shirt pocket, patted it once, and smiled at them. Gorty winced, making me wonder if he'd been interested in Sparks, or even involved with her.

At a nearby table, an elf whose clothes were a mix of Faerie finery and Bordertown rags said, "You're well?" When I nodded, he added, "Pestilent mortals."

"C'mon. Not all of us," Sparks said. "It's the Pack, mostly—"

"*They* are honest rogues at least, I give them that." He turned back to his tablemates.

Sparks shook her head.

I wrote, Do elves have to pass Condescension 101 before they're allowed out of Faerie?

Sparks smiled. I hadn't realized quite how cute an overbite could be.

Pizza and milk arrived then. While I cut a slice for Sparks, she said, "What's with the Packers?"

I shrugged.

"Kids fooling around," she answered herself. "Probably doesn't mean anything."

I glanced at the Packers. The leader was watching us while Gorty and the skinny black guy laughed. Beyond them, on the sidewalk in the flickering light of Godmom's neon-and-faerie-dust sign, something pale darted by, a dog racing past or a sheet of paper tumbled by the wind.

"You haven't said what happened. How you became Wolfboy."

I pointed at my writing hand, which cradled a thick slice of pizza.

"You've got two hands. Right now that gives you the advantage." She stuffed pizza into her face. When I didn't respond, she swallowed and said, "You don't have to tell me anything if you don't want to, you know."

I hate it when people are understanding. I shifted my slice to my other hand, took a bite, and wrote, LEDA HAPPENED.

Sparks frowned. "I thought she went back to Faerie."

I wrote, SHE DID. I looked at that sentence and didn't know what to add.

When I thought about Leda, I remembered three people, and though I tried, I couldn't merge them into one. They all looked the same: a small elf with silver-blue eyes and a cloud of mist-white hair. One was the efficient leader of the Strange Pupae, the largest mixed gang of humans, elves, and halfies that Bordertown had ever seen, the gang I hung with when I first ran away to B-town. One was a kid who never turned down anything that could get her high. One was a Dragon's Tooth

Hill princess in new silks and leathers who sneered at poor kids in Soho. I'd had a crush on the first Leda, and I'd felt sorry for the second, but I hated the third.

"And?" Sparks asked.

I crammed a pizza crust in my mouth and scribbled, AFTER THE PUPS BROKE UP, I SAW HER WITH SOME DRAGON'S TOOTH ELVES. THEY WERE GROUSING ABOUT HUMAN MANNERS, ETC. I WAS THERE WITH SOME WHARF RATS. I SAID SOMETHING CLEVER, LIKE "YAP, YAP, YAP, YOU ELFLANDS BITCH." FELT GOOD AT THE TIME.

"I can imagine."

LEDA SMILED LIKE SHE'D RECOGNIZED ME FROM THE OLD DAYS—NOW I'M NOT SO SURE. SHE SAID, "SINCE YOU'RE SO INTERESTED IN DOGS ..." THEN SHE SAID SOMETHING IN ELVISH THAT SOUNDED LIKE A COMMAND.

I stopped writing, held out my arms, and gestured at myself.

Sparks said, "And a star was born."

I stared, then barked a laugh. Sparks's sense of humor always took me by surprise.

Her smiled disappeared. "You were right. What a bitch."

I wrote, I WASN'T MR. DIPLOMACY.

"That makes it okay?"

I wrote, MAYBE WE WERE BOTH HUNTING TROUBLE. I WON. SHE'LL GET HER TURN, ONE WAY OR ANOTHER.

Sparks sighed. "Poor Leda."

I wanted to ask her how she could have so much sympathy for people whose lives were so much better than hers. Before I could ask anything, I saw another movement in the street.

Sparks turned to stare where I was looking. "What?"

I rose, making a *Stay* motion, and hurried out through Godmom's heavy wooden door.

Two steps brought me from a bright and busy room

to a dark and quiet street. The nearest buildings were skull-like ruins. The sky was cloudy, hiding the stars. The moon was a misty sliver from a silver coin. Godmom's windows threw two large squares of light onto the sidewalk, but that light only reached a few feet into the night.

The air smelled of wood smoke, roasted meat, and fried vegetables from Godmom's kitchen, and, under that, something clean and damp that meant rain within a few hours. Odors of dog shit and cat piss told me what animals had been by recently, but there were older scents from the droppings of other creatures, too: raccoons, rabbits, birds, humans, even a horse or a mule.

A little music and conversation came through Godmom's front door. A little more came from the clubs and warehouse theaters several blocks away, near Ho Street. A dog howled somewhere, and I was tempted to answer, just to say, *You're not alone, there's someone else awake, helping the moon watch over the world.*

A couple of bikes sped by. The spellbox powering the first sounded like a gasoline engine, smelled like one too. Among the bikes of Bordertown, it was not especially distinctive.

I stared at the second, which had no wheels. I had heard of Dead Warlocks, suicidal show-offs who race floating bikes through a city where magic doesn't always work. I had never seen one before. This one's engine smelled like cinnamon and sounded like the spaceships in those movies where no one knows or cares that there's no sound in outer space. I watched it pass and wondered what drove anyone into choosing to live like that.

If I hadn't been so interested in the Dead Warlock, whom I never saw again, I might've paid more attention to the first bike. It had a sidecar, which is rare in Bordertown, and its driver and passenger both wore full-coverage helmets, dark and glistening like the bike. The passenger turned a blank faceplate toward me when they rode by. I waved. As the bike turned onto another street, the passenger lifted a gloved hand in reply.

Grinning, I watched them go. From the alley behind me came a small voice. "You should get a bike, Woofboy."

I turned. Under all the smells of the street lay a trace of peppermint soap that I should've recognized.

"You wou'n't have to worry about takin' care of it, once you got one. I'd help. An' it wouldn't have to be a big bike, either. It could be a little, ugly bike that no one would ever want to steal. You could teach me to drive, an' we could make trips into the Nevernever on it. It'd be stone cool. Don't you think?"

I crooked my finger for her to come closer.

"I di'n't mean to follow you," Florida said, stepping nearer. "Not all the way here, anyway."

I rolled my eyes.

"Well, okay. I jus' wanted to see how your date went."

I bared my teeth. I must've told her twenty times that this wasn't a date.

"Sparks is nice, huh?"

I nodded resignedly and pointed away, toward the Mock Avenue clock tower and the bookstore called Elsewhere.

"Do I gotta?"

I sighed, picked up a rock, and scrawled on a square of cement lit by Godmom's window: DATE FINE. WINDOW PEEPER NOT. GO HOME.

I heard Godmom's door open behind me, but I was still scratching a third line under HOME. As Florida nodded, someone said, "What you doin' with one of ours, fairy lapdog?"

I recognized the Packers by the smell of their leather jackets and the sound of their leader's voice. Before I could straighten up, one of them shoved me hard, rolling me toward the alley where Florida stood.

"Trying to steal a human child?" That was the skinny black Packer. His head seemed too small for his body, an effect exaggerated by his height and his slicked-down hair.

Florida started forward. "Ron!"

The leader stepped between Florida and me. " 'S all right, kid. That thing won't—" She yelled then, in surprise and pain. Florida drew her Bowie knife back, ready to jab the Packer's other buttock.

I roared, " 'O!" and charged forward. I meant it as a yell of *No!* to Florida. No one understood me. Both of the other Packers, the skinny guy and Gorty, tackled me, pinning me on the street.

The leader caught Florida's shoulder and yanked her forward, saying, "Why're you protecting that— Oh."

Florida stood near me in a square of light. She held the Bowie knife in front of her with both hands. Its sheath hung from a beaded belt wrapped twice around her waist.

A moment earlier, she could've been any little kid in dirty jeans, a baggy T-shirt reading HOME IS WHERE THE ART IS, and a shapeless multicolored cotton hat. Now the hat had slipped to one side, and her short, dyed brown hair did not hide her silver eyes or her pointed ears.

The Packers' leader touched her own butt, looked at the blood on her fingers, then looked at Florida. "We're too late. It's a changeling."

Florida, keeping the knife in front of her, said, "That's stupid."

The leader stepped toward her. "Drop the knife, and we won't hurt you."

"Jus' go away."

The leader smiled. "What, you *want* to make us hurt

you? I don't understand elves." She took another step closer.

The other two still held me. Since I hadn't resisted, they watched the contest for the Bowie knife. Florida waved it at the leader, saying, "I mean it! Ge' back! I'll stick you hard this time!"

I twisted and rolled free. Gorty yelled, "Hey!" then lunged for me and missed. I pushed him into the skinny guy, who called, "It's loose! Watch out!"

The leader looked over her shoulder. I ignored her and ran to stand by Florida.

The leader shrugged. "So, Fido, you want to do this the hard way?" Her hand was back in her jacket pocket, and she smiled, scared and cocky. Then I realized who she looked like. She looked like one of my cousins, Maria or Lupe.

I glanced up at Godmom's windows. Several diners were laughing loudly, without any idea that anything might be happening in the street.

I shook my head.

"Good. Give us the knife, and we'll let you go. Is that a deal, or what?"

I had a theory why the Packer had started this. I'd frightened her when I'd sauntered into Godmom's. Now she wanted to prove to herself that she had never been frightened at all.

I held my hand out to Florida. She looked at me. I nodded. Biting her lower lip, Florida set the handle of her Bowie into my palm.

"That's more like it," said the Pack leader.

"Yeah," said Gorty. "That's more like it." His patter hadn't improved since he'd left the Strange Pups.

The leader reached for Florida's knife. I drew it up by my ear, and she ducked. I brought it down fast and released it, sending it spinning past the Packer and into my target, Godmom's wooden front door.

It would've been more impressive if it'd stuck there.

The handle banged the door once, loudly, and the knife clattered onto the stoop. A moment later, fifteen or twenty faces were pressed against Godmom's windows. A moment after that, kids came pouring into the street. The first four were elves in red leather.

"What's this, then?" said one.

"A little fun with friends from Faerie?" asked another, the only one smiling.

"We can improve the game," said a third, a girl as tall as any of the guys.

"Or end it," said a fourth. A switchblade dropped into his hand.

Before he thumbed it open, Sparks pushed through the crowd and past him, her eyes wide, her breathing fast. She looked at me, then at Florida, then at the elf with the blade, and said, "Listen, don't do this. It's stupid."

Florida nodded. "That's what I said."

"Do what?" said the fourth True Blood. "Have we done anything?" His unopened switchblade was still in his hand.

"No," said Godmom, a backlit figure in her doorway. "There's coffee and cheesecake for everyone willing to keep it that way."

"You think—" one of the elves began.

"Anyone who starts a fight in my place"—Godmom looked at the Pack leader—"or near enough that I hear about it, will not be welcome here again. Understand?"

The Trues looked at each other. One said, "Cheesecake is good."

The others nodded. The switchblade had disappeared.

The Packer looked at her buddies, then said, "We thought the girl was in trouble."

"Yeah," said Gorty, who must have had a parrot for a parent. "We thought the girl was in trouble."

"We didn't know she's an elf," said the black Packer. "They tricked us."

Godmom looked from the Packers to me. "Did you?"
I shook my head.

Florida said, "Woofboy's my friend." She indicated the Packers. "*They* think elves'd steal human kids and substitute elf kids for 'em. How stupid can you get?"

The leader of the Packers winced. Looking at me, she said, "If you set us up, dog meat—"

I held my hands out wide and shook my head. The Packer just glared.

Sparks blinked at Florida's dyed hair and said, "Florida?"

Florida grinned. "Yeah. Hi, Sparks."

Gorty gaped at her. "Flor—"

Florida frowned. "I 'member you, Gorty. Why'd you jump us?"

"I—" Gorty looked at me. "I went after that thing. I didn't go after you."

"You hurt my friend, you hurt me."

Gorty looked at his hands. The Packer leader tapped Gorty's shoulder, then began to limp into Godmom's, following the crowd.

Sparks saw the dark stain on the back of the leader's black jeans and said, "You're bleeding!"

The Packer nodded. "It's a human thing."

Sparks said, "I've got a friend who's a doc. You don't want to risk an infection."

The Packer stopped at the door. "Let me get this straight. You expect me to pass on cheesecake so *more* people can poke things in my ass?"

Florida giggled. Sparks said, "After the cheesecake?"

The Packer looked from her to Florida, then back to Sparks. "After the cheesecake."

CHAPTER TWO
Magic Rules!

The Packers ate Godmom's free dessert at their table. The leader perched on the edge of her chair with one leg straight out before her but otherwise didn't seem to be bothered by her wound. She laughed with Gorty and the skinny guy and never caught me watching her.

At our table, Sparks ate chocolate ripple cheesecake, Florida ate plain with strawberries, and I ate plain, plain. While I wondered whether Florida thought this was what dates were supposed to be like, she and Sparks talked about people we'd all known during our Castle Pup days.

Sparks told us, "Rave—Star Raven—and Durward returned to the World. They want to see if they can sell artwork from the Borderlands. I don't know why, but I don't think they'll be coming back."

I nodded; I thought I knew why. People who decide to chase money rarely decide to stay in Bordertown, and they never decide to stay in Soho. I also knew

Sparks understood that, so I didn't try to write anything for her.

She said, "King O'Beer and Jeff are still together. They're taking free classes at the University Without Floors."

I nodded again. It's always good to hear that people you like are happy.

Florida said, "They're nice. Jeff told me to read *Half Magic*, an' it's funny."

Sparks scraped the last of her cheesecake off the bottom of her plate with her finger, then licked the finger clean. "What about you guys?"

Before I could write anything, Florida said, "Ron an' I're living at Elsewhere, now. We might have to move, 'cause Mickey and Goldy broke up, an' neither of 'em wants to run the store without the other."

"I'm sorry to hear that. About Mickey and Goldy, and about Elsewhere."

"Yeah," Florida said firmly. "Mickey might sell it. Goldy's a bouncer at Danceland with Strider and Sai now, and I miss him." Before Sparks or I could do or say anything, Florida laughed. "Everyone calls them the Terrible Trio. Pretty funny, huh?"

Sparks glanced at me and grinned. "Yep, pretty funny."

"Did you hear Wiseguy had her baby?"

Sparks shook her head.

Florida nodded. "His name's Mooner Ronald Uriel-Green. He's got brown skin like Wiseguy, and pointed ears an' silver eyes like Leander. He's beautiful."

I sipped coffee and listened to them talk and thought about friendships and time and vaguely sad things, the sort of things you think about when you're trying to decide whether you want to get romantically involved with a pal when you're also attracted to someone who just tried to beat you up in the street.

Which is better than thinking about whether you want

to get romantically involved with anyone when you're a monster.

Which is better than thinking about whether you want to get romantically involved with anyone when you're a seventeen-year-old virgin and everyone else in the world who's your age seems to have been having sex for years.

Watching Sparks, I wished I could decide who I wanted her to be. She noticed me watching and smiled, quickly and shyly. I smiled back and decided not to decide anything yet.

When the waiters began stacking the chairs and mopping the floor, we got the hint. I paid our bill with a handful of old coins, and I left extra for the waiter I'd scared.

The Packers exited without us, but Sparks ran into the street, calling, "Hey, c'mon! My friend'll fix you better than new in a couple of minutes. Isn't far."

I winced, because I knew life would be simpler if she'd let the Packers go their way. Then I smiled, thinking Sparks was the sort who'd always be taking home strays. Then I winced again, wondering what she thought I was.

Sparks stopped about fifteen feet ahead of Florida and me; the Packers stopped ten feet beyond her, about to get on their bikes. Another bike rolled by on the street, and the beam from its headlamp swept across them. The city was wet from a shower that'd fallen while we all ate dessert. It looked like the Making-Streets-Look-Like-It's-Rained trucks had prepared the stage set.

(That's kind of a joke, for a couple of reasons. Video almost never works in Bordertown. Photography isn't much more dependable—if you manage to develop your film, it hardly ever shows what you thought you'd shot. Magic doesn't like some kinds of technology. Don't hold your breath for a Bordertown show every week on TV.

(And it's kind of a joke because if you look at the world right—or maybe, wrong—everything's a set. You get to decide whether you're a star, a villain, a supporting character, or a walk-on.

(Okay, maybe I should've warned you that you can skip paragraphs that're in parentheses. Here's the deal: I won't waste words on weather and landscape, and you'll tolerate my occasional attacks of motormouth, so long as they're plainly marked.)

It was only after the bike had gone by that I noticed it, dark and gleaming, with a passenger in its sidecar who looked back at us until we'd disappeared into each other's horizon. I thought it was a coincidence, seeing the same people twice on the same night. But this was Bordertown, where there are many coincidences, or none, depending on how you see it.

"Well," said the Pack leader. The three looked at each other, then the leader glanced back at us. "Who's this doc?"

"Milo Chevrolet."

The leader's eyes went wide. "I don't think my butt needs major magicking."

"C'mon," Sparks said. "You don't want to let a knife cut go till morning. Not when there's an easy alternative."

"Well . . ."

"It's free. He likes company."

The leader nodded. "Okay. I'm Taz." She jerked her chin at Gorty, then at the skinny Packer. "Gorty says he's met a couple of you already. Mr. Smoothtalk beside him is Q. Paul."

"Yeah," said Gorty, looking at one of the bikes.

"Happening," said Q. Paul, grinning at Sparks.

Sparks said, "Sparks, Florida." She looked at me, and

I couldn't tell what she was thinking as she added, "Wolfboy."

Gorty jerked a thumb at me. "I've seen my share of strangeness out of Faerie, but nothing like Wolf-face there."

I put a hand on Florida's shoulder and gave him my toothiest grin.

Gorty shivered. "I dunno, Taz—"

"That's true," she said. "We like you anyway. Hey, it's my butt on the line."

Florida said, "You were tryin' t' hurt Woofboy." She put her hand on her Bowie knife. "He wasn't tryin' t' hurt you."

Q. Paul laughed. "Little lady, when you've put on ten years and fifty pounds, you come carry me off to Faerie, hear?"

"Humans can't cross the border." Florida spoke with the exasperation of explaining what everyone knows.

"Not by themselves." Gorty looked at me. "Keeps *you* safe. But you can cross when you want, steal our women, take our kids."

I probably would've said something like *You've got a problem with elves 'cause you can't get a girlfriend?* Sparks just said, "Where're you from, Gorty?"

By Bordertown standards, that's a rude question; your past belongs to the World or to Faerie. Gorty glanced at her. "Thunder Bay, Ontario, Canada. Why?"

"Why didn't you head for Toronto or New York?"

"I went to Toronto. If the first thing someone says about a place is it's clean, it's dead dull."

"If you hate elves, why come to Bordertown?"

Gorty stabbed a finger at the street. " 'Cause this is ours! Humans built this city!" He glared at me. "I've got more right to it than any of you!"

I stared, thinking he'd back down. His hand plunged into his pocket, but Taz slapped it away, saying, "I can't take you anywhere."

Q. Paul said, "Gorty's heart is good, man. He's more the Scarecrow than the Tin Man."

Florida squinted at me. I made a mental note to borrow a copy of *The Wizard of Oz* from Elsewhere's shelves for her.

Sparks said, "The elves say this was theirs, before. Now they've returned, it's theirs again."

Gorty moved closer to her. "Course they say that, Sparks. Why do *you* say it? You hate yourself so much you have to love *them*?"

She said quietly, "I'm trying to be fair. That's all. You got along with the elves and halfies at Castle Pup."

Gorty said, "They were different. The fact they were at Castle Pup said they were different. Didn't last. As for the rest of 'em—"

"What's it mean that you're in the Pack now?"

"I'm not—" Gorty shook his head, as if to clear it. "I'm hanging with my own. Got a problem with that?"

Q. Paul said, "Ease on, Gort-man. Some see it clear, some don't."

Taz looked at me. "What do you make of this, Kennel King?"

I shrugged. I wasn't in the mood for one of those arguments in which everyone knows no one will change their mind.

Florida took my hand. "Woofboy's human, an' he's my friend."

The Packers stared at me. I shrugged and touched Florida's shoulder again.

Gorty said, "Funny kind of human."

Taz said, "A curse?"

"A curse?" Gorty repeated. Then he said it louder. "A curse?" He began to laugh, and told me, "Your little buddy there put a—" He looked at Florida and stopped laughing. "Don't mess with me, Florida. I always treated you decent."

Taz was still watching me. "And you still hang out with elves, even—"

Sparks said, "Florida didn't—" She stopped when I raised my hand.

I nodded at Taz.

"Why not?" said Q. Paul. "Once they've turned you into a dog, what can they do that's worse?"

"Take him to the vet and get him fixed," said Gorty, grinning again.

Taz glanced at him. "Try being the strong and silent type, Gorty."

He said, "For two simpleminded elf-lovers and one little elf? Why—"

"Now," said Taz. She swung a leg onto her bike, a black Moto Guzzi with a gray spellbox wired into the engine. "Where's your doc?"

Sparks said, "Corner of First and First."

Taz nodded. "You got bikes?"

Sparks shook her head.

"Ride with us."

Gorty straddled a dented brown Kawasaki racer and rocked the throttle, making the engine scream once. Then he looked at Florida. "Willin' to ride with me?"

She looked up at me. I shrugged.

Gorty said, "If I'd known it was you, Florida, I would've jumped your shaggy bud that much faster. We didn't know he was friendly."

Florida lifted both shoulders very high, dropped them, and said, "Oh, okay."

Q. Paul swept his hand toward a dark green Ariel and told Sparks, "My steed awaits, m'lady."

I frowned as Sparks laughed. Taz snapped her fingers; when I looked, she said, "Okay, Nanook of the North, you're with me." I sat behind her, not quite sure what to do with my hands. "If you don't bite, I won't either. Hang on."

Q. Paul passed his helmet to Florida. Taz put on hers,

black with a black scarf glued to its top. Gorty didn't have one—big surprise, that.

The bikes were loud; the night was cool and dark. I sat with my arms tight around Taz and wondered if I liked that more than I disliked Sparks having her arms around Q. Paul. We cruised part of the way up Ho Street, past the clubs and the crowds. A few people gaped at me, so I grinned and waved.

Bordertown's business section is usually dead at night. This night, I didn't even see any Silver Suits on patrol. We might've been in the city right after the Change, when people had fled from the newly returned Elflands and no one from Faerie had begun to explore the World.

We headed up North First. Q. Paul laughed, pointed, and shouted, "Isn't exactly shy, is he?"

An entire city block was lit by huge overhead lights—not the usual glow of magical lights, but the glare of electrical ones. Most of the block was a lake of concrete. At one end, seven or eight old automobiles in excellent shape were parked next to a low building with unbroken plate-glass walls. On top of the building was a sign that said, MILO CHEVROLET—ALL OFFERS CONSIDERED!

I felt like I was looking at a piece of Bordertown's past yanked into the present. But I wasn't: In the World, that lot would have been full of this year's vehicles, and no one would've crossed out ALL and neatly written above it, NO.

Taz said, almost sounding nervous, "Will he be up?"

Sparks grinned. "It's night. Of course he's up."

The Packers parked their bikes on the sidewalk instead of rolling up to the building. Milo Chevrolet was supposedly one of B-town's best magicians. We were all on our best behavior.

My fur tingled as I stepped onto the lot—a Magical

Early Warning system is part of the Wolfboy package deal. I looked around quickly. Nothing had changed, not the world, not me.

"Coming, Woofboy?"

Deciding I was just tired, I nodded at Florida. As we passed the parked cars, I slowed to admire them and read their names: Rambler, Thunderbird, Mustang, Terraplane, Hawk, Roadmaster. It was like discovering a dinosaur zoo, complete with live dinosaurs, right behind your favorite restaurant.

I loped after the others. Within the boxlike building's mirrored windows, shadowy versions of ourselves approached us.

Sparks pulled open the front door to call, "Milo? Up for some company? It's a chance to play doctor."

We heard his voice first. "Why, Sparks, I'm always ready to play doctor with—"

A halfie in a white lab coat stepped from behind a metal shelf at the far end of the room. His skin was as pale as any elf's, but he wasn't any taller than I am, his ears were just a little batlike, and a true elf would never have worn glasses with boringly practical frames and thick lenses.

He blinked at us all, then removed his glasses and wiped them while finishing his sentence, "—whatever injured kitten you've brought me."

I looked from the halfie to Sparks. I could imagine how he'd intended to end his sentence before he saw she wasn't alone. I didn't like that, or him, just then.

Taz said, "Meow." She turned around and cocked her hip. The wound had opened again. Below the cut through her jeans was a dark stain as big as my hand.

The halfie said, "Oh," put his glasses back on, said, "oh, my," quickly began to remove the glasses, then stopped, nodded once to Sparks or to himself, and settled the glasses back onto his nose. "This is in a professional capacity, yes?"

"I thought you'd be grateful." When he glanced at Sparks, she added, "It didn't seem important enough to wake anyone at the Free Clinic."

"What caused that?"

Florida held up her Bowie. "This did."

"Confused her with a pincushion? I'm not sure which of you I should treat." Milo nodded. "Come in." He turned and walked toward the back of the building.

We passed row after row of high metal shelves heaped with books and obscure electronic gear. Something whistled overhead. I glanced up. A model train, a perfect replica of the Bordertown Express that'd brought me from the World, ran on tracks laid from shelf to shelf.

Florida said, "Ooh, cool."

Facing the main room were five or six smaller ones, each with a door to provide privacy and a window to prevent it. A rumpled bed and a wardrobe were in one; a refrigerator, a tabletop stove, a hot plate, and an electric wok were in another; a computer with a huge monitor was on a desk in a third; a workbench with painted lead figurines was in a fourth. Milo took us to a fifth, which held a dental chair and a doctor's examination bench.

Taz stopped at the doorway. "I get a discount if everyone watches?"

"There's no charge," Milo said fiercely.

"I meant—"

"Oh." He went into the room and drew a curtain across the window for privacy. "Enter freely, and of your own will."

Taz looked from him to Sparks. Sparks nodded. Taz shrugged and walked in. The halfie closed the door behind her.

We looked at each other. Florida yawned; I suspected I'd have to carry her home. Q. Paul went to a shelf and began to flip through a book on the paintings of Richard

Dadd. Gorty, watching the model train circle the room, said, "I thought this Chevrolet guy was some hot magician."

Sparks said, "He is."

"So where's the magic? This place could be smack in the middle of the World." Gorty gave a smug smile, convinced that he'd made his point. I agreed with him, though I didn't say so.

"Exactly," said Sparks.

"Huh?" said Gorty.

She laughed and indicated the whole room with a sweep of her hands. "*Where* are we?"

I understood it then. My fur hadn't tingled because magic was present when I'd stepped onto Milo Chevrolet's lot. It'd tingled because magic was absent. The magic that washed in waves over Bordertown swirled around this one city block.

The first thing I felt was admiration for Chevrolet. No one could use magic against him when he was home. He could run his automobiles on his lot without needing to make spellboxes strong enough to power them. He could use electrical lights without worrying that they'd fail or explode. In a place where magic and science were undependable, he'd created a secure place for a magician by deflecting all magic from his home.

The second thing I felt was pity for myself. Even in a place without magic, I was still the Wolf. The magicians I had consulted about Leda's curse were right: The spell was remarkably stable. What I'd feared had been proven a fact: Only Leda could turn me back into the geeky human kid I'd been. Only Leda, if anyone.

The third thing I felt was fear for Florida.

I walked to her side so casually that I must've been extremely conspicuous. She was looking through a pile of comic books. I took her by the shoulders and turned her away from the others so she faced me, and then, with my very best grin, I shifted her cotton cap to a rak-ish angle.

She frowned, but I ignored that. I rolled up the right sleeve of her T-shirt and then, holding my breath, the left.

Three moles formed a perfect triangle on her shoulder.

She stared at them. Still grinning, I shook my head in warning, rolled the left sleeve down, then the other, and gave her a thumbs-up of approval. Still she stared at me. I kept smiling as if everything was fine and shoved an *Archie* comic at her.

(For those of you who didn't read what I wrote in *Elsewhere*, and for those who haven't read it recently, let me say that some people were searching for the heir to the throne of Elflands, an elf recognizable by three moles in a triangle on one shoulder. A friend had helped us hide Florida from them by magically moving the three moles. The reappearance of the moles on her shoulder made me more nervous than I dared to show.)

Gorty, watching me adjust Florida's clothing, said, "Do I look good enough for you, Dog?"

Q. Paul said, "You don't look good enough for anyone, Gort-man. But it didn't bother us before; it won't bother us now."

Gorty swatted at Q. Paul with an open hand. Q. Paul laughed, jumped backward, and swung at Gorty, also openhanded.

Before the fight could properly begin, Taz said, "I can't take you guys anywhere." She and Milo stood in the examining room doorway.

Q. Paul said, "How's your butt?"

Taz said, "Excellent, as always." She glanced at Milo. "You sure I don't owe you anything?"

Milo shrugged. "A little antiseptic, a couple of stitches. It's nothing. Stay away from cactuses in big green T-shirts." Florida giggled. Milo continued, "If it was a favor, it was for Sparks."

Sparks said, "You wish."

Taz nodded and looked at Sparks. "Do I owe *you* anything?"

Sparks blinked. "What? Of course not."

Milo said, "I have tea."

He announced it as if he had a rare disease that he was rather proud of. Sparks recognized it as an invitation. She shook her head, then jerked her chin toward Florida. "It's late. We should go."

"Oh." Milo looked at Taz. "If you want to step off the lot, I could restore your pants to their pre-pincushion glory. And make that cut stop hurting you. I could make it disappear entirely, but it's safer to let injuries heal themselves, when that luxury's available."

"Why off the lot?" Taz asked.

Gorty said, "Because magic doesn't rule here. Obviously." He smirked, and Q. Paul laughed.

Taz squinted at them. "Since when've I been hanging with the Einstein twins?"

Gorty nudged Q. Paul with his elbow, and they posed side by side, arms akimbo, grinning widely.

Taz told Milo, "Thanks, but it doesn't hurt much. And I kind of like the way the pants look." She smiled at Florida. "Hey, fashion samurai, ask permission 'fore you do any more alterations, hear?"

Milo walked us to the front door. "Would you like to see my cars? They're gassed and ready—"

Sparks said, "It is late."

"Oh. Yes. It is. But if there's anything—"

Sparks glanced at me, and Milo followed her gaze. "Oh. Wolfboy, you're not from these parts, I gather?"

I nodded.

Sparks said, "He's human. There's a curse on him."

Milo's spine suddenly straightened, adding a couple of inches to his height, and he smiled delightedly. "Oh!

Really?" I was afraid he was going to start rubbing his hands together and cackling.

I nodded again.

"When did this happen?"

Notebook time. I pulled it out and wrote, A FEW WEEKS AGO.

"Have you seen anyone about it?"

I wrote, A KID AT MAGIC FREDDY'S. AND MS. WU.

Milo said, "The kid *is* Magic Freddy. He or Ms. Wu have any suggestions?"

I shook my head.

Milo nodded with satisfaction. "When you walk around town, does the spell weaken at all? Do you become more human sometimes without any warning? If you hit a place where magic isn't working—"

I shook my head again.

"What happened when you came onto the lot?"

I wrote, A TINGLING. I GET THAT SOMETIMES WHEN PEOPLE ARE DOING MAGIC NEAR ME. I DON'T SEEM TO CHANGE PHYSICALLY.

"Mmm."

Sparks said, "No suggestions?"

Milo said, "I didn't say that."

"Well?"

"You know who did this?"

I wrote, SHE'S GONE TO FAERIE.

Milo said, "Too bad."

Sparks said, "Why?"

Milo stared through me, as if he was seeing an interesting equation instead of me. "Well, if you can't get her to lift the curse, and no one else is able to, and the curse doesn't go away when magic is absent . . ."

"Rrr!" I growled.

Milo blinked, and it was as if a person had stepped in front of his blackboard. "Well, um, I guess it'd depend on how badly you wanted to break the curse."

"Why?" said Sparks.

"Well, I don't know anyone who's tried this. Which is probably why Ms. Wu didn't mention it." He shook his head. "Forget I said anything."

Florida said, "If Woofboy could help *you*, Milo Chevrolet, he would."

He glanced down at her. "It's not that I don't want to help. But I forget, sometimes, that actions have consequences." He waved at the surrounding walls. "That's why I live here, where I have to leave the lot or let magic flow back in before I can cast a spell."

Taz said, "Hey, he's a big boy, Milo. Tell him and let him worry about his own consequences."

He smiled sadly at her. "Isn't always that simple."

Taz said, "Yes, it is. Doesn't matter what we know. Only matters what we do with what we know."

Milo said, "This magician is in the Elflands?"

I nodded.

"Then it doesn't matter, anyway."

Sparks smiled and encouraged him to continue speaking by making *Come here* motions with both hands.

Milo shrugged. "Ever hear anyone say, 'Speed the caster, speed the spell'?"

Sparks frowned.

Q. Paul slapped his thigh. "Doo-dah!"

Gorty exhaled loudly. "Sheesh. Fruity magician's talk. What's that mean?"

Taz looked at me. "Means, to end the spell, end the magician."

"End?" Gorty said, and then, "Oh."

Milo nodded sadly.

CHAPTER THREE
Finders, Keepers

(Digression. Don't complain; this is in parentheses.

(I'd thought I'd accepted being the Wolf for the rest
of my life. In novels and movies and especially on TV,
people decide to change the way they think about their
lives, and ka-zang! they're changed forever. From that
moment on, they're brave or honest or loyal, they're no
longer tempted by drugs or alcohol, they're true to their
lovers or kind to their kids, they no longer have doubts
about God or work or life.

(In the real world, it's not like that. Trust me. If
you're ever turned into a werewolf, no matter how well
you think you've accepted it, some days it's going to
bum you big time. It's the backslider's blues.)

Sparks gaped at me, saying, "You couldn't!"

Milo said, "There's no guarantee it'd work."

Florida said, "I liked Leda."

Gorty said, "Leda did this? Man, I'm glad I never
ticked her off."

I grinned, which didn't reassure anyone, then wrote,

RELAX. LEDA DID ME A FAVOR. I GOT THE BEST HAIR IN B-TOWN NOW.

DON'T MAKE ME TELL YOU THAT AGAIN.

Gorty, reading over Sparks's shoulder, said, "I don't know about the hair. If you gotta be something creepshow, I'd pick Dracula. Who needs daylight, anyway?"

Taz said, "Oh, fur's nice." She touched the back of my arm. "Ummm."

Sparks smiled, not jealous or condescending or anything, just like she thought Taz was doing something kind. I jerked my arm back and wrote, DON'T PITY ME.

Taz read that and laughed. "Pity? I'd trade places in an instant."

Gorty gaped at her. "You got to be kidding."

"Nah. It'd be way fine."

Gorty shook his head. "Freak City." When I looked at him, he added, "Nothing personal, Rover."

Taz said, "Who's not from Freak City? Best to be the freak unique."

Q. Paul said quietly, "A lone wolf hasn't got a pack, Taz."

I clapped to get their attention, then tilted my head, rolled my eyes upward, and held out my open hands in exasperation.

Taz said, "Okay, El Lobo, we'll stop talking about you in front of you. Right?"

Gorty and Q. Paul shrugged and nodded.

Milo opened the front door. "Sure you don't want a ride around the lot before you go? I just bought the Mustang from someone who found it in a basement garage. It's a 'sixty-four, so it fishtails some, but—"

Sparks kissed him on the cheek. "It really is late, Milo. Thanks."

I followed her out the front door. The halogen lights slew my night vision, but on the breeze I smelled hot metal, gasoline exhaust, and a dash of burned oil.

And none of Milo's cars had been driven recently.

I turned on the pad of my foot, bumping Florida in the doorway and sweeping her back into Milo Chevrolet's home. The others stared. All I could do was waggle one hand in reassurance.

Sparks stood exposed in the open lot. "What's wrong? Forget something?"

I nodded quite calmly and beckoned for her to return. She shrugged and came back. I pulled the door shut behind her.

Milo looked expectant as I scribbled. That changed to disappointment when he read, WHERE BACK DOOR?

"This is a trick question, right? It's in the back. You want—"

I nodded.

Milo looked at Sparks, who shrugged. Gorty asked, "This have anything to do with us?"

I shook my head.

"Good." He reached for the front door. "Let's ride."

Taz shook her head. "Nothing but sleep waiting back at the flat."

Q. Paul said, "Too true. Who's out there?"

I shrugged.

"But someone is."

I nodded.

"You know what they want?"

I thought I did, but I shrugged again.

Milo said, "If you'd like to know who you're fleeing, I have a pair of military-spec Night Peepers with a two-hundred-times zoom."

I smiled. Milo smiled back. It was the first real clue that we could like each other a lot if we didn't do anything stupid like fight over Sparks.

Gorty said, "If you've got any ground-to-ground missiles among the army surplus, we could solve a lot of problems."

"Ooh," said Q. Paul. "You be the target?"

Milo had disappeared behind some shelves. Florida stood nearby, watching me solemnly. I made a circle with my thumb and forefinger, and she nodded. " 'S okay, Woofboy."

Sparks said, "If you'd let us know what's going on—"

I nodded, but as I reached for my notebook, Milo reappeared with a heavy old pair of Night Peepers. I motioned for patience, balanced the Peepers awkwardly on my nose, and looked through them into the street.

As the Wolf, I see shapes and motion better at night than I used to. But looking through the Peepers was like looking into a grayscale monitor—the world existed in sixty-four distinct shades. Textures and shadows were impossibly crisp. In the far wall, I saw each pit in the surface of the bricks, each swirl in the mortar.

I zoomed out and panned the street. A tailor shop and a barbershop had windows like steel walls; there was no light within them for the Night Peepers to magnify. A couple of cars were parked on the street, but they were rusty, wheelless hulks from before the Change. A cluster of bikes were parked in front of an apartment building that some gang had reclaimed, but no one stood around them. The apartment building was as dark as the shops near it.

In the alley between the apartments and the tailor's was a familiar dark motorcycle with sidecar. Its driver and its passenger had removed their helmets to watch Milo Chevrolet's place.

I zoomed in. The driver was a female elf with short, pale hair and a wry smile. Her passenger was a male human, dark haired, with sharp features that almost made him look elfin. He stared at Milo Chevrolet's windows as if he could see me. He didn't smile at all. His eyebrows were drawn together in concentration or pain.

I handed the Peepers to Milo. I'd seen the human the day before, at Elsewhere. He'd bought some books, but

I couldn't remember the titles. One had been the auto-biography of a detective that had a cover like a how-to book. Maybe the kid was tailing us for homework.

Everyone was staring at me. I wrote, 2 KIDS—RODE BY GODMOM'S EARLIER. IN THE ALLEY, WATCHING US.

Q. Paul said, "We didn't do anything to 'em."

Gorty said, "We could, though."

Taz sighed. "Give it a rest, guys."

I wrote, MAYBE THEY PICKED US AT RANDOM, TO FOLLOW FOR A LARK. I didn't believe that.

Taz said, "Let me look." She stared through the Night Peepers, then said, "Cute guy."

"Yeah?" Sparks accepted the Peepers from Taz. "Yeah."

Milo, a bit irritated, took the Peepers and studied the watchers. "He looks like a hundred kids you'd see on Ho Street. She's cute, though."

"Yeah?" said Gorty, grabbing the Peepers. "Oh. An elf." He continued to stare. "I've seen 'em somewhere."

Q. Paul said, "My turn?"

"Oh, right." Gorty gave him the Peepers.

Q. Paul whistled. "Ah. The Finder."

I glanced at Florida. She had her nose against the window as she stared into the lot. She was rubbing her left shoulder with her right hand, but her face was calm. My heart Bungee-jumped.

"The wha'?" said Gorty.

Q. Paul said, "Didi pointed him out at Homegirl's, remember?"

I tapped his shoulder and took back the Peepers. In the alley, the human kid was frowning and shaking his head; a lock of dark hair moved across his forehead. The elf touched his shoulder, but he shook her hand off, almost angrily. She smiled that tolerant elven smile that could mean anything, and they continued to watch Milo's lot.

I gave the Peepers to Florida. She looked into the alley, then said, "I dunno 'em, Woofboy. Friends?"

I held up one hand and waggled it from side to side.

Gorty snapped his fingers. "The Finder! Yeah. What a racket."

"What's he find?" asked Sparks. "Besides girls' hearts?"

Taz snorted a laugh, said, "Stuff. If you can't find something and you've got trading goods, they say he can help sometimes. Or will help. I don't know which."

Q. Paul said, "Didi said a friend of a friend lost her dog once, and he found 'im right away."

Gorty grunted. "Guy prob'ly swiped the dog in the first place. Doesn't the elf have some racket, too?"

Q. Paul grinned. "Yes! Finder and Fixer." He frowned. "But what's she s'posed to fix?"

Sparks said, "What he finds?"

No one answered that. Milo said, "Still want the back door? I could turn off the yard lights if you'd rather go by the front."

I wrote, COULD YOU SEE FLORIDA BACK TO ELSE-WHERE? and showed it to Sparks.

Florida peeked from behind her to read it and said, "Hey, no way!"

I wrote, YES WAY.

Florida said, "I c'n get home by myself."

I shook my head and wrote: IS IMPORTANT. STRIDER WOULD AGREE.

She glanced up at me when she read Strider's name. I growled quietly, "I' o'ay."

She said, "Really okay?"

I shrugged, then nodded tentatively, then cocked my head to one side to say, *Maybe. I think so.*

"Where're you going?"

About the only thing I know about dealing with kids is you should never lie to them. I pointed toward the watchers in the alley.

Florida said, "I'm comin'."

I wrote, HAVE I EVER ASKED FOR A FAVOR?

She shook her head.

I wrote, GOOD. GO WITH SPARKS.

She said, "Woofboy, that's a totally stupid fa—"

I clasped my hands together and rolled my eyes upward.

She nodded. "Okay."

Sparks flicked her eyes at Florida and asked me, "They're after her? Why—"

I shrugged again. Florida said, "I'll go with you, Sparks. You don' want to be alone if those're bad people."

Sparks looked at me, then looked back at Florida and nodded. The favors were piling up fast.

Florida said, "Be careful, Woofboy. I'll tell Mickey you'll be back soon. Okay?"

I nodded.

Sparks said, "R—Wolfboy, what're you planning?"

TO FOLLOW THE FOLLOWERS FOR A CHANGE. THAT'S ALL.

After reading it, she passed that note to the others.

"That's all?" said Gorty. "Shoot, let's go out, grab 'em, and make 'em talk."

I shook my head. MIGHT GET AWAY. IF THEY TALKED, COULD WE BELIEVE THEM? LET THEM SHOW WHAT THEY'RE UP TO.

Milo said, "You want to scare them away?"

I wrote, & NEED WAY TO FOLLOW THEM.

"Easy," Taz said. "Ride with me."

I blinked at her. When Sparks had agreed to take Florida home, I'd felt a twinge of relief that was only partly about Florida. I'd thought it meant that for another day at least, I wouldn't have to worry any more about what Mickey calls "the whole hearts-and-groins thing."

Taz just shrugged. "Night's young. Why break up the party?"

MAYBE THEY'RE BIKE THIEVES. YOURS WOULD SELL FOR A FAIR BIT.

Taz lifted an eyebrow as if she'd watched too much "Star Trek" as a kid. "They would've made a try for it by now."

I JUST DON'T WANT ANYONE HURT FOR SOME BRAIN-DEAD IDEA I HAD.

Taz grinned. "You spoiled our fun once already. You owe us."

I looked at Sparks, who smiled helplessly.

We made our plan then. Here's how it went:

Florida and Sparks waited in Milo's home, ready to scoot out the back a few minutes after we went out the front. I explained that by saying the watchers might not've spotted everyone, and there was no point in giving them a second look at anyone till we knew what they were up to.

At the door, Florida hugged me. Sparks gave me a kiss on the cheek. I caught the tail end of almost everyone's reaction to that: Gorty seemed annoyed, as if he didn't think any human should be kissing me. Milo seemed interested and annoyed, as if this was more data for a problem that he had thought was already solved. Q. Paul seemed interested and amused, as if he wondered about his chances with Sparks and displays of affection made him grin. Taz just seemed amused; I couldn't guess why.

At the last minute, Sparks said, "You've got to let me know how this ends, you know."

"Big ditto," said Florida.

I nodded, then Milo, Gorty, Q. Paul, Taz, and I sauntered out under the halogen lights. Milo was saying something technical about his cars. I think Taz was the only one who understood him, and she didn't seem to be paying close attention. We were all avoiding looking into the alley.

Realizing that, I looked into the alley. The Finder and the Fixer were still there, motionless in the darkness. I glanced away before they could know I'd seen them.

Milo slid behind the wheel of the biggest vehicle on the lot, a black Roadmaster, a tank of a car that looked like it should have had gangsters with tommy guns leaning out its windows and crouching on its running boards. The three Packers and I strolled over to their bikes.

The watchers had to know something was happening, but they couldn't know if we were planning to race around Milo's lot or drive someplace interesting. They would certainly be getting ready to ride, whatever we did. That was part of the plan.

Milo waited until Q. Paul and Taz put on their helmets. The Roadmaster started immediately and idled with a tiger's purr. Milo pulled into the center of the parking lot, pointing his grille toward the street. The rest of us had mounted by then. Taz, in front of me, nodded once.

Milo revved his engine, a dragon's roar, and popped on the headlights. The beams carved a path for the Roadmaster, straight through the lot, across the street, and into the alley, where a human kid gaped and an elf looked very grim.

Milo dropped the motor into gear. I saw his face lit from beneath by the dashboard lights: He wore a tight, determined grin. That made sense. He was about to test two extremely different skills.

The Roadmaster leaped like a panther after prey. Trapped in its headlights, the human kid started to rise, as if he was going to abandon the sidecar and run. Then the elf stood and kicked the bike's starter. The human dropped back into the sidecar. He had more faith in his partner than I would've.

As the Roadmaster's engine crossed the edge of Milo's lot, it coughed and died. The headlights went blind. But nothing altered the Roadmaster's direction or momentum: It was crossing First Avenue at something like seventy kilometers an hour, aimed at the mouth of the alley. The watchers' choices were to drive forward to meet it or race backward to escape it—but Milo had said the alley dead-ended in less than thirty meters.

Just as I began to imagine the Roadmaster rolling into the alley while people screamed and metal crashed, the watchers' bike whipped into the street. The shriek of its spellbox filled a vacuum of sound. The elf and the human leaned into a tight turn within inches of the Roadmaster's front bumper. I wanted to close my eyes but couldn't.

Maybe Milo used magic to slow the car at the last moment. Maybe the elf was as fast as we'd hoped she'd be. The Roadmaster's bumper kissed the elf's back tire, making her slew sideways. Then her wheels gripped the road, and she shot toward Soho.

"Ee-hah!" Gorty yelled. His Kawasaki was first from the lot. Q. Paul grinned and followed.

Taz said, "Hold like it's true love," and we chased the screaming engines into the night.

Since there was nothing to do after that except worry, I worried. I worried that we were doing what the watchers wanted: While we chased them, someone could grab Sparks and Florida from the street as they made their way home. I worried that we shouldn't be doing anything at all. I worried that we were following the best plan, but the Packers and I were the worst choices to carry it out.

Then I told myself we were the only available choices to carry it out. Odd how that thought wasn't comforting.

Taz and I fell farther behind Q. Paul and Gorty until we were a full block back from them, maybe three blocks behind the kids we were chasing. The Fixer turned onto Market Street. As soon as they were out of sight, Taz mumbled something. Our lights shut down, and so did the sound of our engine.

We rolled silently through Soho's dark streets. At Market, we turned too. Gorty and Q. Paul's taillights were bright before us. Taz brought her Moto Guzzi's throttle back full, and we raced ahead. The streets outside of Soho are kept better than the ones within. On smooth pavement, our only sound was the wind we made as we rode.

The Fixer knew Bordertown well or was very lucky. None of the alleys she took came to dead ends; none of the streets held impassable pits or makeshift walls. After the fifth turn, her lights disappeared.

I thought we'd lost her, but Gorty, in the lead, turned decisively. We followed. As he passed Riverview, he blinked his taillights once, and he and Q. Paul rocketed onward. Taz and I turned onto Riverview.

We couldn't muffle the sound we made knifing through the wind or, firmly announcing our return to Soho, bumping over potholes and rubble. Neither could the Fixer and the Finder. Their noise should've made it impossible for them to hear ours. Unfortunately, the reverse was true.

I tapped Taz's shoulder twice. She slowed. I listened. Something moved in the distance. I tapped her again. We shot forward. I tried not to wonder how good Taz's night vision was.

Seeing a black shape moving in the road, I tapped Taz twice again. My eyes were probably better than the Finder's, unless he had Night Peepers, and might have been better than the elf's, but there was no point in taking chances.

And no need. I had their odor now: the petrochemical smell of their bike, the leather smell of their jackets, the wildflower scent that one of them wore. I grinned, and I only stopped because I imagined my teeth reflecting light from the occasional bright window. It would look like some demonic canine relative of the Cheshire Cat was flying through Bordertown's streets.

The Finder and Fixer stopped in front of a two-story

townhouse in Soho. Taz and I waited a block back until they'd entered. Then I hopped off the bike, made a *Stay!* motion at Taz, and ran forward.

I was thinking about what lay ahead when I realized that Taz was riding beside me. I made a *Shoo!* motion, and she whispered, "I'll wait at the next corner. How many minutes?"

I rolled my eyes, then held up both hands with all of my fingers splayed wide.

She nodded. "Good. I've got a short attention span."

A light went on in the second floor of the building that the Finder and the Fixer had entered. I leaped onto the wall and climbed up. My claws sounded loud to me as I jammed my fingertips into the cracks between the bricks, but then, so did my heart.

I hesitated by the window, thinking, *Spider-Man, Spider-Man, does whatever a—* Then I heard an elf say, "Clearly, my understanding is more limited than I'd thought."

"Oh?"

I peeked over the sill. The Finder sat at a table cluttered with magazines, books, loose sheets of paper, a couple of apples in a wicker bowl, and a shiny silver toaster with its cord wrapped about itself. His face was cradled in his hands.

"Yes." The Fixer handed him a mug and kept one for herself, then filled them both from a metal thermos. "I thought that when you follow someone, your quarry is supposed to stay in front of you."

"Oh, all right, we'll try it that way next time." He sniffed the mug and straightened up. "Ah! The staff of life."

"Espresso beans, m'lad," the Fixer said. "That staff will drub a good deal of life into you." She sat across from him, picked up the toaster, smiled, and set it aside. "Found what appears to be cream in your icebox. You try it first."

"Wish I hadn't taken this job."

"Oh? Have I heard that said before?" She pushed a small clay pitcher toward him.

The Finder sniffed the pitcher, splashed milk from it into his cup, sipped, and smiled. "Yes. Then you said, 'You must answer what's within you. To deny that is to slay your soul.' "

She kept her satisfied smile. "I did?"

"It was after a few beers. After we'd both had a few beers."

She nodded. "An odd way to ask the way to the toilet."

He looked across the table, still quite somber. He had the kind of steady gaze that makes girls talk about their loves and guys talk about their fears. "Elves. They do everything obliquely."

"Is't true?" She lost her amusement. "Then, purely as an exercise, I'll ask, What now?"

My fingers and toes were growing tired, but the Fixer's question made me forget that.

"Tell 'er we found the kid with three moles. Get our money. And not have to take another job for months."

"As though you hate doing this." She had pulled a Swiss Army knife from her pocket and was dismantling the toaster, so her eyes did not meet his.

He grimaced. "If I can't stop it, I might as well make a living from it."

She held up something from the innards of the toaster, then began to scrape it clean. "Make a living, or make a life?"

He said, "C'mon, Tick-Tick." She glanced up at the name, and he said, "Do I ask you that?"

"No, I grant you, and would bless you for it, could we soulless folk bless anyone." Tick-Tick was already reassembling the toaster. She pressed the lever once, and it sprang up obediently. "Was this for me?"

"Took it in trade for finding a National steel guitar.

Easiest job I ever had. Told the kid the directions to Folk Yourself, and she gave me the toaster. It's a working antique—"

Tick-Tick muttered, "Now."

"—from Bordertown. One of the truckers at the market'll give us something for it. Be worth something back in the World."

I wanted to scream, *What about the kid with three moles?* I wondered if Taz were still waiting, if Florida and Sparks had made it to their respective homes, if anyone in the neighborhood had noticed that there was a werewolf clinging to the outside of someone's window.

The Finder finished his coffee and went to a shelf. I saw books, jewelry boxes, clothing, old record albums, and kids' toys, all neatly placed as if waiting for their owners to fetch them. The guy picked up a hand mirror, which seemed odd, and then spoke to it, which seemed odder yet. "Mirror, mirror, on the ball, who's the vainest of them all?"

"Very funny," someone said. I glanced at the Fixer, Tick-Tick. She was sipping her coffee and watching the guy. I wondered if she was the best ventriloquist I'd ever seen. Then I shivered: My fur was screaming a warning at my skin. The Voice was coming from the hand mirror.

"Found what you want," the kid said.

"Oh?" The Voice had an Elflands accent, but so did a quarter of the elves in Bordertown.

"Wasn't easy. The pull kept disappearing. Every time I had to ask for it again, I got the most amazing headaches—"

"Orient. We agreed on a price," the Voice said.

Orient? At first I thought it was a command, then realized it was the Finder's name, or maybe his title.

"All right. But I want you to know what you're paying for."

"I'm paying for an elven child with a triangle of birthmarks on one shoulder."

"Right you are," said Orient. "Which isn't very specific, which is probably why the pull kept fading on me. What I did—"

"Do you have our child?" the Voice demanded.

"What I did," Orient repeated quite calmly, and I rather respected him then, even if he was in the middle of dooming Florida, "was triangulate on the fix whenever I got it. And eventually I narrowed it down to a couple of areas. And tonight, we got lucky."

"Yes?"

"Direct fix while I was looking right at the kid. Can't be much surer than that."

"I believe you. Where is the child now?"

"Well." Orient looked at Tick-Tick, who shrugged. I wondered if I should attack them both somehow, just to distract them, but I also wanted to know everything they knew. If they kept talking, I might learn the identity, and maybe even the location, of the Voice.

"I am waiting."

"I'm not sure, exactly," said Orient.

"I expected something more than this."

"And I expected a lot less, dammit! Finding a missing elf ought—" Orient brushed his loose locks of hair back and said, more calmly, "Look. It'll be easy now. Your kid seems to be around Mock Avenue fairly often. And I can give you an exact description, as of this evening. Good enough?"

"It will have to be," said the Voice. "But do not expect payment until we have our child."

Orient glanced at Tick-Tick, and they shrugged simultaneously. Orient said, "No prob. The reason you never spotted the elf with the birthmarks is 'cause someone did some serious magic. You're now looking for a medium-height kid who looks remarkably like the title character in *I Was a Teen-Aged Werewolf.*"

I fell off the side of the building.

CHAPTER FOUR
Night of the Hunter's Moon

If Leda had tried to turn me into a cat, maybe I would've landed on my feet. Mutt-man was lucky he didn't bust his butt. I just sat there on the leaf-strewn sidewalk looking stupid until I glanced up and saw someone in the window above. A lock of moon-white hair told me it was Tick-Tick, and her voice confirmed that. She said, "Speaking of—"

I scrambled to my feet and ran. It was probably luck again that took me toward Taz instead of away. If luck's finite, I was using mine up awfully quickly.

My mind was like a bike stripped of high gear. I was thinking frantically, but answers wouldn't come. I saw one thing clearly: Now that the searchers thought they were looking for the Teen Wolf, Orient could find me anytime, anywhere. If they caught me and realized I wasn't who they wanted, they might let me go. Or they might not. Either way, if they got that close to me, they'd be one step from capturing Florida.

Taz was waiting on her bike at the corner. I began to

realize I'd done a few things wrong. I should've tried to break the magic mirror that let Orient talk to his boss. I should've stolen or sabotaged their bike. But if I'd tried either, Orient and Tick-Tick might've caught or killed me, and things would have been even worse than they were.

Whatever else I do, I worry better than anyone I know.

I realized another thing. If I was in danger, anyone with me was in danger. I made a shooing motion with one hand as I ran past Taz. I had a destination then. Sometimes that's a reasonable substitute for a plan.

Riding beside me, her bike quiet and its lights out, Taz said, "Training for the Olympics? I 'spect you'd get the gold as the only entrant in the werewolf-runs-through-town-and-doesn't-explain-a-bloody-thing race."

I made the shooing motion again.

"Anyplace you're going, I can get you there faster."

She was right. I didn't like that; it meant I had to trade a little of Taz's safety in the hope of winning more for Florida. I nodded. As Taz slowed, I hopped on back, then jammed my finger forward in the air several times, pointing ahead.

"Go fast?" Taz asked. "Like, there's *another* way to travel?" She cranked the throttle.

I kept my left arm around her waist as we raced. With my right hand, I tapped her shoulder whenever I thought she should turn, then pointed in the proper direction. After a couple of turns, we settled on a system; tap right shoulder for right turn, tap left for left.

And after five or ten very long minutes, I pointed at a black cinder-block building. If you squinted, you could tell that it had started life as a bus station. Since I'd last been there, a spell-driven neon sign had been mounted over the front doors so even tourists could know they'd found Danceland.

There are always kids hanging out by the doors if the

club's open. When bands like the Unwanted or Lord Dunsany's Nightmare are playing, the street is as packed as the interior. I could tell we'd arrived after the last show: The only people on this end of Ho were a couple of elf and human kids who sat talking together on the curb. They glanced at us as Taz pulled up to Danceland's front doors, and they kept talking. At another time, I would've been pleased that I was becoming a common sight in some parts of Soho.

Taz said doubtfully, "Least it's not an elves-only joint."

I jumped off, gave her a grin and a wave in the hope that she'd go, and headed for the front door. I heard her kickstand drop behind me, and then her bootsteps trailed me to the front doors.

They were locked. I pounded on the wooden planks that'd replaced the glass long ago, and ignored someone yelling from inside, "It's over, go home, find some more money and bring it to us tomorrow night!" After half a minute, the same person said, "All right, all right, if it's not an emergency already, I warn you, it shall be one."

The door opened. Beside me, Taz took a small step backward, a reasonable response to Goldy when he's in bouncer mode. The tight coils of metallic hair and the weightlifter's shoulders are part of it, but when he sets his dark features in an I'm-going-to-eat-you-for-lunch-and-I'm-still-going-to-be-hungry look, smart people want to get out of his way.

I pushed into the doorway as Goldy said, "Wolfboy? Something wrong with Mickey?"

I shook my head quickly. At my heels, Taz said, "I'm with him."

Goldy said, "Nothing's happening now, we're shutting—"

I said, " 'I'er."

Goldy squinted; he'd regained his impassive look af-

49

ter I'd said Mickey was all right. "Strider? He's mopping the dance floor, I think."

I ran inside with Taz and Goldy in tow.

A lot of the glamour departs from a club when the overhead lights are bright and the customers have gone. In Danceland, the black wall paint wanted renewing; the ceiling neon, turned off, was a grotesque jumble of wires and tubes. The room stank of stale smoke and stale beer. The owner and her main bartender were wiping down the counters and gathering dirty bottles, Sai was pushing a beer keg on a dolly across the dance floor, and Strider was mopping the bare stage. For some people, it's disillusioning to see behind the scenes. For me, it's a different kind of magic. It's the magic of being trusted with the truth.

The owner, a wiry woman called Dancer, looked our way. So did Valda, the bartender, who always reminded me of my grandmother. Goldy called, " 'S cool. The Wolf's a friend."

Dancer nodded, and she and Valda kept working.

Sai grinned, parked the dolly at the bar, grabbed me around the waist in a hug, and whirled me into the air. "Hey, Woof-woof, how was the Nevernever?"

I wriggled a bit, wishing she'd set me down. As soon as Goldy said, "Something's up," she did.

"Oh?" She looked at Taz.

"Just taxi service," Taz said cautiously. Maybe she wasn't sure what to make of a half-Asian, half-elven woman who still had the biceps of her boxing days. I preferred to think Taz wondered what Sai's hug meant.

Sai nodded, bouncing the short mane of black hair about her head. "Come after pay and a tip?"

"Nah. Finding out what this is all about will be enough pay."

Sai glanced at me. I winced and shook my head a tiny bit.

Taz caught that. "But if I'm not wanted—"

I grabbed her arm as she turned away. She spun back fast, angry. I raised both hands in surrender, then one finger for patience, then pulled out pen and paper: NOT MY PLACE TO TELL. ISN'T ABOUT ME.

Taz said, "Yeah, right," in a hard voice.

If I could've talked, I would've said *Fine* in the same voice. I wrote, SORRY. BUT I CAN'T DO ANYTHING ABOUT IT.

She gave me the deep eyeball search. It wasn't easy to stand there meeting her gaze, but I did, and she nodded. "Okay, Wolf. See you."

She started toward the door. I ran after her, tapped her shoulder, and crooked my finger to draw her back toward the center of the room. Strider had joined the others, so the Terrible Trio awaited us in all their glory: a slender elf with his white hair tied back in a samurai's knot, a stocky halfie, and a broad-shouldered human, united only by green Danceland long-sleeved T-shirts and identical expressions of grim confidence.

I grinned and, bowing a bit, pointed both hands at Strider, then waved them to point at Taz.

Strider caught on, as I knew he would. I expected him to answer in Prince-of-Faerie mode, but he had his Bordertown manners down: "Strider. Hope you had better luck with your *nom de guerre*."

Bordertown style undoubtedly made Taz more comfortable than Elflands would've; Strider knew more about manners than I did. Taz smiled. " 'Tasmanian Devil' didn't last, thank God. Taz."

Sai said, "Sai. I fought pro for a year or so. When I quit, I lost the *the*."

"The Soho Sai!" Taz grinned. "I saw you tie with the Dragontown Kid. I thought you were better'n him."

"Course she is," Goldy said. "Call me Goldy. For reasons that must be evident."

Taz nodded. "You've all got business. I'm gone." She

made a pistol of her thumb and forefinger and fired it at me. "See you."

I watched her disappear around the front hall, wondered if I would see her again, and scribbled, CAN WE GO? PEOPLE ARE AFTER ME WHO BELIEVE I'M THE HEIR TO FAERIE. I DON'T WANT THEM THINKING DANCELAND'S IMPORTANT.

I expected Strider to laugh, but Goldy was the only one who began to smile. He saw I was serious at the same time Sai called, "Dancer, okay if we finish up early tomorrow?"

Dancer waved a hand in dismissal. "Get. Come in at the usual."

Valda added, "Hey, have some fun for me!"

The Trio grabbed jackets, and we exited through the back door into the alley. A midnight blue Harley with a flaring windshield was parked there, next to a dented red Honda scooter. Sai got onto the motorcycle, saying, "Isn't it beautiful? It's the Batcycle."

Strider got on behind her. "A wedding present. Who needs money when you have wheels?"

Goldy started the little red scooter. "Where to, Lupo?"

I got behind him and showed him my latest note: SOMEPLACE WHERE WE CAN TALK THAT WON'T COMPROMISE ANYONE. "Compromise" made me feel like Spywolf.

The Trio said simultaneously, "Hard Luck."

I nodded; I should've guessed that.

We rolled all of half a block up Ho Street, and I wondered whether Florida and Sparks had gotten home, and how soon the Voice would send people after me. That kept me from paying attention to Ho itself, which is usually a shame. Ho's where you go when you want to see something happening, or to be something happening.

The Hard Luck Café is where you go on Ho when

you're thoroughly tired of things happening, and all you want is food or conversation or a few minutes of relative calm. I say "relative" because the Hard Luck's where everyone else goes who's in search of a salsa-and-mushroom grilled-cheese sandwich, coffee that'll wake the dead and kill the living, or a chance to see who else is playing nighthawks-at-the-diner.

This night, that consisted of a couple of chess players near the window, a couple of girls holding hands across the table at a booth, and a few loners, human and elf, at the counter. We took the corner booth without consulting. When the waiter yelled over the music from a seedybox, "The usual?" Sai told her, "All around."

I hardly noticed the coffee cup that appeared at my elbow, and when the waiter asked about food, I shook my head. I was writing. By the time the waiter returned with a bowl of blueberries and yogurt for Goldy and a huge cinnamon roll for Strider and Sai to share, I'd written this:

HUMAN CALLED FINDER A.K.A. ORIENT AND ELF CALLED FIXER A.K.A. TICK-TICK WERE PAID TO FIND ELF KID W/ 3 MOLES. TONIGHT, FLORIDA, SPARKS, & I WENT TO MILO CHEVROLET'S W/ SOME PACKERS: TAZ, GORTY FM. CASTLE PUP, & SKINNY GUY CALLED Q. PAUL.

MAGIC DOESN'T WORK AT MILO'S. SO MOLES WERE ON KID'S SHOULDER. SO FINDER TRACKED US MAGICALLY OR SOMETHING. GOOD NEWS IS I WAS STANDING IN FRONT OF FLORIDA THE ONLY TIME ORIENT GOT A LOOK AT HIS QUARRY, SO HE THINKS I'M THE HEIR.

THAT'S THE BAD NEWS, TOO.

Goldy shook his head. "You have some kind of luck, kid."

Strider said, "Who knows what happened?"

I wrote, ME. & YOU GUYS. OTHERS JUST KNOW SOME KIDS WERE TRACKING US. THEY HELPED ME FIND ORIENT: 2ND FLOOR, 231 MORRISON.

Sai said, "Where's Florida?"

Elsewhere, I hope.

Goldy said, "You haven't checked?"

Ms. Wu's spell should be hiding her again. Nothing's hiding me if this Finder starts tracking werewolves.

Strider said, "He is."

Sai glanced at him.

Strider said, "They want the heir. As quickly as possible. Any idea who hired 'em?"

A voice came through a mirror Orient used. Sounded female. Elflands accent, not B-town.

Strider grimaced. "Crystaviel."

I shrugged. I didn't need to write that I thought so. There were thousands of female elves in Bordertown, but only one had tried to kidnap Florida before.

Strider stood. "One way to find out for sure."

I gulped coffee, Goldy gobbled a last spoonful of yogurt, and Sai stuffed the last crust of cinnamon roll into her mouth. Strider gave the waiter a pass good for any Danceland main stage show; she said, "Oh, that's too much," and gave him a Ren and Stimpy pin in change, which he pinned to Sai's jacket.

Sai said, "You'll spoil me."

Strider answered, "Never enough."

Back on the street, Goldy said, "Shall I go with you?"

Strider said, "No. Check on Florida."

Goldy nodded and left on his scooter. To state the obvious: Appearances are always deceiving in Bordertown. Prime example: there's no relation between the size of a bike and the power of a spellbox. Goldy rocketed.

Sai said, "Do we tell Leander and Wiseguy?"

Strider shook his head. "No time to assemble the forces of good, m'love. The three of us will have to do." He looked at her bike, then at the two of us. "Damn."

So we made our plans, and once again, you may assume they worked out, at least at first, 'cause I'm not going to tell them to you now. A minute or two later, my notes safely burned so no magician could learn my side of the conversation, Sai and I were on the Harley, taking a speed tour of Bordertown.

(That's a parenthesis at the beginning of this sentence: A digression starts here. This is your last warning.

(I like a lot of things about writing down what's happened to me. It sorts out parts of my life, helps me see things that didn't make sense at the time. It also makes me look smarter than I am, as if I was figuring these things out as they happened, instead of doing whatever seemed right and hoping for the best.

(But I hate it when I have to tell about something that I already told about, like Ho Street at night. Sure, I love it, and sure, the kids who're still up are dressed in wild clothes, and sure, the stars are impossibly beautiful over Faerie, and sure, passing an open club gives you a burst of picture and a snatch of sound like cruising through TV channels. But after a while, I just want to give it a rest. Like what I'm telling you about now: Sai and I rode through Soho. It was grand, even though I worried about how everything would work out, and sometimes Sai would laugh simply 'cause she likes to race through the night. But do I really need to tell you about all that?

(I think not.)

We assumed simplemindedly that because Orient's finding talent was the surest way to track me, Crystaviel's people would stay together to follow Orient's instructions. At a major intersection in the scandal district, we had an unpleasant surprise. Three silent bikes whipped out of a dark alley, each with two riders. All six wore burning helmets, and fire raced from their tires.

Beneath rippling flames, mirrored faceplates hid their identities. They were equipped like part of Dragonfire, the rich brat elf gang from Dragon's Tooth Hill. Their bikes, jackets, boots, and helmets were sleek and new. Each helmet burned in a different hue: orange, purple, blue, green, yellow, and red.

"The Inhuman Torches," Sai said.

Which was more fuel for fretting. The Hill gangs, human and elf, can be scary; any gang can be scary. But most Dragon's Toothers are posers, rich kids who live in comfort on the Hill and come down to Soho when they're bored. The Inhuman Torches, though, may be the baddest of B-town's baddest. They're famous for hating humans and halfies, and they like to pretend they're an advance guard for an army that'll someday come from Faerie to conquer Bordertown and the World.

The orange Torch shot right at us, clearly intending to knock us over if we didn't stop and trusting their gear would protect him and his passenger. On the blue Torch's bike, the rider flipped open a makeup compact like it was some Super-spy toy and said into the mirror, "It's the dog kid."

Sai said, "Hang on," as if I had a choice.

We leaned low. At first I thought Sai was trying for a tight U-turn, but as we began to skid, I thought she was simply going to slam into the approaching bike and see who could do the most damage. But the orange bike, trying to sideswipe us, went down first, spilling its riders. Sai's Harley peeled rubber as we narrowly dodged them.

Someone screamed from the downed bike. Trying to ram us had been a stupid move. Someone was going to have a bad case of road rash, and maybe much worse. Whether they deserved it or not, I hated the sound of people in pain. If I'd been driving one of the other bikes, I would've stayed behind to help my mates.

Either the other drivers were caught up in the thrill of the hunt or Crystaviel's orders were to be obeyed at any cost. The two remaining bikes stayed close behind us.

Since there was no longer anything to be gained by trying to lead Orient all around Bordertown, Sai shot back toward Soho.

I looked back as we passed under a working streetlight. Behind us, burning globes hovered over wheels of fire, then became humanlike bikers. Flames, stars, and streetlights glinted within their faceplates and from their dark blue patent leather boots, jackets, and gloves. The Torches showed no skin; they could've been mechanical men or demons made of flame.

The remaining Torches seemed to remember that I was supposed to be the heir. They made no attempts to ram us or throw things at us. Sai had the Batcycle's throttle wide open, but their bikes must've been equipped with the best spellboxes to be found in town. We couldn't outrun them.

Every block or two, the passenger on the blue Torch's bike screamed street names into the mirror, keeping Crystaviel or someone up to date about our precise location. I imagined bikes from all over Bordertown converging on us, and I wondered how many people Crystaviel had to call upon.

Sai had a better idea of where we were than I did, until I saw oil lamps burning on poles in an open field. The Endless Rave happens at the edge of Soho proper. Some people say the first humans to return to Bordertown decided to celebrate by dancing there, and the dancing has never stopped. The dancers come and go, of course, and so does the music: Sometimes it's made by seedyboxes, and sometimes by B-town drummers gathered to jam, and sometimes by a dancer or two stamping a rhythm and humming a tune. No one knows how large the Endless Rave has been, but everyone swears there's always at least one kid dancing there.

As Sai and I came closer to the field, I saw there must've been two or three hundred kids dancing—mostly humans, but some elves stood to one side, watching, and at least one had joined the dancers. A band was playing at the center of the Rave: a drummer on a trap set, another on congas, a trumpeter, a flautist, a harmonica player, and four or five singers. It looked like an impromptu band. It looked like fun. It looked like we were going to ride right into the heart of the Rave.

Appearances aren't always deceiving. We did.

Sai flashed her headlight and let her engine scream, and I felt us slow a little before we left the street for grass and dirt via a gap in the curb that Sai must've known was there. I closed my eyes. I figured the next thing I'd experience would be shrieking and broken limbs, most notably my own.

The Ravers were too deep into dance trance to run away. They opened a path, flowed around us, and closed behind us, swallowing us in their rhythm, incorporating us into the Rave. Sai killed her light and her spellbox's motorcycle growl, and we wove through the Ravers' patterns, circling with them around the musicians.

One set of Torches were lost in the Rave as we slipped away. The last two, on the red bike, had circled the block. The passenger pointed at us just as we turned down Market Street. I took some consolation in noticing that they had no mirror. I would have given almost anything to know what the blue Torch's passenger told Crystaviel while they were trapped in the Endless Rave.

Our race continued. Without headlights, we hit several potholes, but none so badly that Sai lost control. We passed a few people on the street, and a bike or two going the other way, but there was no danger of colliding with anyone. No one stayed in the path of the speeding fireballs that followed us.

Then I noticed a bike with a single rider coming up fast behind the Torches. I started to tap Sai so she'd look, and I stopped as I recognized the newcomer.

Taz whipped by the last set of Torches as though they

were on a Sunday cruise and she was late to a very hot date. Two flaming helmets turned in unison as her headlight announced her approach; she passed them before they could finish looking back. The movement of their heads was small, but it told me enough about their surprise. When Taz drew alongside us, she called, "If I help you shake 'em, you'll owe me big time!"

Sai glanced over her shoulder. I nodded.

Taz and Sai conferred briefly, then Taz shut down her headlight, too. We veered into a dark tangle of narrow residential streets. From the Flames' point of view, their prey rolled from dimly lit streets into a solid wall of shadow.

The Torches' headlights pierced the wall, but our bikes were beyond their light. They rolled through cavelike darkness, undoubtedly wondering if they had lost us, when suddenly they saw a single bike's headlight snap on in the distance and heard the growl of its engine. That light and that sound sped away, rapidly becoming more distant.

The Flames slowed then. What alternative was there? If they followed the headlight, the bike they wanted might slip past them. They listened, and they watched the shadows to see if the second bike had stopped or had turned onto a branching street. And because the blue Flames listened carefully, they heard rubble spray under the wheels of a second bike that was picking its way toward Soho.

And they followed that dark, quiet bike.

Sai and I raced on as quickly as Sai dared. Then she turned off her headlight and her engine's roar. I stared back into the darkness. We had lost Crystaviel's agents—for the moment.

CHAPTER FIVE
Understandings

Sai left her bike by the curb. (Nah, I'm not going to tell you where we were. Wait for it.) The front door was ajar, so we stepped cautiously into a quiet hallway, then climbed the stairs. The apartment door showed no signs of having been forced. No one was in the living room, but an oil lamp was burning on an end table. The kitchen door opened an inch, then swung wide, and Strider grinned as he saw us. "You're the first to arrive, kids."

He and Sai met in the middle of the room and hugged. Sai asked, "Any trouble getting here?"

He shook his head. "Like strolling through a park on a glorious afternoon. You?"

"I'll bore you later."

I heard the door below being wrenched open, leaped into a stuffed chair, and landed with my arms folded and my legs stretched out on a hassock. Strider gave me a thumbs-up; Sai rolled her eyes and whispered, "Boys."

They both went into the kitchen and let the door close softly as a small gang of people charged upstairs.

Orient entered first. His eyebrows unfurled, as if a toothache had gone away. Nothing else about him said he was glad to see me. "My own apartment," he said. "Cute."

"Too cute." The Voice lost a lot of its mystery when it came from a hallway instead of a mirror.

Tick-Tick was standing behind Orient, but this wasn't ventriloquism. She smiled at me, as if she admired my style in leading Orient on a hunt to his own home. Since I admired it, too, I winked at her as she stepped aside to let the Voice by.

Hope you weren't expecting a surprise—it was Crystaviel. I wouldn't have recognized her in another setting. Her hair was in tight white braids, like the head of a mop, and half of her face was painted like the skin of some beautiful reptile with glittering blue scales. Her jacket, pants, and boots were all made from alligator hide.

Behind her came her second in command, a too-familiar elf whose name I didn't know. His presence probably helped me recognize Crystaviel: His short, tangled hair was dyed in shades of blue and white like a fire made of ice, and his eyes were the color of frost. He wore the dark blue leather of the Inhuman Torches. I wondered if he'd been driving the bike that we'd left caught up in the Endless Rave.

Several more elves in new leather and designer denim followed them. Crystaviel had us outnumbered and outdressed; I had to hope we had her outthought.

Tick-Tick said, "Please, no violence. Be it ever so humble"—she glanced around the room; Orient's house-keeping did not inspire respect—"and it is humble—Orient calls it home."

Orient said, "So fix me a vacuum cleaner someday, hey?"

"I think there's no need for violence," Crystaviel said.

I nodded, wondering if Strider and Sai were making out in the kitchen and had forgotten that I needed someone to make an entrance real soon now.

"He's older than I expected," Ice Hair said.

"Larger," Crystaviel said, studying me. "Perhaps an effect of the wolf spell. Perhaps more time passed in Bordertown than we realized." She suddenly dropped to one knee and bowed low. All of the elves, excepting Tick-Tick, followed her example. "It is a most excellent disguise, Your Majesty."

Tick-Tick blinked, a major loss of composure for an elf, but remained standing. Orient scowled, saying, "You never said I was hunting—"

Crystaviel finished, "Not once did I suspect your identity when we passed in the street."

I shrugged modestly; no one saw that. The kitchen door opened. One hand gripping the door frame, the other on the handle, Strider leaned into the crowded living room and laughed. "Long time, no see."

Ice Hair lunged at Strider, but Crystaviel, standing, stopped him with a hand against his chest. "Patience, my hound." She glanced at me just after she said it.

Strider laughed again. "Relax, Tavi. Wolfboy's no one's hound but his own."

Ice Hair sneered at him. "I never thought to see you sink so low. Bordertown trash."

A smile stayed on Strider's lips, but there was none of it in his voice. "You yap, little lapdog. Do you bite?"

Sai grabbed his shoulder and yanked him back. "Sheesh, you sound just like Prince Bozo there."

Strider's cold look moved from Ice Hair to Sai. I remembered that we weren't doing this for an evening's entertainment. People could get hurt, and the hurt could be stranger and more terrible than I'd imagined. Then Strider laughed again, lightly, without a hint of the Elflands to his voice, and said, "I do? I never thought I'd sink so low."

"Enough." Crystaviel looked from Strider to Ice Hair. "In the presence of His Maj—"

"Wrong," said Strider.

Crystaviel glanced at Orient, who shrugged and sat at the table where he'd been when I spied on him earlier. "You wanted an elf kid with three moles. The signs pointed to yon Wolfboy." Orient smirked just a bit; I think he saw we'd pulled something on Crystaviel, and approved. "Then you wanted a kid who looked like a wolf. 'Less there's more'n one in town, I did that, too. My job's done."

Crystaviel addressed me. "Your Majesty, these traitors seek to use you for—"

Strider said, "You got it wrong, Tavi."

This had gone on long enough. I stood, pulled up my left sleeve, and parted the matted hairs to show her a dark blotch on my skin, then another, then a third. If you connected them with a pen, they'd make a perfect equilateral triangle.

Crystaviel pointed at my shoulder. "Did I? The proof—"

"Evidence," Sai said. "As in, circumstantial."

"An elf child—"

"Human," Strider said.

I nodded.

Crystaviel moved closer to me, to within an inch or two of my face, and studied my eyes, then my ears. "Shed this form," she said.

I shook my head and noted that she hadn't said, "Your Majesty."

"He can't," Strider said, with just a trace of kindness.

Crystaviel laughed. "You cannot expect me to trust *you*?"

Strider said, "I still have some fondness for you, Tavi, for all we may've been opponents beyond the

Border. I wouldn't have you return to Faerie with a disguised human. It'd ruin you."

Crystaviel said, "You are too kind, m'Lord."

Sai said, "I can vouch for 'im. I knew the kid before he became Wolfboy. He was as human as they come."

Crystaviel said, "And who can vouch for you?"

Sai shrugged. So far as I knew, there were only two elves that Sai liked, Strider and Leda. Crystaviel wasn't improving Sai's opinion of the race.

Crystaviel asked Orient, "Is it possible? A transformed human is no elf, whatever the pattern of birthmarks."

Orient repeated Sai's shrug. "I don't know how it works. Maybe the kid you want isn't in Bordertown, but Wolfboy was close enough to your conditions that I came up with him. There's certainly something of Faerie about him."

Tick-Tick said quickly, "No refunds."

"No," said Crystaviel, "you'll have the rest of your pay." She said something in Elvish then.

When I didn't answer, Strider said, "I told you."

Crystaviel said something else, more forcefully. A burning wind swept my fur, and my bones twisted to new shapes inside me. I screamed.

The pain left a moment later. Strider had one hand around Crystaviel's throat, Ice Hair had a jeweled switchblade at Strider's neck, Sai had one hand on Ice Hair's wrist and the other cocked in a fist. They reminded me of the *Laocoön*, that statue of the family wrapped around with snakes.

Orient, still in his chair, said, "Uh, let's all be very cool, hmm?"

Strider glanced my way. I was still the Wolf. I felt as if nothing had happened; magic can be like that. I nodded, and he and Sai backed away from Crystaviel and Ice Hair. The switchblade disappeared, which made me feel better.

"Well," Crystaviel told me. "Your spell's very well wrought; my compliments to your wizard. Be flattered, human. For several minutes, I thought you my superior."

"Whom you'd have used," Strider said.

She looked at him from the corners of her dark gray eyes. "Whom I'd have restored to the throne of all Faerie, Your Highness. Since you know where the heir is *not*, do you know as well where the heir *is*?"

"No." Since Goldy hadn't reported whether Florida was back at Elsewhere, Strider's answer was scrupulously honest. "If the heir's in Bordertown, surely you would've discovered that with or without the Finder's aid." I noted that when Strider ventured into half-truths, his Elflands' diction returned.

Ice Hair blurted, "Then why're you in Bordertown?"

Strider gave him a thin smile. "I like the music. Why are most elves in Bordertown?"

"You seem well informed about the heir," Crystaviel said. "And especially well informed about my search."

"Oh, that." Now that he'd completely left the land of truth, Strider spoke pure Bordertown. "M'mate, Wolflad there, sees he's being followed by some kids. So he returns the favor and finds they're talking into a mirror about him being an elf with three moles.

"No dummy, he spots a major case of mistaken identity and, proving he's no dummy, comes to me. I spy a bit of the truth right off. In Faerie, I heard rumors: an heir born with three moles in a triangle on one shoulder. But the heir's missing, no one knows its name, sex, or hiding place, and there are whispers about assassins—"

"You speak of the distant past," Crystaviel said.

"Well, if your memory can still reach a few hours into this evening," Strider said, "I decide we should set these kids straight before life gets too complicated for me good bud. No one's home when we arrive, so we

settle in. 'Magine our surprise when you stroll through
the door. It's Old Home Week."

"Why the ride around Bordertown before you came
here?"

Strider smiled. "You're the ones playing hide-and-
seek. Just thought we'd give you a last bit of fun before
the game was over."

"Is it over?" asked Ice Hair.

Strider shrugged.

Crystaviel looked at him and said nothing, then gave
me the same treatment. She reached into her jacket
pocket, and I tensed. She pulled out a bulky leather bag
and slapped it into Orient's hand. As he began to open
its drawstrings, Crystaviel turned on her heel and left
the apartment.

"See you!" Strider called.

Ice Hair smiled at him. "Yes. You shall." Then he
followed, and the silent goons trailed him.

Orient whistled once. His palm was full of golden
coins.

"We didn't break anything," Sai said.

Tick-Tick nodded, almost disappointedly.

"We just wanted—" Sai began.

Tick-Tick said, "To show them how wrong they'd
been to suspect your friend. Which you did."

Orient looked at me. "Sorry about—" He made a circle with his hand, and I shrugged.

Sai handed two Danceland passes to Tick-Tick, who
frowned, then smiled. "Ah yes. Wild Hunt's playing
next month. Thanks."

"It's late," Strider announced.

"Early," said Orient, looking out at the lightening
sky. He looked at Tick-Tick. "French toast in the Re-
naissance?"

She shook her head, said, "Scrambled eggs at the
Hard Luck," studied us, then said, "Join us?"

"Maybe some other time," Strider said.

"On us," said Orient. "Since we inconvenienced you."

"Faerie gold," said Tick-Tick. "Have to spend it before it turns into sticks and leaves."

Almost everyone laughed: Crystaviel's gold was almost certainly good. That is, if she expected to keep a decent reputation in Bordertown.

Strider looked at Sai, who nodded and looked at me.

I smiled, shook my head, then turned my head to one side to lay it on a pillow that I made with my hands.

"Gotcha," said Orient.

"Some other time," said Tick-Tick.

We headed into the street. It wasn't dawn yet, not properly. The air was clean and damp with dew. To the east, the night sky was rimmed in a paler shade of blue. I heard birds calling, "Wake up, wake up, it's a beautiful day; let's all go out and eat some worms."

"Need a ride?" asked Sai.

I shook my head. I love Bordertown in the early morning, when it belongs to the few who are still awake or just rising, and Elsewhere was only a ten- or fifteen-minute walk away.

Sai told Strider, "You can drive the Batcycle."

He blinked and stared at her.

"It's cold. 'Sides, this way I can snuggle." She got on behind him and gave him a tight squeeze. "Scratch the paint, you die horribly."

Tick-Tick told Orient, "Don't get any ideas about who drives *this* bike."

Orient hopped into the sidecar. "At this time of the morning? It's a perfect vacuum up there."

I looked at my hands. At times like these, I wanted a chalkboard. I just lifted one hand to wave.

As Strider started the Batcycle, Sai called, "Hey, Wolfboy, there's someone at the University Without

Floors teaching sign. I was thinking about going. Interested?"

I nodded.

"Good. Florida said she thought it'd be fun. We could talk even when the music's turned to eleven."

Strider said, "Be careful." He meant that Crystaviel was going to wonder why her efforts to track the heir kept bringing her into contact with me, and now with Strider, too.

Everyone waved, and they disappeared around the corner. The smell of their exhausts dissipated. Since their engines were only cranked loud enough to warn people in the street that they were coming, that sound faded as quickly as the smell. The city was entirely my own.

The Mock Avenue Tower chimed the hour, which didn't mean anything—it rang thirteen. I wasn't the only one up. A skateboarder rolled by and nodded cautiously at me. Far away, someone was playing the violin, some energetic and melancholy Flash Girls' tune.

A couple of blocks from Orient's pad, six or seven dogs came out of an alley. Dogs never know what to make of me. I held out my hand, and they sniffed it, and sniffed the rest of me, deciding I was okay. I was down on all fours, horsing (dogging?) around with them, when I heard a bike approach.

Taz said, "Should've known. Leader of the pack."

I stood up. The dogs circled me, wondering if their new friend had an enemy.

"Saw a whole bunch of elves leave the Finder's place. They didn't look happy."

I shook my head and smiled.

"They going to be after you anymore?"

I lifted both hands in helplessness, then turned my head slowly from side to side.

"Just 'cause you're different." She spit to one side.

I shrugged.

"That elf and that halfie stick up for you?"

I nodded.

"Good." One of the dogs, some kind of shepherd mix, was by her leg, so she patted it, then laughed. "Those damn Torches never did catch up to me. I led 'em down by the river and ditched 'em."

I stepped closer and gripped her shoulder once, then released it.

"Listen," she said. "You want to go somewhere?"

Maybe that didn't mean anything more than it seemed to. That was one thought that sped through my mind, and another was, Yes, I would love to go somewhere private with this strong girl and do my very best to see that one thing leads to another.

Then I told myself I was reading too much into her question. I was reading *everything* into it. I thought she couldn't be interested in me since I was a wolf kid. I thought she was interested in me *because* I was a wolf kid. I thought I could put up with that.

And then I remembered Florida. She may not have made it back to Elsewhere. And Sparks was expecting to know how my evening ended, and Mickey would probably be worried, and Goldy, who hadn't seen Mickey for a week, not since he moved out, might be waiting up at Elsewhere for news.

Taz said, "Or maybe just a ride home?"

I nodded. She gave me a small smile, and I realized that there had been a lot in her first question, but the answer I had given her was okay, too.

The first thing I noticed when we got close to Elsewhere was the smell of noodles baking at Wu's Worldly Emporium. That always makes me feel like I'm coming home. When we turned the last corner, I saw the row of shops. A light burned in Ms. Wu's, but the bookstore and the Gallery of Fine and Not-So-Fine Art were still dark.

As I hopped off her bike, Taz said, "I'd say be good, but I guess you are. If you feel like being bad sometime, look me up."

I grinned and waved as she rode away, and I thought, This is all right. We can be friends. I like that.

I knocked very lightly on the front door, rapping out the secret rhythm to let me through Elsewhere's magical security system, then reversed the rhythm to start it up again once I was inside. Neither of the cats came to meet me; the cynical little fakers knew it was too early for me to feed them. I walked through the canyons of bookshelves, and at the stairs, I thought, You simple-minded git, you should've taken up Taz's offer. What are you, scared?

And I answered: Nah, I'm not scared. I just don't want to be pitied.

It seemed a good-enough answer. I removed my sneakers and padded down into the basement. Halfway down the steps, as my feet entered the dim illumination from a night-light, I heard, "Woofboy?"

Before I could try to say anything, the kid had dumped poor Doodle off her lap and charged from her cot into my arms. The cat calmly curled up in the warm spot where Florida had been. After one of her stomach-crushing hugs, Florida said, "Sparks an' I got back fine. Everything's okay?"

I nodded.

"Good." She giggled. "You go to sleep now." She dove back into bed, scaring Doodle again. "G'night, Woofboy. I love you."

I tapped my chest, then pointed at her. Turning away, I frowned. I wouldn't have woken her if she'd been asleep, but finding her awake made me realize I wanted to tell someone about the night. Yet she was right, we were both tired. I could write a proper account for her the next morning, if she was still curious. And if she had some secret, I could learn it the next morning, too.

I climbed upstairs, thinking, Of course, the kid's okay—you knew you could trust Sparks to deliver her safely. You should've gone with Taz. So what if it turned out she was using you? Couldn't you use each other?

The living room was dark. Something smelled odd, but then I recognized Goldy's and Sparks's scents. I imagined them up here, having tea with Mickey and worrying about how I was doing, and I felt a little better.

I saw light under Mickey's door. Thinking to tell her I was back, I stepped up to it and raised a fist to knock. Then I realized that Goldy and Mickey had resolved their differences, at least for the time being, and I moved away quickly, a little pleased and a little embarrassed.

I started to put my sneakers back on, because I owed Sparks the story of the night. She'd probably have coffee and freshly baked bread. If her housemates were up, she and Jeff and King O'Beer and I could sit around until my eyes were so red that I had to trek home for vampire sleep. It would not be a bad end for the night.

I decided to hit the bathroom first. There, I washed my hands and my face, and since they had served their purpose, I washed off the three marks that Sai had drawn on my shoulder during our only stop on the B-town Tour. I dragged a brush across most of the hair on my head and the backs of my hands, then stepped into the hall, ready for the last trip of a very long night.

The door to my room was ajar. A light flickered within it.

I remembered Strider's warning about Crystaviel, and then Florida's giggle. Did I want to disturb Goldy and Mickey when the only thing inside might be one of Florida's crayon drawings? Did I want to walk boldly in when the room might be packed full of some kind of ninja elf assassins?

Telling myself that Crystaviel wasn't going to do anything horrible to me just 'cause I'd made her look stupid, and almost believing that, I touched the door. It swung back, slowly, silently. I peeked around the frame.

Sparks was lying on her stomach on my futon, reading her copy of Oscar Wilde by candlelight. Her jacket was draped over her shoulders like a shawl. Her green-and-yellow dress clashed with my purple-and-pink quilt, but I noticed that less than the way the thin cotton draped her legs. Her feet were bare; her blue cowboy boots stood beside my desk chair.

I wanted to watch her, 'cause she looked so peaceful, and I wanted time to unravel my suddenly quite tangled emotions. But she gasped and sat up. "Ron, you're back! Mickey said I could nap in here if I really wanted to wait for you. But I couldn't sleep. Do you mind?"

I waved one hand in a very cool dismissing gesture.

"I'm glad." She plucked a spiral-bound notebook and a fountain pen from the floor beside the futon and held them out. "Tell me about it?"

I took the pen and paper and tried to think of how to begin. When I looked at her, wondering how much I could tell her, she said, "You don't have to."

I snorted a dog laugh and wrote, EVER NOTICE WHEN PEOPLE SAY "YOU DON'T HAVE TO," YOU DO?

"Not if you don't want to."

SOMETIMES YOU DON'T KNOW YOU WANT TO UNTIL YOU'RE TOLD YOU DON'T HAVE TO.

"Mmm. How's that apply here?"

I shrugged my frustration. She laughed like that was hysterical, and I laughed 'cause she was laughing. She didn't seem to mind hyena chuckles.

"What don't you want to have to do?"

EVERYTHING.

She laughed again. "Ooh, rebellious youth. That's too easy, Ron. That's why you came to B-town."

OH.

"So, what don't you want to have to do?"

PRETEND.

She almost gasped, she looked so shocked. "You don't have to pretend with me!" There was the slightest pause before she added, "With any of your friends!"

I KNOW.

She leaned closer to me. "So, what do you pretend with us?"

I waved one hand: *Drop it.*

"No, really."

THAT I DON'T FEEL LIKE A FREAK.

She stared at that. "What'd you feel like before you came to B-town?"

I smiled. TOUCHÉ.

"What're you pretending now?"

NOTHING.

"Excellent." She took my hand. "That true?"

No.

She laughed. "And?"

Sometimes you have to take chances. I'M PRETENDING IT'S NO BIG DEAL TO FIND SOMEONE IN MY BED.

She said quietly, "I'm pretending it's no big deal to be in someone's bed."

I looked out the window. It was definitely dawn. A couple of pigeons sat on the opposite rooftop, as if they expected us to entertain them.

"What is it?"

That was one of my brother's bits of advice: Sometimes you have to take chances. I touched the back of her hand. She put her other hand over the furry back of mine and tilted her head up a little, as if to see me better. Her lips parted a little, as if to speak.

Look, our first kiss wouldn't win any awards, okay? It took me a little practice to figure out what to do, but it really wasn't all that difficult. I began to fumble at her clothing, and it seemed like my fingers didn't work nearly as well as they usually did.

"Wait," she whispered. "There's no hurry."

I wanted to say, *I know that*, but I hadn't been acting like I knew that. I'd been acting like a little kid with a new present. My brother had given me another bit of advice that I'd never had a chance to use: When the time comes, don't worry about your fun. Worry about the other person's fun. It's twice as good that way.

(The rest of this chapter is in parentheses so you can skip it, if you want. All it's about is sex. It's totally gratuitous and has nothing to do with the struggle over Faerie's heir. You can safely skip to the beginning of the next chapter, honest.

(It has occurred to me that I should stop with our first kiss, then start the next sentence, "Afterward—" Or maybe I should write one of those vague scenes where Sparks says nothing but "Yes yes oh yes" and no one's quite sure what's happening, including the writer.

(There are at least three reasons to avoid writing about sex. It's embarrassing, and the act of sex is always less important than the consequences of sex, and if this is ever published in the World, there may be people who'll want to censor it.

(But one thing my favorite writers do is tell me that I'm not alone when I feel stupid and awkward and inept. So I'll try to return the favor: If you're about to have sex for the first time, or for the first time with someone new, and you're a werewolf, it's okay to be embarrassed. The other person's probably embarrassed, too.

(And details are important. If I'm telling about losing my virginity—or rather, about choosing to leave my virginity behind—I should say something about what I learned. Either you'll learn something, or you'll be amused, or you'll be bored and skip to the next chapter. What's to lose?

(As for censors, they're insane. You can't guess what little thing might set them off. They believe people have to be guarded from knowledge. Yeah, right. Talk to some of the pregnant runaways at the Free Clinic about what ignorance did for them. Censors don't realize that if you want people to stay out of a room, they need to know what's in the room and why it might be a bad idea to go in.

(Hmm. After all that, you're going to expect extremely explicit details. Tough. Here's what you get:

(I remembered that ears were supposed to be an erogenous area, so I licked Sparks's. She laughed, saying, "That tickles!"

(Feeling like a total loser, I stopped immediately. Sparks looked at me, then said, "Hey, it's okay. I like it." She smiled. "This is supposed to be fun, y'know."

(I hadn't known that. In movies, people roll around desperately without talking, like they're doing something they have to but not something they're enjoying. Relieved and grateful, I nuzzled her ear and under her jaw, and she laughed a little and began to make a cat's sound of contentment: "Mmmm." And when I paid attention to what inspired that sound, she added things like "Oh, my," and "That's nice."

(As clothes and sheets became a tangle around us, I began to think less about Sparks and more about what I wanted to do next. Suddenly she was pushing against my chest, saying, "Whoa, whoa, whoa."

(I didn't know what I'd done, or hadn't done. I sat back, feeling angry because I didn't want to stop, and stupid because I didn't know what I'd done wrong, and disappointed because this was all such an awkward and oddly unromantic process.

(Sparks said, "I'm not, you know, I didn't—" And then she pursed her lips and said, "If we're going to go any further, I want you wearing a rubber."

(I stared. None of the things I wanted to do right then included hunting for a funny-looking synthetic sheath and putting it on.

(Sparks said gently, "Neither of us needs a kid. And

we both think we're disease free, but one of us might be wrong. It's for both of us."

(Then I remembered, and I grinned as I reached into my jacket pocket.

("Gee," Sparks said, "We'll have to thank Gorty." I looked at the rubber, and Sparks said, "What?"

(I tossed it to her. It was no longer a useful trade item: The wrapper was cracked and stiff from age. Sparks shook her head. "Poor Gorty. If he'd learn to be nicer to people—" She tossed the rubber at the trash can beside my desk.

(My big opportunity seemed to be over. I decided that was a relief, since the mood was completely broken. Then Sparks reached into her jacket and came out with a foil-wrapped disk of her own. I was astonished at how quickly the mood came back.)

(Afterward—hey, I'll leave some details for you virgins to discover and you nonvirgins to wonder about—I remembered to hold on to the base of the rubber when I withdrew so it didn't fall off, and I threw it away because you're not supposed to use them twice. Getting the textbook details of sex is easy. But textbooks don't tell you what to do after you've had sex and you're filled with doubts about whether any of it went like it was supposed to.

(Sparks, curled up against me, draped an arm over my chest and said, "Mmm."

(I said, "Mmm," too, because she seemed to expect that. It had all been messier and more awkward than I'd expected, with arms and legs getting in the way, and almost everything I had tried had required fine-tuning by Sparks. It hadn't occured to me that movie love scenes are as carefully choreographed and rehearsed as dances. Now that we were done, I wanted to move away from Sparks and lie perfectly still until I felt dry or fell asleep.

(She hugged me tighter. "Some guys are too insecure to just lie there and hold you afterward."

(I gave a little shrug. It *was* nice lying there with someone I liked beside me. My left arm tingled as it fell asleep under her, but I didn't want to move it. The sun was bright outside our window. The pigeons had gotten bored and flown away.

(Careful not to disturb Sparks, I reached for my notebook, propped it on my knee, and wrote, THANK YOU.

("No, no, my dear Alphonse," she said. "Thank *you*."

(I tapped what I'd written. She tapped it, too, and then we engaged in a flurry of jabs at those two words, until our fingers linked, and then we were holding hands. Which was nice, but I couldn't write, so I let go and wrote, I REALLY LIKE YOU.

(Her face became still, which I had not expected. "Is that followed by a 'but'? I'm used to it, you know."

(I wrote, STATEMENT OF FACT.

("Good." She moved her hand through the hair on my chest. "I really like you, too. As you might've guessed."

(WHAT'LL THIS DO TO OUR FRIENDSHIP?

("You want to pretend this didn't happen?"

(I shook my head.

("Then that's a remarkably stupid question."

(I wrote, A BOY QUESTION?

(She laughed. "Exactly. Males and females are alike in every important way, except guys are idiots."

(I kissed her, then wrote, APPRECIATIVE IDIOTS.

(She said, "Well, the best of them are." Then she reached across the futon for her jacket. I figured she was cold, until she said, "Guess what a girl who's prepared carries at least two of?")

CHAPTER SIX
Fast Forward #1

If you want, you can skip this whole chapter and pretend it consists of a single sentence: Time passed.

There's nothing in here about Crystaviel's hunt for Elfland's missing heir. (I ask you, how many writers provide this kind of service for their readers? I sure hope you didn't steal this book.) For the first month after Orient's attempt to find Florida, I watched for Crystaviel in every dark place, and I thought every unexpected sound was announcing her return. In the second month, I began to relax: Maybe she had given up. In the third month, I may have been more vigilant than ever before; I decided Crystaviel would never give up, and she was only staying away to get us all to relax our guard.

I asked Strider when we'd know Florida was safe.

He said, "Never."

I wrote, THANKS HEAPS.

He said, "When Florida is an adult in the Elflands, she'll be as safe as anyone can make her." I asked him when we'd know that Crystaviel had given up. He said that question had the same answer as the first one.

By the fourth month, we had all relaxed our guard. We knew that Crystaviel would always be searching, and we knew that an elf's sense of urgency is much more leisurely than any human's, but we relaxed anyway. We had to. It's called getting on with life.

Mickey and Goldy got back together and stayed back together. They fought some more, of course. Given their personalities, I guess that was inevitable.

Mickey's obsession with being independent must have been tied to losing both her arms in a farm accident. When she was nineteen, she came to Bordertown against her parents' wishes, using money she'd earned herself, with no more help than a kid who agreed to be her hands for six months in exchange for a one-way ticket to B-town and two meals a day. By the end of the six months, the kid had gone back to the World, but Mickey had started Elsewhere, B-town's finest bookstore, in my not-so-humble opinion.

Goldy's obsession with independence had something to do with being picked on for being fat and weak when he was a boy. So he'd started working out, and when he wasn't exercising, he read: He'd decided to be strong in every way he could. When he was seventeen, his mother expected him to join the army and be prepared to kill people he didn't know for reasons he didn't understand. He discovered he was strong enough to live with her disapproval, and he came to Bordertown.

I wasn't going to ask either of them for details about what went wrong and what went right between them. I was just glad they decided they could be independent together.

Sai and Florida and I took sign language at the University Without Floors. Sai dropped out after learning a few basics, but Florida and I kept it up. In the evenings, when we came home, we'd teach Mickey what we'd learned—she didn't need hands to read us, after all. To my amazement, Goldy started taking lessons too. He said it was to talk with deaf customers at Danceland.

After a couple of months, I moved out of Elsewhere. That wasn't an easy decision, but I decided I wanted a place of my own. Since I kept working part-time at the bookstore, I still saw a lot of Mickey, Goldy, and Florida.

The place of my own was an office in an abandoned factory. The steel doors had been locked when Faerie returned, and never reopened. A few looters had found their way in the same way I did: going through a skylight that you reached by climbing to the top of an oak tree, then tossing a rope or jumping about fifteen feet. You got out by reversing the process. If you missed the tree, it'd be ugly.

I lived in an enormous room where supervisors and accountants and secretaries must've watched huge machines work forty feet beneath them. I spent a day shoving all of the desks, chairs, shelves, and modular walls to the back wall. Since I never figured out an easy way to get a futon in there, I made a bed of blankets in the center of that room where I could lie, surrounded by windows. Though the panes were thick with dust on the inside and dirt and pigeon droppings on the outside, I could look out at Bordertown, the Mad River, or the woods of the Nevernever whenever I wanted to.

I also joined a band. Sergeant Furry and His Howling Commandos—hey, I didn't name it—released one tune on the B-town club circuit. "Music of the Night" was mostly drums, a little strings, and me making the sounds I make best. We were a novelty act, I wasn't very musical, and we were all egomaniacs who couldn't see that a band whose main strengths were visual had *muchas problemas* in a place where film and video aren't dependable. But it was fun practicing our tunes and planning what to tell the press when we were megastars.

The Howling Commandos and the sign classes kept me away from Sparks. She wanted to take sign with me, and I said I didn't want her to do anything just for my sake, and she asked why it was okay for my other friends to do stuff for my sake, and I walked out on her.

Sometime later, she suggested we could find a flat to share, and I said I wasn't ready to make a commitment to anyone, and she said, "Who's asking you to commit? We're spending all of our free time under one roof; why shouldn't it be *our* roof?" I got a book and didn't talk to her for a couple of hours. She didn't bring it up again.

We finally realized that if we wanted to stay friends, we'd better stop being lovers. That was my decision. I felt very mature.

The Commandos opened for several hot bands at Danceland and Homegirl's; we knew we were going to be B-town's biggest, baddest band. After breaking up with Sparks, I slept with a couple of groupies, and while I didn't like either of them very much, they were real, honest-to-God groupies, even if they were rather sad kids who measured their worth by the fame of the people they slept with.

Right after "Music of the Night" came out, you couldn't walk into a Soho club without hearing the seedy, or walk down a street without passing some kid gripping an impression ball (the magical equivalent of wearing headphones—the ball feeds the music to you through your skin). I think we were the hottest band in B-town for three and a half days. Then Wild Hunt released a new song, and we were old news.

Our main singer said if we were serious, we'd make a tour into the World, where some lame band's lame cover of "Music of the Night" was white hot, and bootlegs of our seedy were making lots of other people rich.

I told her if I left the Borderlands, I'd be human again and we'd lost our novelty shtick, or I'd be your standard run-on-four-legs-and-eat-his-own-feces lapdog. She thought it was worth the risk—I could wear a fur suit if I turned human, and a singing dog would have loads of novelty value in the World. She said I could be Wolf the Wonder Dog.

I just don't have a show-biz soul. I walked.

By then, Sparks was living with Milo Chevrolet. I visited her once and asked if we could get back together. She said she couldn't do that to Milo, and they were real good for each other, and I'd been right all along, we should stay friends. I cried, and she held me and cried, and eventually we gave each other very chaste kisses and went our separate ways.

But we did stay friends.

After that, I had a short involvement with Vangogo, a deaf painter from the sign class. I think that didn't work because we didn't trust each other. Sometimes I was afraid my only attraction was that I'd been famous for a week, and sometimes that it was that I was a freak and it didn't really matter whose mind was behind the Wolf's eyes. Vangogo was convinced that a hearing person could never truly understand a deaf one. I was going through a cynical phase then. I answered, WHO CAN TRULY UNDERSTAND ANYONE? ISN'T IT OK TO HAVE FUN? Looking back now, I see that affair was doomed. It still hurt when it ended.

There was also a night when I ran into Taz at Homegirl's. We hung out together, we danced, but nothing happened. The night that she helped fool Crystaviel had probably been my one chance with her. If we'd slept together, I doubt we would've lasted a weekend.

Besides the relationship with Sparks, the best part of my life during that winter was my relationship with *Surplus Art*, one of Bordertown's homemade art mags. The publisher-editor was a girl named Jiff who had a small, hand-powered press in her basement. The staff was always changing; I played poetry editor for a couple months.

Through *Surplus Art*, Orient and I began to hang out. He wrote essays and short stories about life in B-town. I mostly wrote poems, but I was working on a novel about an elf detective that Orient thought was hilarious. I never told him it wasn't supposed to be funny.

Our friendship grew from our knowledge of what it's like to have people think we're strange. He'd discovered his finding talent in the World. It'd scared people there. Teen Wolf had an advantage that Li'l Finder never did: People see me and know I'm different, then they get to know me, and I'm just a guy who goes through a lot of shampoo.

But in the World, people saw Orient and thought he was like them. Then they learned he had something that they didn't, and they felt he'd betrayed them. You never learn until too late that everyone's passing for normal.

Orient, Florida, and I made a day trip into the Nevernever once, to lie by a lake and swim. Florida told us the waves were calling our names, and Orient laughed. And as he did, I saw him looking at her bare left shoulder.

Ms. Wu's spell was working, but even if it hadn't been, I wouldn't have worried about him. He said, "You're lucky, having a sister." For the briefest second, I wanted to scrawl in the sand, DIDN'T I TELL YOU I STARTED LIFE HUMAN? ISN'T IT OBVIOUS TO ANYONE WHO LOOKS THAT SHE'S ELF? Then I saw his smile. I looked at Florida running toward us with a turtle in both hands, and I nodded. Yes. I was lucky.

I gave up on love after my second failure. I didn't give up on being in love: I had crushes on Sai, who was only interested in Strider; and Tick-Tick, who was only interested in machinery; and Jiff, who wasn't going to sleep with anyone she was working with " 'cause you can't let good sex confuse you about good art." Heck, I had crushes on every talented female musician in town. At least I had plenty of subjects for my poems.

Sorry if I sound like I'm whining. I'm not. It was a good time. I had friends and a family in B-town. That meant I shared a lot of pain, like when Wiseguy's second pregnancy ended in a miscarriage, and when Florida fell and needed fifteen stitches at the Free Clinic.

I also shared a lot of joy. When Florida was Puck in the Ho Street Players' *A Midsummer Night's Dream*, Goldy, Mickey, Strider, Sai, and I sat grinning through the thing like opium eaters.

I kept busy. I clerked at the bookstore, and I filled in at Danceland sometimes as a bouncer or a bottle washer. I helped do almost everything on *Surplus Art*, from laying out pages to running the press to selling copies on the street. Sometimes I'd go into the Padded Cell Studios when a band needed prime howling on a song. After I started doing music reviews in *Surplus Art*, half the clubs in town let me in free.

But I also had a way to escape when life got too busy. I made several trips into the Nevernever for Ms. Wu, hunting herbs, artifacts, and oddities.

Those trips always began the same way. After checking with Ms. Wu for last-minute changes in her shopping list, I'd say good-bye to the Elsewhere gang. Mickey usually told me to take a book she'd read recently. If Goldy was there, he'd give me a loaf of bread or a jar of vegetables from his garden that was "going to go bad if somebody didn't eat it," then tell me to watch out for wild elves. Once he added, "Especially the female ones," and winked, but Mickey kneed him in the butt and he never did that again.

Florida always followed me out into the street and signed, *You have big fun.* I'd back away and sign, *No, you have big fun.* She'd sign, *No, you have big fun.* And we'd repeat that at each other as I walked backward down the street, each time adding stress to a new word and putting more stress on the ones we'd already emphasized until our arms were flying furiously as we tried to see who could have the last and grandest fare-well before I turned the corner onto Ho Street.

I should tell you about the Nevernever. Problem is, time and space are strange near the Border. The lands change as you go through them, and so do the seasons. You might walk from summer to fall or from desert lands to ice fields by going around a hill or through a clump of brush. Once I was gone for weeks from the city and came back to find that only a few days had passed there. Once I was away for six days and found a month had passed in B-town.

I made maps during my first explorations, but they never did me any good on later trips. It's as if the land-marks move or change, as if space and time are as whimsical as magic is here. Maybe the gods of Faerie have incredibly stupid senses of humor.

The Nevernever was scary at first, I admit, and it continued to be scary at times. Most good things are worth a little fear.

Before Leda turned me into Wolfboy, I hadn't thought much about nature. (Okay, there's a long list of things I didn't think about back then.) Now I began to wonder about my place in the world. No answers, mind you, or I'd write them here. But I found I loved running through the woods and swimming in the lakes. I felt I was part of the natural world, and the natural world was part of me.

Which is enough simpleminded philosophy for this chapter, and maybe for the whole book. The Heir of Faerie Affair resumes on the very next page, shortly af-ter my return from one of those trips.

CHAPTER SEVEN
Danceland Blood

It was springtime in Bordertown, I had just made a very profitable run into the Nevernever, and Wild Hunt was finally going to give their hungry fans a live gig after canceling three previous engagements. I sauntered down Ho Street, ready to howl.

"Wolfboy!"

I started grinning before I looked. At the curb near Danceland, Orient was sitting in his usual place in the sidecar. He was smoking an herbal cig that smelled of coltsfoot and comfrey. The tips of his dark hair had been dyed red since I last saw him: He was out to steal hearts tonight.

I didn't see Tick-Tick. Since she'd parked across from Snappin' Wizard's Surplus and Salvage—"More bang for the buck, more spell for the silver, more toys for the trade"—it didn't take an Elflands magician to guess where she'd gone.

Orient was talking with a quiet kid I hadn't seen before. Given the extremes of dress in any Danceland crowd, this small girl should've been invisible, but she wasn't. She wore gray denim jeans and jacket, and a black cap with a gray pheasant feather in its band. The clothes were too new, and she didn't know how to wear them like they didn't matter. I smelled runaway. I wondered whose floor Orient was offering her.

"Wolfboy, I'd like you to meet Caramel."

She offered her hand as if I'd bite it off but that'd be all right if it made her part of B-town. I clasped the hand and smiled.

"Pleased to meet you," she whispered, then looked at Orient. "Guess I should go . . ."

He nodded. "You don't want to miss the first song."

As Caramel edged into the Danceland crowd, Orient said, "Lord, Lord. Perfectly nice Friday night, and *I* have to get pinned down in the street by some poor little thing with the dust of the World still behind her ears."

I laughed and patted his head.

"Oh, go chase cats. I even gave her a name, for crying out loud."

I gave him the You-know-you-want-me-to-ask look.

"Well, what was I supposed to do? Camilla," he muttered. I thought it was pretty, but Orient added, "Lordy," and he was probably right. Your name's part of the first impression you make. Some names can destroy your life if you're not strong enough, and *Camilla* sounded like one of those. Whatever his motive, Orient had given Caramel a much easier identity to form in town.

Which made me remember running off to B-town. I'd wanted to call myself Starbuck, like a sci-fi hero with a blaster on his hip. Mickey had warned me in time. It was amusing to wonder if Ron Starbuck would have ended up as Wolfboy.

Orient tapped out a second cig. I shrugged and took it. If I got hooked, I could always have the fun of quitting. Orient lit it without saying anything; the Wolf's hands are stronger than those of the kid who wanted to be Ron Starbuck, but they aren't as nimble.

"You been out of town?"

I grinned, drew a bulky leather wallet from my back pocket, and flipped it open: twenty-two perfectly preserved four-leaf clovers. See 'em and weep.

"Oh, my stars and garters." He sighed. "Well, if I need to borrow money I'll sure 'nuff come to you. You gonna sell 'em inside?" He pointed to Danceland.

I flipped the wallet shut and nodded as I stuffed it into my back pocket.

"Offer one to Goldy. He's going to need it."

I gave him the high eyebrows.

He explained, "I just sent that runaway to him."

I laughed and shook my head. A couple of Packers glanced my way; I suppose there'll always be people wondering when I'll turn rabid.

"I don't suppose you'd trade one of those little green beauties for the latest copy of *Stick Wizard*, would you?"

I grinned: *Dream on.*

He pulled an issue of the mag out of the sidecar's map pocket. On the cover, stick figures flickered in faerie-dust ink: The Wizard was flying off a beat-up cycle that'd hit a wire held by Tater and Bert, the cigar-smoking elf delinquents. Tater and Bert are great. Villains are always more interesting than heroes.

I forced myself to shake my head. With luck, someone would give me a copy. Orient smiled and put it away. He has a sadistic streak.

"Here's a fine convocation of riffraff," Tick-Tick announced behind us.

My Tick-Tick crush clicked in when I heard her voice. Her short hair was dyed dandelion-yellow, with a lock in front that hung to her eyebrows. The evening's gear consisted of a long gray leather coat, matching tight pants, low red boots, a charcoal-gray suit coat, a white shirt, a red tie, and three garnet earrings in one ear. Poor Caramel—this was the woman she wanted to be.

"Boil me in lead," Orient said blandly. "She's back before morning!"

"Oh, shut up. Hi, Lobo."

I grinned. (See the importance of names? *Lobo*. It's got dignity.)

Tick-Tick loaded a paper-covered bundle into her bike's top cargo box. "Goodies?" Orient asked.

"Well, not that you'd think so. A little replacement stock, wire connectors, and that sort of thing. And a toy or two."

"Or eight or ten."

She shrugged. "So, anyone here want to rock the moon down?"

"Me! Me!" Orient leaped from the sidecar, and I gave my best party howl. As Orient checked his hair in the bike's rearview mirror, Tick-Tick said, "Yes, yes, you're just breathtaking. Come along."

The crowd inside was even thicker than the crowd outside. Maybe that was possible because the laws of physics aren't consistent in B-town. The stage lights were off, but the band's equipment was up and waiting, and the spellboxes powering the amps gave a steady red glow. Tick-Tick headed for the pool tables, and Orient and I squeezed up to the bar.

Valda was setting bottles of beer on the counter three at a time to meet the demand. Orient yelled over the din of conversation and recorded music, "Val, precious Val, did the coffee come in yet?"

She looked at him and started to shake her head, but as his face fell, she smiled and said, "You're a lucky boy." He blew her a kiss, and she headed to the end of the bar to pour a cup.

She set it in front of Orient, and a bottle of beer in front of me. Orient pried a silver stud out of his wristband and said, "That's for both."

I glared at him; I had trading stock, which wasn't always the case.

He nodded toward my wallet of clovers. "So pay me back when you've made your killing in good luck."

Orient had a major coffee jones. He held the cup under his nose and savored the fumes. Since this was one of the times when coffee was rare in town, I forgave him.

A dark hand tapped his shoulder, interrupting his bliss. A familiar voice said, "Watch that stuff, young man."

Goldy was in uniform, the standard green long-sleeved Danceland T-shirt, which he wore that night with silver-green trousers and gleaming gray pointed-toe shoes. The shirt doesn't scream *Bouncer*, since you can buy them at the bar, but when he's wearing one and makes a request of a customer, it gives him an extra degree of authority.

"Goldy. What it is. Watch what stuff?"

He narrowed his eyes at the coffee cup. "That's a dangerous intoxicant, Orient, my friend. I fear you may get high as the Tooth and tear the place up before the night is out."

"Call me Mr. Coffee Nerves."

"Or perhaps I might toss you out now and save myself a bit of trouble. It'd be no more than you deserve."

"Me? Oh, you got my present, then."

"If you mean your runaway, yes, you snot-nosed little mutant, I did. What am I supposed to do with her?"

"Talk her out of doing all the stupid things we did at her age."

"Except for continuing my acquaintance with you, I've never done anything stupid. I assume you Found her?" Something in Goldy's voice, a pause, a bit of stress, let us know that "Found" had a capital *F*.

"Course not. Though I suppose you could say I found her nickname." Goldy frowned, so Orient added, "Well, she was complaining about her real one. I guess it worked as well as a direct request."

The ceiling lights fired up in bursts of light, electrical and magical, forming alien symbols that clearly meant, *You're born to have fun; start now.* "Back to the fray," Goldy said, then signed to me, *Enjoy*, and moved into the crowd.

The stage lights came up. Dancer walked to the center microphone, and Orient nodded at me. (When Dancer introduces the band, it's something special. And when she saunters slow and pleased, making us wait, you know it's something extra-special.) I gave Orient the thumbs-up, and we charged up front toward the stage. Along with half of B-town.

Orient and I made it to the middle of the dance floor before the press of bodies became an impenetrable wall.

Dancer waited for silence, then brought her lean hands up, paused, threw back her head and laughed, shaking her curly ponytail of black hair, and finally said, "I give up. Ladies and gentlemen, Wild Hunt!"

What more did she need to say? All of Soho had been hearing their recordings for months. At long last, we were going to get the real thing, to finally see the people who made the music we loved.

An elf in white leather leggings and a white sleeveless tunic ran onstage. She was paler than Strider or Tick-Tick or any elf I'd seen. Her eyes were coins of polished silver. Her hair, the color of milk lit by moonlight, had been cut close on the left side and lengthened as it circled her head. Her left eye was daubed in blue paint that ran from her nose into her short white hair.

Add another to my list of crushes.

While the rest of the band, all elves and halfies, took

their places, the elf in white slung a Fender Witchfire bass over her shoulder. Faerie dust in the paint job made star formations that went supernova within seconds. Light flared from silver rings on her fingers as she slammed down on the bass strings.

Everyone recognized "Shake the Wall Down." Everyone screamed. Everyone danced.

(For you music mavens, some tech specs: The keyboard player had a Fairlight Sorcerer. The lead guitarist played an eight-stringed custom ax with ease, at least partly because he had six fingers on each hand. The drummer bopped around like a madman, but his beat stayed steady and complex. As for the halfie on elfpipes, well, I wished there were some elves fresh out of the Elflands to hear it, 'cause they would've thought it sacrilege. I thought it genius.)

My hand was grabbed by an elf with green hair, a sweet grin, and a red jewel on one cheek. You got to live. I picked her up by her waist, whirled her once, and we dove into the crowd to see if we could dance on the ceiling.

Sometime during a wild, mad version of "Heart's Desire," I spotted Orient dancing with Sai. She was in a Danceland shirt, too, which meant she must have been on break. Strider stood near the bar, but I don't think he saw me. His eyes kept panning from the crowd to the band to Sai.

Someone waved—okay, lots of people waved, but I spotted a hand and saw it was attached to King O'Beer, who was dancing with Jeff. They drove their fists into the air in time to the tune, and so did I. I signed, *Flying!* and the King signed, *Yes!*

Wild Hunt moved into "Running on the Border" without a pause. The crowd quieted, but no one left the dance floor. Everyone was swaying in place and singing along. The halfie on elfpipes stopped playing to lead the crowd in double handclaps like on the album.

Then the crowd rippled because of a sudden intrusion: Across the dance floor strode an Elflands elf in an odd seventeenth-century brocade coat that kept changing color and pattern. His pale hair was pulled back in a braid that hung to his waist.

I moved toward Orient and Sai in time to hear Sai say, "My, my. Weeds of Elfland he doth wear."

Orient kept a grip on her arm. "Calm down, he hasn't done anything yet."

"Couldn't I just warn him a little?"

"No."

I suppose she sounds like a madwoman when I record her words without her tone of voice, but Sai's hatred of elves was mostly a joke that we all shared with her. We watched the elf in brocade stalk to the edge of the stage, but we didn't know there'd be trouble until he shouted something Elvish, maybe a name.

Wild Hunt kept playing, but you could tell they weren't happy. When the Elflander screamed and pounded his fist on the stage, the singer hit a jarring chord on her bass, then stopped playing. The rest of the band let the song flop about for a couple of seconds and die. Sai began forcing herself into the crowd.

The singer clicked off her mike. In the silence, probably half the club could still hear her. "Leave me alone," she said in a fainter version of the other's Elflands accent.

The elf in brocade balled his fists and said something else, even more angrily.

The singer answered, "No! I told you no. I am not—I *will* not go."

The Elflander said something more, including the Elvish words for *family* and *Faerie*. From what I could tell, he wanted her to come back with him, he wanted her to come back now, it was important, and her life in Bordertown wasn't. Which must've really endeared him to her.

She turned away, as if to leave, then turned back. "Are you, now?" Whatever he thought of himself, she thought very little of him. "Well, not me. Maybe all *those* pretty sheep"—she pointed north, toward the Border—"but not me." She stalked away.

The elf grabbed the edge of the stage to jump up and follow her. Then Strider arrived as if from nowhere— he'd avoided the crowd by crossing under the stage— and grabbed the Elflander's shoulders, spun him about, and shook him by the lapels. Strider wasn't happy. I don't suppose any of us were.

Suddenly he released the Elflander and stepped back, as if he'd been hurt. They each moved sideways, measuring the space between them. Strider spoke an Elvish word, very tentatively.

The Elflander lifted his chin even higher. "You are not permitted to be free with my name."

"You're over the Border now. That name doesn't mean piss-all here." When Strider was working, he was always polite. Something was very wrong.

The Elflander sneered at Strider's shirt, which looked as if someone had driven over it several times (which, in fact, Strider had), and his raggedy blue jeans. "Little more than a savage. You embarrass all in whom the True Blood flows."

"Yeah, well, you set a fine example for the race, rich boy. Go make trouble in somebody else's place." Strider reached for the Elflander's arm.

The stranger pulled something from his coat that looked like a metal antenna, a weapon you'd expect to see in the hands of Wharf Rats and the worst of the Packers. He casually snapped it open to maybe a meter in length, and as everyone watched, slashed Strider's face.

Sai screamed something. I couldn't see Goldy, who was undoubtedly caught in the crowd like the rest of us. People backed desperately away from the Elflander, but they ran into people who were trying to get closer to see what was happening and whether they could help.

Strider fell back against the stage with blood smearing his face. The Elflander kept after him—a lunge took Strider in the arm, a swipe sliced through his T-shirt's Danceland logo.

I was part of the crowd trying to get forward, fighting the crowd trying to get away. We were like waves rolling back from the beach only to crash into new ones coming ashore, and Strider was somewhere out in the calm ocean, dying beyond our reach.

He fell to his knees, holding his bleeding chest and still raising a fist. Sai burst through the crowd then, almost within reach of the Elflander's Faerie blade. Strider gasped, "No."

Sai stopped still, to everyone's surprise, and waited for Strider's explanation. The Elflander backed away, letting the tip of his blade lower a little. Behind him, Goldy stepped from the crowd with a baseball bat dangling from his hand.

Strider shook hair out of his face. "This is an honor fight. Nobody gets this son of a bitch but me." Sai stiffened, but Strider ignored her. "And I *will.*"

The Elflander turned his back on Strider, which seemed brave, and on Sai, which seemed foolhardy. He saw Goldy and drew back, but Goldy smiled and bowed, indicating the door. The crowd made a wide path for the Elflander.

At the door, he turned. His cutter was back in his gaudy jacket. He called, "We shall continue this matter sometime soon."

"Damn straight," Strider agreed.

The Elflander smiled. "Yes. Soon." He bowed with a flourish and left.

Sai and Orient helped Strider to his feet. I opened the door to the back hall for them, and we went to Dancer's office. They set Strider on the couch, but he refused to lie down.

Strider grunted as he peeled off his shirt. Orient, wincing, filled a bowl with water at the office sink and brought it with some towels to Sai, who dabbed at Strider's face. The only sounds were our breathing and Strider's occasional burst of swearing.

Goldy leaned into the office. "Is it as bad as it looks?"

Sai frowned, but Strider shook his head. "I'll live. Mostly slashes, and none of them deep. Bastard knew what he was doing." He grinned suddenly. "When he drew on me, he'd lost it for a second. But when he started cutting . . ."

"What was that objectionable little tool of his? Any idea?"

"It's a goddam dueling toy in the Elflands," Strider replied.

Sai streaked Gold-N-Rod Creme across Strider's cuts. He swore some more, and if he hadn't been in such pain, I would've admired his inventiveness. When Sai did his face, she had to hold him by the hair to keep his head still.

The cream drew the edges of his skin together as we watched. Oil of goldenrod works best on elves and halfies. In Faerie, it probably works instantly and prevents scars from forming; that'd explain the Elflander's flawless features, given his habits. But maybe he was just very good with his fencing toy.

We weren't in Faerie: Strider was going to remember the Elflander's attack for the rest of his life. Every time he looked in the mirror, he'd see a white seam across his nose and cheek.

Goldy said, "Strider, my lad, are you quite sure you don't want me to find him, cut off his pretty braid, and see that he eats it?"

Sai said, "The hell you will! If he doesn't want to do

it himself, I'm gonna—you hear me? Oh, shit." She looked away and hit her thigh with her fist.

Strider squeezed her shoulder. "Hey, all of you, why don't you take a walk? I don't feel like talking right now. Okay?"

Sai looked up at him.

"Yeah," he said kindly, "you, too."

She nodded and stood. Orient and I were already leaving. Sai followed, closing the door, and we all stood in the hall feeling useless. I thought, *Okay, everyone's talking crazy to blow steam. It'll be all right now.*

As if to prove me right, Goldy said, "Ah, well. Friday night, a band that'll draw half of Bordertown when the word gets out, and only two of us on the floor. Nothing we can't manage, yes?"

Sai pursed her lips, then lifted one finger.

"Oh, dear," said Goldy.

"Please, Goldy? I gotta get out of here. I'd just take this out on some poor jerk out front."

He sighed. "Very well. Don't do anything foolish, will you?"

She grinned wearily and headed for the back door.

As we went back to the main room, I tapped my chest. Goldy said, "You'll fill in?"

I nodded.

Goldy shook his head. "If there's any more trouble, wait for me, hmm? You may look like Captain Fangs 'n' Fur, but you're a pussycat in real life."

I growled at him, and everyone smiled a little.

The crowd had stayed. The band was onstage, tuning up, though the singer wasn't back yet.

Tick-Tick met us by the door. "I'll buy."

Goldy said, "Thank you, but no. I'm going to need every wit I have left. And as of this moment, all my breaks are canceled." He signed, *Thanks, Big Dog,* gave us all a little salute, and left.

I glanced at his back, then headed up front to get a

shirt from Val so everyone would know I wasn't just any pushy creep, but an official pushy creep.

Jeff and King O'Beer met me while Val was finding a shirt. "How is he?" they asked, not quite in sync.

I signed, *He lives.*

The King said, "Good." Jeff added, "Thank God."

I pulled a three-by-five card from my pocket and wrote, WHY DO KIDS THINK SCARS ARE ROMANTIC?

The King whispered, "Oh."

Jeff said, "Too many pirate movies, I guess. Scars are a symbol of experience. Kids don't know they're a symbol of *bad* experience."

The King touched Jeff's lips to quiet him; he knew my question had been rhetorical. I quickly signed, *It's okay*; I knew they were each being considerate in their own ways. I wrote, IMPORTANT THING IS NO SERIOUS DAMAGE DONE.

"Yeah," said Jeff.

"How're Sai and Goldy taking it?" asked the King. For Jeff's sake, he repeated my answer aloud, "Goldy, working. Sai, not working. Both, talking like mean dogs."

Jeff said, "Why'd that guy go after the band?"

The King, as my lips, said, "After the singer. Lovers' spat?"

Jeff said, "I understand why people want to hurt other people. Who doesn't? But when they know they're going to lash out at whoever comes along, why don't they—" He shook his head. "One of those questions, eh?"

Wild Hunt played a good, long set that lasted at least two hours. It's easier working as a bouncer when there's a great band; everyone's concentrating on the music and no one's looking for something to do.

Wild Hunt did one encore, then had to come back for another even after Dancer turned the lights on. They finally got people quiet and ready to go home by doing a ballad, "Jenny on the Hill." The vocalist put down her bass and sang it, so simply that only afterward did you realize how much skill it takes to hide that much skill.

Tick-Tick helped herd people out the door. Orient was lounging near the stage, probably hoping for another chance to see the singer. Valda called his name and held out a push broom. "So, you want to stay after closing, like the employees?"

"Oh, Lord." He sighed and began sweeping. I joined him in stacking chairs, all except the one Goldy flopped into and refused to leave.

"That bad?" Orient asked.

"I doubted I'd live to see this moment. I don't suppose you'd be so kind as to fetch me a beer?"

"The dying bouncer's last request." Orient handed me the broom. I snarled at him.

When he returned with a moist bottle, Goldy said, "Seen your little runaway lately?"

I'd forgotten Caramel. Orient said, "No."

Goldy shook his head. "We may've lost her, then. I'm afraid that the events of the evening scared her away."

"Can't blame her for that."

I looked up then. Wild Hunt's singer was approaching us.

She smiled. "May I sit?" I grabbed a chair and offered it with a bow. "Thank you," she said, and I was in love again.

"You—all of you—were wonderful," Orient said. It was fun watching him try to be appreciative and aloof at the same time.

She laughed. "That's very sweet of you."

"And very true," Goldy said.

She smiled again. "We don't often play in concert, and it's difficult for me—I feel very shy in front of an audience. But everyone here was so excited, so kind to us . . ." She gestured helplessly. She wore three rings on her right hand, all of silver and sapphires, with only her middle finger and thumb bare. She wore none on her left hand; they'd have scratched the guitar neck.

Goldy said, "There was a little too much excitement tonight, I'm afraid. For which I am heartily sorry."

She looked down. "I'm sorry, too. The one who made the trouble . . . he was my fault, I think."

"Your fault?" Orient asked.

"He . . . we were lovers, for a short time. He is not willing to leave it at that. How is the fellow he hurt?"

"Healing," Goldy said, with no enthusiasm.

"None of us meant for things to occur as they did."

Goldy waved that away. "Tonight's business fit our job description."

No one spoke until Dancer and Tick-Tick came up to us. Dancer told the singer, "Good show. Damn good show." She was carrying the bag that held the night's receipts: pay time. We all returned to work.

Orient was by the door when the singer left. I'm sure that was a coincidence, uh-huh. I was far enough away that a normal human wouldn't have heard them. Maybe I should've given them some privacy, but I wasn't in the mood to let the cleaning wait.

"Will you be all right?" he asked.

"What? Oh, yes, of course. You mustn't worry about me."

"If *he's* out there waiting for Strider, you could be in trouble."

"He won't hurt me. But I'll watch for him and be careful. You're very kind. Perhaps I'll see you again?"

"I'd like that. People around here usually know where I am."

"But who would I ask them for?"

"My name's Orient."

"Orient. And mine is Linden." She touched his hand again, then slipped into the night.

He leaned against the door and watched her go. I grinned when he met my eyes. He walked over. "I was only asking if she'd be all right."

I gave him a blast of the coyote giggles, and he blushed.

Valda called down the counter, "Guys? One more favor of you? Can you take the bottles back to the alley?"

I spread my hands wide and bowed: *But of course.*

She had loaded the empty bottles into the crates. The brewer would pick them up in the morning from the alley. Orient and I hoisted three crates each and headed for the back.

As we passed the office door, I wondered if I should check on Strider.

Orient slowed down. "Oh, hell, why not? If he objects, he'll just break my face, right?" He knocked. No answer. He knocked again, then opened the door a crack, then stuck his head in.

When he pulled it back, he said, "He must be all right. He's gone."

I considered that, then shrugged. I hoped he'd gone to meet Sai; that'd have been the best thing for both of them.

We went through the door at the end of the hall that opens into Danceland's private garage, and through that to the alley, which is properly a small cul-de-sac rather than an alley. Danceland's back door is at the closed end. When there's no moon, you can't see a thing back there. Tonight, there was a moon.

I knew something was wrong—I smelled blood. I'm not as good as my rep; I didn't know what kind of blood. I smelled a lot of things, most of them alley things, some of them things people do as they die. I attributed those to the alley at first. Maybe dogs had been fighting there.

Something caught light from the back door. I recognized the stupid Faeriecloth coat, wondered why the

Elflander had ditched it, then grinned, thinking someone had swiped it from him to teach him a lesson about Soho etiquette.

I was still grinning when I saw that the Elflander was in his coat, lying like he was resting. His hands were folded over his stomach. His legs were straight out before him.

I was still grinning when I saw what had been done to him while he was in his coat. My grin withered on my face. I grunted and set down my load of empties, and wished for some way to warn Orient of what he was about to see.

CHAPTER EIGHT
Silver Suits and Copper Cards

Orient turned. Then he saw what I was looking at, and we both stared for a little longer, then he went to the side and threw up. I wish I could say I was staring to see if the Elflander might still be breathing, but I wasn't. There was no chance that he was living. I was staring to convince myself that a person I had seen alive was now a corpse in Danceland's alley.

The Elflander's coat was in ribbons, like his skin, and the moonlight made him all shiny with blood, almost as if he'd been coated with varnish. His dueling toy was still in his hand. His long white braid had been stuffed into his mouth, and a part of my mind was saying that wasn't very original while another part thought that was obscene. A distant part of my mind whispered, *Goldy and Sai both threatened*—but the thought was too weak to live. I don't know why I didn't vomit. Maybe dogs don't vomit for emotional reasons.

Orient and I went into the back room without having to suggest it to each other. Orient leaned against a stack of whiskey kegs and brought up both hands to push back his hair, or maybe just to massage his temples.

We stood there, trying to breathe casually and trying to understand what had happened. At last, Orient said, "Strider's in trouble."

I grunted.

"Can we cover it up?" That was phrased as a question mostly out of habit, I think, of being considerate of me. He answered it himself. "No way. Might get Dancer in trouble with the coppers if we wait. Might get Strider in more trouble. Hell." He looked at me then, with his face pale and controlled. "I'll tell Dancer. It's her alley, after all."

I nodded. It was nice to be able to pass on the decision.

I can guess what thoughts were going through Orient's head as we went to find Dancer:

Strider did it. No, Strider'd meet the Elflander near the river or in a bombed-out house or in a deserted theater, and they'd fight until honor was satisfied or Strider was dead. Strider wouldn't kill someone he'd defeated. He'd forgive him. That's how Strider thinks, the simple git.

Sai did it, then, to protect Strider from the stranger who had cut up her lover for fun. No, Sai wouldn't jump someone in an alley, and Sai wouldn't go after him until she knew Strider was fine. Then she'd arrange for the stranger to be without his little dueling toy— have some of her friends surround him, or something. And she'd show him why she had been Soho's middleweight champion for a season and a half, until she decided she was too pretty to stay a boxer. Sai wouldn't kill, either. Not deliberately, not like this, anyway.

That meant Goldy did it, because he was frustrated that he couldn't do anything else to show he cared for Strider, because he felt that he should have stopped the stranger sooner somehow, because he stepped outside to

grab some fresh air and saw the Elflander waiting for
Strider—

And that didn't work either, because Goldy's not like
that, no more than the rest of us are. More likely, Goldy
would take a certain delight in tossing the Elflander
to the coppers for a night in the B-town jail. Wouldn't
do that with a local, but with a Faerie lord in a silly
coat . . .

And that left Orient with one last suspect, Wild
Hunt's lead singer. He wouldn't like that, 'cause he had
a mad crush on Linden. But Orient's smart. He'd weigh
the possibility, and it wouldn't work any better than any
of the rest. You don't carve up a crazy boyfriend; you
just wait patiently until he finds someone else to pester.
And it couldn't've been self-defense, not considering
what had been done to the body.

We stepped into the main room and Orient said, "The
elf that made trouble tonight . . ." I was the only one
who knew why he stopped, but everyone could tell
something was wrong.

Val came over and put her arm around his back. Just
'cause she's twice our age, she thinks she's everyone's
grandmother, sometimes. Sometimes we all appreciate
it. "What?"

"He's dead. In the back alley. He's all . . ." Orient
winced, ". . . cut up."

"Shit," Goldy said. Goldy never swears.

Dancer and Tick-Tick went back to look while Orient
tried to describe it to Goldy and Val. His words didn't
do much to tell it, but his tone did. I was glad I couldn't
talk, myself.

"We call the coppers," Dancer said when she returned.

"No," Goldy whispered, and I thought there was going to be worse trouble.

Dancer didn't hear, or maybe she's wise enough to
know when to pretend she didn't. "Val, tell Strider and

Sai what happened. Tick-Tick will tell the coppers."
She glanced at the Ticker. "Better take the avenues to
the cop shop, 'cause the shortcuts might not be safe this
time of night. And I wouldn't be surprised if you didn't
even leave for another five minutes or so. Bikes can be
so hard to start, sometimes."

Tick-Tick smiled a tiny bit, more in recognition than
in humor. Goldy nodded, said, "Yes. That's right."

Dancer brewed a pot of coffee while we sat around,
not really talking about anything important. Orient said,
"Good band," then quoted Tick-Tick so softly that I
may have been the only one who heard him, "Oh,
shards and splinters."

Goldy said, "Bastard deserved it."

Orient whispered, as if testing the sound, "To dine on
iron needles."

Goldy said, "If anyone deserves what they get, that
bastard did."

Orient said, "Damn it to *hell*."

Goldy nodded. "Yeah."

Dancer poured coffee for us all, and I realized that
was another first. Not the freebies, 'cause Dancer can
be so generous I sometimes wonder how she stays in
business. But she never worked behind the counter. Val
made decent coffee, and Goldy brewed great coffee.
Dancer's tasted like she was the one who taught Goldy,
but even Orient's "Good coffee" sounded perfunctory.

Val came back and said Sai and Strider weren't
home. I didn't like that. Then Strider came in. I liked
that less. He was pocketing his key to the place and
saying, "Anybody seen Sai?" He stopped, stared at us
staring at him. "What'd I say?" When no one answered
immediately, he added, "Hey, if my part's crooked, I'm
sorry, I lost my comb." His hair, as usual, was a perfect
white mane.

Goldy shook his head.

"That's a joke," Strider said, moving toward the bar

where we had gathered. Then he stopped and said quietly, "Something happened to Sai."

"No, Strider," Goldy said. "Not that we know of."

"It's that elf," Dancer said. "He's dead back by the empties. Cut up bad, like someone hated him." That was obviously a warning, not an accusation. "Tick-Tick's gone for the coppers. I told her to. If I didn't, they'd shut me down."

Strider's pale face went paler, which is some trick. The new scar was like a lightning flash on his cheek. He sat on a stool and whispered, "Oh, to sail a sunless sea." It took me a minute to realize that was a Faerie oath, and before I did, Strider sounded more like himself. " 'S all right, Dancer."

"I told her to stall. You could get out—"

He shook his head. "And go where? This is Bordertown. I'm Strider. I don't want anything else."

"Don't be a bigger fool!" Goldy hit the table with the flat of his hand, and our cups danced.

Strider smiled slightly. "Hey, Goldy, don't give me that. You know."

"Yeah, you bastard." Goldy turned his back. His shoulders shook, and no one spoke for a minute or two.

"He's dead," Strider said, not quite asking.

"Yes," Orient said.

"Fine. Then I don't have to see him." He glanced at Dancer. "Coffee, please?"

"Yeah, sure." She slid him a cup.

"Goldy?" he asked, lifting the cup to his lips.

Goldy grunted, sounding like me, I suppose. He didn't turn around.

"Tell Sai I love her. Tell her not to do anything stupid. And don't you do anything stupid, either."

Goldy's bright head bobbed in a nod.

"Got any poems for me, Wolfboy?"

I shook my head. I hadn't written anything in three weeks, but I knew I'd write something soon.

"You're innocent," Orient said, and his voice was accusing and angry.

"Maybe."

Orient looked upward in exasperation. "You could say so, then."

Goldy said, "He doesn't have to."

"No," said Orient. "I guess not."

Tick-Tick came back with the coppers soon after that. I didn't recognize them as coppers, not immediately. There's not a lot of law in B-town, and you almost never see the Silver Suits in uniform in Soho. Law only comes in for important things, like an ugly killing that too many people will hear of.

The woman was about Dancer's age. Her hair was a sun-bleached brown with flecks of white, combed straight back from her forehead. Her skin was lighter than Goldy's and darker than Tick-Tick's. She wore a loose cotton jacket cut from a pattern of tropical flowers, black slacks, and black loafers. Her eyes were hidden behind silver glasses, probably Night Peepers. She kept one hand in her slacks pocket, maybe 'cause there was a weapon there, maybe 'cause it made her jacket hang better. The elf was less conspicuous, in a sea green suit with his white hair cut close to his skull.

"Name's Rico," the human said, not smiling. "My partner's Lieutenant Linn. Anyone want to see a copper card?" I've always wondered about that name, 'cause the only c-card I ever saw was brass.

"It's all right, Sunny," Dancer said, and Goldy snickered.

"Good," Rico replied, looking at Dancer. "Sorry you're in this." Her head didn't move at all as she asked Goldy, "Something amusing?"

"Yeah," he said. "Sunny." Once we had a talk about why coppers were called coppers. Goldy had said that was because you could buy them cheap.

"Named for my cheerful disposition," Rico said. So far her face hadn't been any more expressive than her silver glasses. "Think it's funny, Walter?" Goldy didn't answer. At another time, the whole exchange would have been hilarious, but it wasn't now. I think Rico agreed. She said, "Everyone stick around, okay? You"—she pointed at me—"show me the body while Linn takes statements."

I can't say that she did anything more significant than we did. She lit the place with a torch spell, which impressed me until I saw that it only made everything more obvious and more ugly. Rico whistled a low note as she looked at the Elflander. She walked around and studied things, not touching anything. Then she stood quietly, and I figured she was doing what I was doing: trying to imagine it.

When she was ready to go, I stepped in front of her. I pointed at the body, pointed at the alley, and shrugged. Rico's about my height, so she looked straight at me in that way they must teach at copper school. "Aren't I going to do something more? What do you want? I should take fingerprints? I should try a spell to sense what happened here?"

I nodded.

"Right. Look, Lobo"—it must have been Tick-Tick who told her my name—"even if we had the murder weapon, we probably wouldn't sense anything more than rage, quick heartbeats, and a real sick pleasure. And that last is a guess, so don't quote me. As for fingerprints, don't make me laugh. No murder weapon. In an alley, anything else is circumstantial. The whole case would probably end right here, if it wasn't for two things." She held the back of her hand toward me and lifted her index finger. "Your friend made some crazy threats in front of three hundred people." She raised the next finger. "Someone killed Tejorinin Yorl."

I tucked my chin slightly to show her I didn't understand.

"I don't know either," she admitted. "Not exactly. He's some elf kid who just inherited something important in Faerie. Don't know why he came out here. Usual reasons are vacation, business, and politics. Doesn't matter which was Yorl's. He was rich and important, and we got to get someone for his murder."

I could have hit her then.

"I don't like it," Rico said. "Not at all. Dancer's told me about most of you, and I questioned Tick-Tick before we followed her here. Sounds like you're all okay, for B-town kids. But facts are facts. If we can find who's responsible, everything'll be fine. If we can't . . ." She shrugged and headed back into Danceland.

I stood there and thought about it till she called back, "C'mon, Lobo. I know you write. Linn'll want your statement, too."

I went in and listened to the last couple of stories. Strider said he'd been walking around, just thinking. Goldy claimed to have been moving around the floor all the time, but the cops knew he could've ducked out for a few minutes while claiming to be in a back room or on the balconies. They wrote down the names of the members of Wild Hunt but didn't seem too excited about getting anything from them. About the only time no one had been watching the band was while Yorl was slicing Strider.

"What about Sai?" asked Rico.

"She went walking, too," said Goldy, not too happy.

Rico nodded. "It's a houseful of great alibis."

I sat there, scribbling on some paper that Dancer lent me. I could have interrupted the statements, I suppose, but I wanted to write out my theory in full. So I did, and it was short:

THE KILLING WAS THE WORK OF A GANG, THREE AT

LEAST, PROBABLY MORE. I SAW YORL WHEN HE WAS CUTTING STRIDER ON THE DANCE FLOOR. YORL LOOKED LIKE HE'D STUDIED THAT DUELING GADGET FOR YEARS. HE WAS TOO GOOD TO LET HIMSELF BE CARVED UP BY ANY ONE PERSON. AND THIS WORK WAS DONE MOSTLY FOR THE FUN OF THE CARVERS. YOU SAW THAT. THE BUSINESS WITH THE BRAID. EVEN IF STRIDER KILLED YORL, STRIDER WOULDN'T DO SOMETHING LIKE THAT. YORL HAD TO HAVE BEEN SURROUNDED, AND AS ONE KID DISTRACTED HIM, ANOTHER CUT HIM. SOME SICKIES PROBABLY HEARD TALK ABOUT STRIDER AND THE ELFLANDER AND DECIDED TO KILL AN OUTSIDER FOR FUN, FIGURING STRIDER WOULD GET THE BLAME. EVERYONE ON HO STREET HAD TO BE TALKING ABOUT WHAT HAPPENED IN DANCELAND.

"A gang," Rico said when she joined me at a table.

I nodded.

"You're the only one with this gang theory."

I nodded again and gestured for her to give me back the paper. When she did, I wrote:

ORIENT DIDN'T THINK ABOUT THE CUTS. OR ABOUT WHAT IT MEANS, DOING THAT THING WITH THE BRAID TO A CORPSE. YOU BLAME HIM?

I think she smiled a tiny bit, and that was worse than the absence of expression.

"No, I don't. You want to pin this on the Bloods, the Pack, or the Rats?"

I snorted in disgust and wrote:

YOU THINK THERE'S ONLY A FEW GANGS? MORE LIKE HUNDREDS. SOME REALLY TWISTED BUNCHES HIDE WITHIN THE BLOODS & THE PACK & THE RATS, CLAIMING ALLEGIANCE TO THE BIGGER GANG AND ACTING LIKE THE REST OF THE GANG IS BEHIND THEM.

That little smile came back. "Dancer, Mickey, and I ran with the Go-boys when I was your age. We were part of the Pack. So, who do you favor?"

EVER HEAR OF FINEAGH STEEL? STYLED HIMSELF

THE LEADER OF THE BLOODS? Steel built a little army of elf morons, then jackbooted around Soho for a week or two.

Rico nodded. "I hear he's dead. I hear his gang's scattered. You think this was the work of one of his lieutenants, maybe?"

I shrugged.

"Doesn't work, Lobo." She took off her glasses and grinned at me. Her eyes weren't any friendlier than the glasses. "Why carve a strange elf? If they were jealous of him, they'd rough him up and steal his money, that's all. No need to bring the coppers down on everyone."

I nodded, wishing I had someone better to point at.

She folded up the page I'd written on and replaced her glasses. "Nice theory. No evidence to back it up." When she said that, it was like she'd kicked me, even though her voice sounded kind, for her. "Sorry." Then she tore up my statement and handed me the shreds. I stared at it.

She said, "If I convinced anyone that Strider couldn't have done it alone, we'd just have to lock up some of his friends, too." She patted the back of my hand and left me sitting at the table.

Valda finished giving her account to Lieutenant Linn. He thanked her, then picked up the impression ball that had been on the table, recording everyone's version of the evening, and said, "I, Linn, witnessed the preceding statements on this day." And he gave the date and time, and pocketed the i-ball.

Linn looked at Strider. "Will you accompany us to C Street?"

Strider glanced at all of us. Goldy tensed, and Strider smiled. "I said I wouldn't run or hide. Only thing left's to clear my good nickname." He glanced at Linn. "I assume you're offering food and lodging until my honor has been restored?"

Linn nodded. Rico said, "You'll eat as well as we do.

No promises about the lodging. Someone downtown will decide tomorrow whether we have enough to hold you longer. Unless we find a likelier suspect, we have enough to hold you. Visiting hours are from ten to ten, before your trial."

Goldy said, "And the charge?"

Rico said, "If Tejorinin Yorl has no friends, accessory to suicide. If his friends have some influence with the merchants' council, manslaughter. If his friends have a lot of influence, murder."

Strider looked at Goldy. "Tell Sai they cannot cage my soul, for she has freed it."

Goldy nodded.

Rico said, "Tell Sai we want to talk to her."

Goldy said, "Oh, yes."

Rico and Lieutenant Linn left with Strider when a van and a few Silver Suits showed up. The Silver Suits poked around and fingerprinted us all and did some mystical juju that obviously had as much effect as Rico expected, but now their report would be nice and fat.

When they were done, one of them said none of us should disappear. Goldy laughed at that. The Silver Suits took away Yorl's body in a shiny black bag, and finally Dancer said, "To hell with it. Good night, everybody." And we all wandered out into the good night.

CHAPTER NINE
Losers, Weepers

I woke up around noon Saturday and didn't want to get out of bed. I lay there, thinking the sheets should be changed and wishing I lived with somebody and wondering if maybe Strider had done it. Time does that, lets you see things differently, sometimes in ways you wish it didn't.

Whether he killed Yorl or not, I like Strider. But what did I know about him? He'd been important in Faerie—I'd heard him addressed as "Your Highness" by Leander, who had known him in the Elflands. They were both on the same side of a struggle to control the heir of Faerie, a struggle that would shape the relationship between Faerie and the World. If Strider's side won, Faerie and the World might have a chance to learn more about each other. If Crystaviel's side won, the Wall would remain between them, and trade between them might end.

I didn't care about Faerie's future. I cared about Florida's. Strider seemed to think of her as a person first and as the heir second, but could I say I *knew* that about him?

Maybe the killing had been an accident and Strider thought he had to cover it up. If you accept that, it's not too hard to imagine him doing the rest, forcing himself to do something so atypical that no one could believe he had killed Yorl. Under normal circumstances, all he'd need would be a reasonable amount of doubt and charges would be dropped. He may not have known that the flashy Elflander he'd killed had been someone important.

The day was cooler than the day before, but that didn't bother me. I found my other jeans and a corduroy jacket and decided not to bother with shoes. There's enough broken glass in B-town that that isn't the smartest thing to do, but it makes people think I'm tough. The truth is, I tended to run from trouble before I was changed. Now that I'm stronger and more perceptive, I run even faster.

I went to Sai's. She makes great *huevos rancheros* without the least provocation. And if she didn't feel like cooking for a stray, she might need some company.

She already had company. Tick-Tick was there, sitting a little stiffly on a purple beanbag, maybe aware that it clashed with her red leather outfit. Sai wore a faded man's undershirt and cut-offs. Under her black bangs, her eyes were almost as red as Tick-Tick's leather. I glanced at her knuckles. They were bandaged. A heavy weight bag hangs in Sai's living room where she can kick or punch it whenever she wants. I suspected the bag had been worked thoroughly that morning.

I made a little circular motion with my hand, and Sai smiled a bit, saying, "Hi, Wolfboy. C'mon in. The Ticker toasted bagels, but I'm not too hungry."

Tick-Tick said, "Rico and her faithful elfin companion came by earlier."

I nodded and stuffed an onion bagel in my face.

"They didn't have anything useful to say." She shrugged. "We didn't have anything useful to tell them."

"She said I could visit Strider," Sai said. "You want to come, too?"

I nodded again, and, looking at her bandaged knuckles, decided that Sai had not killed Yorl. His arrogant nose had not been broken; therefore, Sai had not killed him.

I grabbed two bagels and followed. Sai took the Batcycle. I hopped into Orient's usual place in Tick-Tick's sidecar, which made me wonder where he was. I pointed at the seat and frowned. Tick-Tick said, "He hasn't been around. We were supposed to meet. We can swing by his place after seeing Strider."

The B-town Jail isn't particularly better or worse than most jails, I imagine, but I wouldn't want to stay there. Rico had left a note, so we didn't have any trouble getting in. I wasn't too crazy about the man at the front desk, who shook his head as he looked at me and said, "You kids are getting weirder every year."

A couple of Silver Suits walked Strider into the waiting room, then leaned up against the wall as if they were bored enough to sleep. One was bored by each door, and they both had three-foot sting-rods dangling from straps around their right wrists.

"Nice place," Tick-Tick said.

"You should try their breakfast," Strider answered.

"You're such an ass," Sai said.

"I'm glad to see you, too, love."

They kissed. Tick-Tick and I tried to pretend we were as bored as the guards.

"We're getting you out of here," Sai said quietly.

"No whispering," one guard called. "And no, you're not."

"He's innocent!" Sai said.

"You're confessing?" the guard asked. Before Sai could say anything more, he said, "Look, kids. Behave yourselves, and we won't bug you."

"Yeah," Strider said, seconding the guard's advice.

"Okay," Sai said. "Okay. But I don't like this, Strider. I want you out of here."

"No chance for bail," Strider said. "I just hope I don't lose my tan."

"Don't be a pain," Tick-Tick said. "You just make it worse for Sai when you act like that."

Sai quickly shook her head. "No. I understand."

"Hey," Strider said softly, and he stroked her chin with his forefinger. "I'm okay. Maybe I'll get a lot of reading done."

"Rico said the charge is murder," Sai said. "I don't want you to get *that* much reading done."

Tick-Tick's elfin features were very grim as she said, "You won't get any reading done if they take away your memories, Strider. Not until you learn how again. Nor will you get any reading done if they send you to a place where there are no books. And if they pick death—"

Strider turned away. I don't think he was uncomfortable; elves love to talk politely about depressing things. I think he wanted to stop Tick-Tick for Sai's sake. He said, "Trial's weeks away. 'Sides, they'll do what they'll do, okay? You guys better leave now."

"No," Tick-Tick said.

"I can go back to my cell anytime," Strider said.

"You certainly can," Tick-Tick admitted. "That won't help you, and it won't help Sai. Is that what you want?"

"I want out." He smiled. "Hey, Ticker, bring your seedybox? Haven't heard a tune in twelve hours; I'm about to go into major withdrawal."

Tick-Tick glanced at one of the guards, who waved for her to go ahead. Peter Gabriel's "Solsbury Hill" filled the air, loud enough to remove us a little from the prison, though not so loud that the guards couldn't hear us talk. Strider, grinning, began twitching one hand by his leg in time to the music, making little shapes as if a part of him would dance no matter where he was.

I thought about the ways we deal with stress, and my heart took an express for the basement. Then I realized he was finger-spelling. Most of my friends have learned the alphabet in sign, along with a few, much more often useful, rude phrases. Strider was spelling, —I-E-L-C-R-Y-S-T-A-V-I-E—

By my leg, I shaped, S-H-E-D-I-D-I-T-?

He shook his head a tiny bit.

Tick-Tick thought that was to her. "I know. We have to find the killer. The coppers need someone to hang for this one. Maybe literally."

Strider signed, Y-I-S-F-R-I-E-N-D. As I puzzled over that, he glanced at Sai, who looked at her lap. I suddenly knew why Strider was being so stupid. I suspected it earlier, but I knew it then. He thought Sai did it. He was too stupidly in love with her to see that if she had and he'd been arrested, she would've confessed immediately, because she was just as stupidly in love with him. I wondered if she'd considered confessing anyway, just to save him. I decided not to ask. No point in giving her the idea.

And I realized Strider had spelled, *Y is friend.* More specifically: *Crystaviel. Y is friend.*

I spelled, I-N-F-A-E-R-I-E?

H-E-R-E.

B-L-U-E-H-A-I-R-?

Strider nodded.

Tejorinin Yorl had been Crystaviel's ice-haired lieutenant in the search for Florida. What did that mean now? And how could I talk about it in front of the guards? They might spot the finger-spelling at any moment, and if we began to sign openly, they'd throw us out or bring in someone to read what we said.

I pulled out a sheet of scrap paper and wrote out something like what I'd written for Rico about the theory I no longer believed: that it was a coincidence that Yorl was murdered after attacking Strider. I added: PROBLEM IS, WE DON'T HAVE ANYONE LIKELY. ANY IDEAS?

One of the guards read it before letting Strider have it. Strider read it, and his eyes flicked wide from their usual squint. "You sure about this, Wolfboy?"

I held my hands wide, like: *Who's ever sure?* Then I nodded.

Sai and Tick-Tick read the note together. Tick-Tick said, "You should've said something—oops." Her face was still, but I think she was proud of the "oops."

I waved downward to show I'd let that pass, then grabbed the note back and scribbled: RICO DIDN'T LIKE IT. WHERE'S A SUSPECT? WHO'D WANT TO CARVE A STRANGER, EVEN ONE AS BAD AS YORL?

"Wharf Rats, perhaps," Tick-Tick mused. "A chance for fun, and a chance to blame someone else."

"Not all the Rats are like that," Sai said. Her brother's a Rat.

"It only takes three or four like that," Tick-Tick said.

"There were five Rats in Danceland last night," Strider said, and we all got very quiet."

"Is it my turn to call you an idiot?" Tick-Tick asked him.

"No. Hers." Strider pointed at Sai.

"I'll take a rain check," Sai said. "What about these Rats?"

"They had a table up on the left balcony. Near the women's room. I was watching 'em before Yorl decided I was a fencing dummy."

I lifted my hand. Tick-Tick glanced at me, then told Strider and Sai, "After you two left, Lobo filled in on the floor."

"Did you see the Rats?" Strider asked, surprisingly

hopeful for Strider. "One was a little brown-haired guy with tiny round glasses. Wire rims. The rest were, well, Rats."

Rats aren't usually distinctive as anything more than Rats. Sai's brother is a nice guy, but he's a Mad River addict like most of them, and he dresses poorly and smells a little funny . . . I didn't like remembering what my life as a Rat had been like before I was changed. I just shook my head.

"You went by that corner," Tick-Tick said to me, 'cause she likes to test things to see how well they function. "After Strider and Yorl fought. And the Rats were not there."

I nodded.

"Was this when you and Goldy first made the rounds?"

I nodded again.

Tick-Tick smiled. "Rico might like your theory a little better now."

"Yeah," said Strider. "Some Rats did it. She'll love that."

"Still . . ." Tick-Tick said.

"We'll find them," Sai announced.

Strider nodded, not particularly hopeful, and said to Sai, "I thought . . ."

"I know," she said, and Tick-Tick and I looked away again. We talked for another couple of minutes about nothing particularly promising. While we chatted, Strider spelled, W-A-T-C-H-F-L-O-R-I-D-A.

I nodded. Mickey and Goldy needed to know that one of Crystaviel's people had been doing something in Bordertown, even if he was just acting like a dink and getting murdered.

When it was time to go, I gave Strider a four-leaf clover and a poem I'd written late the night before. It was a stupid thing about owls flying over dark forests, but he read it and said, "Nice. I'll put it on my wall."

His own damn wall. That was when I could've cried.

Tick-Tick patted her pockets, came up with the new *Stick Wizard*, and passed it on, saying, "From Orient and me."

Sai looked sad. "I didn't bring you a thing."

"Yes, you did." He kissed her lightly on the lips. Then his mouth quivered a fraction, and he turned and told the guards, "Let's go."

Sai watched him leave, then said, "Where to?"

"Orient," Tick-Tick announced as she headed into the hall.

"He can find a Rat with round glasses?"

"I don't know," Tick-Tick admitted. "But it's worth a try."

In the street, Sai said, "All right, what was the signing about?"

I blinked.

Tick-Tick said, "Are we to think you were both seized simultaneously with Saint Vitus's Dance? That wouldn't be easy, but I suppose I could manage it."

I pulled a three-by-five and wrote, THE DEAD GUY WAS CRYSTAVIEL'S BLUE-HAIRED BOY. For Tick-Tick, I added, THE FOLKS WHO HIRED ORIENT TO FIND ME.

Sai said, "Oh."

Tick-Tick mulled over my message. She and Orient must have known that something more had been going on that night than it seemed, but they'd never asked. She didn't ask now.

I wrote, I DON'T THINK STRIDER DID IT. I THINK HE THOUGHT YOU OR GOLDY DID IT FOR HIS SAKE.

Sai said, "What a jerk," and touched the back of her hand to the corner of her eye.

"We shall save him," Tick-Tick said, opening her arms. Sai may have hesitated a second—Tick-Tick's as elvish as they come—but she accepted the embrace.

I wrote, SOMEONE SHOULD TELL GOLDY AND MICKEY.

Tick-Tick said, "We'll run by Elsewhere once we've

found our good Finder. If you have questions for his former client, he can track *her* more easily than some Rat with round glasses. It helps to have a name."

And it would have been a fine plan, if we could have found Orient. We went to his flat, where no one answered the door, then to Danceland, where we told Dancer and Val most of what we'd learned. Neither of them had seen Orient. Val was annoyed because he'd promised to buy her lunch at Taco Hell.

Then Sai said, "Seen Goldy?"

Dancer said, "No. And he should've been in by now. I don't suppose—" As Sai looked for the rest of the sentence, Dancer shook her head. "Nah. You get Strider out of that damn jail. We can get by without the Trio for a few nights, if we have to. But if there's anything we can do . . ."

"Thanks." Sai saw me pacing as I worried about Goldy. "We better go."

The CLOSED sign was in Elsewhere's window. That wasn't unusual; not many people in Soho keep perfectly dependable hours. I tapped out the rhythm that shuts down the guard spell, then turned the door handle. It was locked.

Maybe that meant Magic Freddy had raised his spellmaking rates and Mickey had decided not to pay him, but I didn't think so. I ran into the back alley, with Sai and Tick-Tick following on their bikes.

The back door was closed but not locked. I looked at the others, and Sai whispered, "Hell." We entered. Snicker and Doodle and the kittens, Ditto, Mimeo, Hekto, and Xerox, let us know immediately that they, at least, were fine, but lonely.

I ran through the bookstore, from the second floor to the basement. No one was in the building. Nothing had been disturbed, so far as I could tell. The cats had food and water in their bowls, but no more than I'd expect to find any day. Bills and coins and magical trinkets waited in the open cash register for anyone to take.

I unlocked the front and ran next door. Ms. Wu was with a customer by the tea and spice bins. She looked at me, told her customer, "You must excuse me," and followed me back into Elsewhere.

Tick-Tick squatted on the floor with a cat on her shoulders, one in her lap, and two of the kittens at her feet. Sai was ignoring a third kitten, who circled her cautiously. Ms. Wu said, "What is it?"

Sai said, "Everyone's missing. Correction. Strider's locked up, and Orient, Goldy, Mickey, and Florida are missing." She hit the side of Mickey's desk with her hand. Doodle ran into the basement.

Tick-Tick told the entire story, as she knew it. I looked at Sai and signed, *Tick-Tick and Ms. Wu ought to be told everything.*

Sai nodded.

Ms. Wu said aloud, "Florida is Faerie's missing heir. Yes, I know." As I gaped at her, she signed, *You never asked.*

Tick-Tick nodded. "The heir. Ah. Half of Faerie may be against us, then."

I stared at her. She was talking casually about a kid I'd sat beside for two nights while she sweated out a fever, a kid who'd made me a booklet for my birthday called *Why Wolfboy Is Wonderful, by Florida.* Then I nodded. She was talking casually about five people we all loved.

The nature of the game was simple: Strider and Crystaviel were the players, Florida was the goal, and the rest of us, by helping Strider hide her, had become his gaming pieces. But now he was locked up where he could not play. His game-pieces would have to win without him.

I looked at Sai. Gaming pieces were expendable. We

could assume that Florida was alive, at least. We had no assurances about the others.

Ms. Wu mumbled something and moved her arms in a way that suggested all mystical gestures are a form of sign language. She frowned. "I don't think anyone's done any magic here lately. Nor have there been any deaths. I'm afraid that's all that I can tell you."

"It's something," Sai said.

"Perhaps we've overreacted," Tick-Tick said, clearly not believing that. "We'll return to Orient's. I have a spare key." She smiled. "And I'm not afraid to use it."

No one laughed. Ms. Wu said, "I'll let you know if I learn anything."

I signed, *Could we break Strider out of the B-town Jail?*

Ms. Wu looked aghast. I thought it was her reaction to a suggestion that we break the law, but she said, "The merchant council pays several magicians, myself included, to set magical wards about that place. Magic cannot free him. Could you free him without magic?"

Tick-Tick said, "Not without bringing every freelance police force and every would-be vigilante after us. Which is to say, no."

Ms. Wu nodded. "Better to prove his innocence."

I signed, *Thanks.* When everyone was outside of the building, I tapped the rhythm that activates the guard spell. I tried the door. The handle did not turn or rattle; the guard spell was working. I began to feel very, very bad.

We raced back to Orient's apartment. No one answered our knock. Tick-Tick used her key, and we went up, quickly and cautiously. As we went, Tick-Tick said, "I'd hate to interrupt him with someone."

Sai said, "I wouldn't," opened the door, and yelled, "Burglars!" No one answered. Tick-Tick went straight to the bedroom door and walked inside while Sai checked the bathroom and I investigated the kitchen.

We met back in the living room. Tick-Tick sighed. "I would have been very pleased to interrupt him, I confess."

"Do we wait?"

Tick-Tick said, "Anything to drink in his icebox?"

I shook my head. This was the first time I'd been glad to find nothing in his fridge.

"A most inconsiderate host," Tick-Tick said, then, "You shouldn't read that."

Sai was reaching for Orient's diary, open on the table next to an empty coffee mug and an ashtray half-full of cigarette butts. She turned the page back, then flipped a couple of pages more. "It's about last night."

"Ah," Tick-Tick said, and she read over Sai's left shoulder while I read over Sai's right.

Most of the entry was an account of the events of Friday night, beginning with meeting the runaway and giving her a B-town name. At Danceland, he didn't see or hear anything significant that I didn't. He came up with a suspect I'd missed; in his list of possibilities, he wrote, EVEN THE TICKER'S ALIBI IS LOW-GRADE. HELL, MAYBE THEY ALL DID IT. THE ONLY PERSON WHOSE INNOCENCE I'M CERTAIN OF IS ME. AND IF THIS GOES ON, I'LL BE ASKING PEOPLE TO CORROBORATE MY MEMORIES.

I looked at Tick-Tick then, and I wondered if she minded being among the suspects. It did make me feel better about doubting Strider.

Here are the last three paragraphs in Orient's diary:

THE SUN'S BEEN UP FOR THREE HOURS. I'D FORGOTTEN THIS PARTICULAR TIME OF DAY EXISTED. I WENT BACK TO DANCELAND AFTER WRITING THE LAST PARAGRAPH. I WANTED A CIG, AND I WANTED MY DAMN COPY OF *STICK WIZARD*, BECAUSE I KNEW I WASN'T GOING TO SLEEP. BOTH THINGS WERE IN THE SIDECAR. THE TICKER PARKED THE BIKE IN DANCELAND'S GARAGE FOR SAFEKEEPING AND WENT

TO WAIT UP FOR SAI, TO KEEP HER BOTH FROM BEING ALONE AND FROM DOING SOMETHING STUPID.

I WENT TO SEE IF SOMEONE WAS AROUND TO LET ME IN, OR IF I COULD GET IN BY MYSELF. I HAD TO GO THROUGH THE CUL-DE-SAC, OF COURSE. I DIDN'T GET IN THE GARAGE, DIDN'T EVEN TRY, BECAUSE I FOUND SOMETHING ON THE GROUND NEAR THE STREET END OF THE CUL-DE-SAC, AND IT DISTRACTED ME.

SO I DON'T HAVE MY CIGS. I HAVE A PHEASANT FEATHER WITH A DISTINCTIVE NICK OUT OF ONE EDGE, DIRTY NOW FROM LYING IN THE MUD. I'VE BEEN PICKING IT UP AND TWIRLING IT OR SLIDING IT THROUGH MY FINGERS, AS IF IT'S AN IMPRESSION BALL, READY TO POUR OUT ITS STORED SONG AT A TOUCH. I HAVE TO SLEEP NOW, WHATEVER I MIGHT DREAM. BUT I WANT TO KNOW WHAT IT MEANS. CARAMEL, WHERE ARE YOU NOW?

Sai said, "This Caramel kid killed Yorl?"
Tick-Tick shrugged. "Why didn't he come get me?"
"He didn't want to wake you?" Sai said hesitantly. "Maybe he didn't want to wake me."
Tick-Tick looked out the window, then said, "I'm spreading the word. I'll tell the Horn Dance, I'll tell Scully, I'll tell Commander X's Kids. Someone must've seen something."

Everyone called in favors. Sai had her brother's friends cruising the wharfs. Tick-Tick spread the word among the Bloods; what with the ones who like her and the ones who admire Strider, there were a lot of elves in red leather cruising B-town. She made a run up the Tooth to speak with Scully and some of the Dragon Fire kids. Dancer and Val talked with the old-timers.

I wrote up the short version of what had happened and carried it around. King O'Beer gave me a hug and offered to tell people in his karate class. Jeff said he'd speak with the Rough Riders; the Leather and Lace League, a.k.a. the 3Ls; and the Dragon Ladies of Dragontown. (Sometimes I wonder if this place would have one or two fewer dragon things if we had some real dragons.)

Then I climbed Dragon's Tooth Hill to the nice little street with the nice little house where one of my many crushes was living. She didn't come to the door. Leander did. He wore dark slacks and a blue blazer; I don't know if he thought he looked like the elfin version of James Bond or a tour director.

He grinned and opened the door. "Wolfboy! Come in, come in! Luce is resting, but I'm sure she'd—"

I always want to despise Leander when he's not around, maybe because he's married to my first B-town crush, the kid I knew as Wiseguy, who he knows as Lucia. But I never can despise him when I'm with him. There's something about him that exudes, *Of course I'm much better bred and much better educated than you or any of your kind can ever hope to be, but I like you ever so much, so our little differences really don't matter at all, do they, old chap?*

I shook my head and handed him the note. In the clothes I was wearing, I felt like I should squat in the yard in the sun and the dust while he read what I'd written. (Actually, the sky was overcast, and the yard was a lush carpet of grass, but you know what I mean.)

He said, "I haven't seen any of them."

I handed him a three-by-five card that I hadn't shown anyone else. He read that Strider believed Tejorinin Yorl to be Crystaviel's ice-haired companion, and he said, "Ah." There was nothing of the tour director about him then.

He said, "It's a frame, of course."

I raised an eyebrow.

"That was the effect. Better to assume it was intentional, then be pleasantly surprised if we're wrong." He shook his head and frowned. "Would that Strider were here. He'd know what to do. Which is, of course, why he is not. Could we post bail?"

I shook my head. No bail for poor folk from Soho suspected of killing rich folk from Faerie.

"Has anyone seen Crystaviel within the last month or so?"

I shook my head. So far as I knew, no one had seen her since she'd hired Orient in the fall.

"The singer's the key. Linden?"

I nodded.

"Do you know what *Crystaviel* means?"

I shook my head.

"It means, 'Cool shade of heart-shaped leaves, flowers of cream and gold.' "

I lifted an eyebrow to ask what that told us.

Leander nodded. "Exactly. Linden."

Do you ever hear a name and see in your mind the face that goes with the name? When Leander said "Linden," I only saw a mask, as beautiful and as unreal as a model's face in any lipstick or perfume ad, but I heard a glorious voice singing a snatch of "Heart's Desire," Wild Hunt's second song that Friday night at Danceland.

I wondered if Strider had been trying to warn me about Crystaviel and Linden with his finger-spelling and decided he had not. We hadn't recognized Yorl. If Crystaviel was Linden, she was even better disguised in her makeup, haircut, and perfume. Who would've looked for her on stage with Wild Hunt?

Wild Hunt, I thought, and suddenly that seemed like another sly taunt. Leander was right. Crystaviel had arranged this, Strider framed in a way that no one suspected her and Florida seized before anyone realized she was the true target.

If Florida was across the Border, we had lost. If she

remained in Bordertown, there was still hope. With each second, hope fled further away.

I wrote, TRY TO FREE STRIDER. CAN YOU CONVINCE THEM TO SET BAIL?

"Without telling who he is? He'd do that himself, if he wished or dared." Leander straightened his shoulders. "I'll pour a stream of gold upon the magistrate's desk until she frees him lest she smother beneath it."

That, I suppose, is an example of why Wiseguy married him instead of running off with me. I smiled and ran back to Orient's apartment, the unofficial command post of the Bordertown Treasure Hunt Society. We'd picked it out of the wild hope that he hadn't walked right into a trap when he'd followed the runaway, and that therefore he'd walk back in sometime soon and wonder why we'd decided to have a party at his place and not invite him.

Bordertown's streets were alive as they'd never been before. We told ourselves we'd find Florida and all of the others, and we'd find the Rats who were in Danceland Friday night too, and maybe we'd even find the person who killed the Elflander. The size of the search made me very proud of this stupid town.

But it didn't help us find anyone.

CHAPTER TEN
Things Go Boom

I woke on Orient's extremely uncomfortable couch to the sound of running feet, and I leaped up. Tick-Tick and Sai were already at either side of the door. Tick-Tick put a finger to her lips, meaning something had told her the person on the stairs wasn't Orient. I tensed up—for action, I suppose. The knob rattled as someone touched the handle, I tensed up more, and Tick-Tick yanked the door wide.

A smudged-gray human-shaped creature fell into the room. It was too solid to be a ghost, too small to be an elf. It looked at me and said, "Wolfboy!"

I recognized Caramel, our runaway, more by her voice and her odor than her appearance. Her clothes were filthy and torn, her dark brown hair and light brown skin were hidden beneath a film of black powder, her cheek and one knee were bleeding, her black hat was gone where all affectations go. I should've congratulated her. She looked extremely Bordertown now.

Tick-Tick glanced from me to Caramel. "Where's Orient?" She touched Caramel's cheek. "Soot?"

Caramel nodded and began, "I—"

Sai said, "Where's everyone, dammit!"

Tick-Tick held a hand toward Sai for patience, then looked at me.

I crossed my arms in front of me, pointing one finger at Caramel, one at Sai and Tick-Tick.

"Intro-bloody-ductions," said Sai. "Sai. Tick-Tick. If you know where anyone is, take us to 'em now."

"Caramel," she said. "I only know where Orient is. Or was half an hour ago. I don't know about anyone else."

"Where? If we find him—"

"Down by the Mad River. There's a bunch of these, um, Rats, and they locked us up in a room. See, he followed me—"

Tick-Tick nodded. "We figured that part out."

"I got out through a chimney—it was too small for Orient. He's in bad shape. I think his wrist's broken, and he was hit on the head, so—I don't know. The Rats left us nothing to drink except a jar of River water, and Orient said if we drank any, we'd be addicts, like the Rats."

Tick-Tick said, "Eh," a small noise telling us she'd had to speak to acknowledge what she'd heard, but no one should think it hurt her. "How did you know to come here?"

"Orient told me to try here first. Then your place, then Danceland."

Tick-Tick nodded. "That's plausible."

"Let's get him." said Sai.

"There's a lot of them," said Caramel. "I don't know how many. And they've got guns."

"Guns don't always work."

"They don't need to *always* work," Tick-Tick noted. "Now and then is nuisance enough."

"Why were you there?" Sai asked Caramel. "Part of their gang?"

"No." She blinked at me, then back at Sai. "I saw the elf in the coat, the elf who'd cut up the other one, go into that alley with a raggedy-looking human kid. They were such an odd combination, you know? And I was a little afraid he'd hurt the kid. So I glanced into the alley as I walked by, not really knowing what I could do if there was trouble, and there were more of the raggedy kids there."

Sai said, "Keep it coming."

"This one with glasses, he held something out toward the elf and said, 'Looking for this?' The elf pulled out his sword thing, but the kids were all over him before he could do anything with it. They had razors and knives, and it was—it was— It made me feel sick."

Sai said, "So they caught you."

Caramel shook her head. "Not then. The glasses guy, he put the thing he'd shown the elf into the saddlebag of his bike and drove off. But two of them were on foot, so I followed them 'cause, you know, you have to report murders—"

"Should've reported it then," said Sai.

"Who to? I mean, you're right, but they were going away then, fast, so there wasn't time to get anyone, and bold, like they didn't think anyone would follow them."

"And they caught you."

"No. I followed them to their place. The glasses guy's bike was in their garage. And I thought if whatever he'd put in the bags was still there, I'd have something to show people, so they'd know I didn't make it up. That's when they caught me, in the garage."

"Tough. The thing in the bag might've been important."

Caramel nodded. "Orient said it was." She held out a silver ring set with a sapphire. I'd seen its sisters on Linden's hand.

Tick-Tick said, "Too small for fingerprints. Nor can anyone confirm your tale."

Caramel did her impersonation of one of those paintings of big-eyed kids. "I'm not lying!"

"No," Tick-Tick agreed. "I meant that this and your story will not free Strider, who's being held as a murderer."

Sai pocketed the ring. "Unless someone's got a better idea, we get Orient, then we worry about this."

Tick-Tick and I nodded.

"Can anyone help?" asked Caramel.

"Maybe," said Sai.

We brought in everyone, people from the Pack and the True Bloods and even Sai's brother and a few of his Rat pals. The only person we left out was Ms. Wu, for fear she'd want to bring in the Silver Suits. If we hadn't known another magician who was supposed to be as good, we would've taken a chance on her, and probably on Sunny Rico as well.

I approached Milo. I felt uneasy walking across the parking lot, which seemed unnaturally lit in the early-morning sunlight. I felt even odder when Milo opened the door, gave me an absent nod, and stalked back through the display room cluttered with metal shelves. I looked at Sai, who was waiting for me on the Batcycle, then I waved and followed Milo.

He sat at his computer and tapped out a burst of something. I held up the letter I'd written and growled. He typed a bit more, said, "Wait, wait," typed a bit more, then looked at me. "Wolfboy, yes?"

I held up the letter again. "Oh," he said, and began to read.

I smelled Sparks before she touched my shoulder. I stood perfectly still until I felt her hand, then I turned to meet her smile.

Her hair was growing out; the two inches closest to

her scalp were dark brown. She wore one earring, a painted wooden parrot that I had given her on her birthday. She said, "H'lo, Ron. Any leads on Florida? On anyone?"

I nodded. Milo said, "Mmm. Yes," and set my explanation on his desk. "A commando raid. Hmm."

Sparks picked up the letter while I nodded at Milo. He said, "This offer of gold—"

I waited, wondering if Milo had been insulted because Leander had offered payment, or because Leander had offered too little payment.

"D'you think he could get O-scale train track? I don't need gold, but I was thinking—"

I nodded, quickly and vigorously.

Milo pointed toward the ceiling. "—that I could extend the track—"

Sparks said, "Milo."

He said, "Oh. It doesn't really matter. Of course I'll help." He stepped to one of the shelves, where an empty water pistol sat on top of several leather-bound books that appeared to be ancient. "The point is to demoralize the Rats, I think, and to make them harmless without harming them in turn."

He pulled a volume from the shelf and slapped dust from its cover, revealing the title: *Secrets of Seven Sages*. He walked his fingers through the pages, paused, mumbled, "To reverse ten years of an enemy's life." His finger swept down the page. "Mmm. Hmm. Got it." He snapped the book shut. "Let's go."

"An enemy's?" Sparks said.

"That means it can't be undone, so far as I can tell from the notes. I won't feel guilty about turning a few Rats into small children. It'll give them a second chance at life." He kissed her cheek. "And I won't change any of them unless I have to." She still looked at him. "This will be *dangerous*. I need to be able to protect myself and the others."

She nodded. "Okay. Let's go."

"You're—" He nodded, too. "Okay. Let's go."

They followed us in the Mustang. You make better time traveling Soho's rundown streets on a bike, so Sai and I beat them to the meeting place, an overgrown park near the Mad River. There must've been a hundred kids waiting for us.

Leander was among them, looking quite out of place in a black polo shirt and black chinos. Wiseguy stood beside him, looking something like her old self in jeans and leather. She said, "Hey, Wolf, don't be a stranger. Young parents need suckers to baby-sit. Uh, I mean, the company of their wild friends to remind them that life goes on."

Leander smiled. "Luce is mistaken about our need for baby-sitters, but never about a wish for your company." He moved his hand wearily over his perfectly combed hair. "I spoke with the magistrate, promising her wealth eternal. She said she wouldn't bail out a pseudonymous Soho murderer, no matter how rich his friends."

I shrugged; I suppose I hadn't expected anything more.

"So I'm here to atone for my failure." He carried a hunting bow and a quiver of arrows; he looked like he was about to enter a college sports event.

I rolled my eyes and slapped his shoulder. Wiseguy ruffled his hair with her fingers and laughed as he grimaced and smoothed his white locks.

Sai's brief speech to the crowd ended, "If the Rats won't let us in, about ten of us are going in anyway. The rest of you circle the place, but you stay back. Your job's to make the Rats know they can't escape. And that's all. Understand? This isn't a video, y'know."

"Yeah!" Gorty yelled. "Video doesn't work here!" I spotted him next to Taz and Q. Paul. They gave me a thumbs-up that I returned, though I felt less and less certain of success as we came closer to acting.

Sai repeated, "Understand?"

Sparks said, "I know that time is against us, but a threat is a threat, no matter how politely you offer it. It might make them feel they have to fight."

"Then we fight," said Sai.

Someone said, "Maybe we should call in the Silver Suits."

Gorty said, "Why? We've seen the same movies they have."

Sai said, "If we can't get in, we'll call the Silver Suits."

Sparks said, "Are you sure this is the best way?" She moved her hands out, indicating the gathered kids. Most were bare-handed, but many had bats, quarterstaffs, and knives.

Sai studied Sparks. "No. Not at all. But it's the fastest." She looked at the crowd and said, slowly and fiercely, "We don't start anything. And we don't leave here until everyone agrees to that."

Several people sounded disappointed, but everyone agreed.

So we moved toward the River. The territory seemed familiar, but that wasn't strange. I'd gotten to know these grounds when I'd been a Rat, even though I'd forgotten most of the details of my life as a River junkie. But a growing suspicion was confirmed when I saw the building where Caramel said Orient was being held. Someone had poured cans of paint down its walls from the roof since I'd been there, but this was the building I'd lived in.

Which meant the head Rat holding Orient, the little guy with the round glasses, was Specs, the King of Spectacles. I should have guessed.

Specs wasn't keeping Orient in a room with a jar of

River to torment him or to turn him into a slave. He was keeping him there to convert him to the joys of drinking the blood-red waters that flowed from Faerie. Some people can't understand that you ought to ask permission before doing anyone a favor.

I made a note for Sai about the probable leader of this group of Rats. She moved into the open and yelled, "Specs! C'mon out! You've got company!"

Someone on the roof yelled, "Whatchawan'?"

Sai looked at me; I shook my head. Sai yelled, "We want to talk with Specs! Tell 'im we appeal to his hospitality and his good sense!"

The sentry yelled, "Specs don't need to—"

Sai lifted her right hand a couple of inches and snapped her fingers. Our people began to show themselves. A few bikes rolled into one street, a few into another. People stepped out of empty buildings, from behind trees. No one said anything.

The sentry disappeared. A moment later, Specs appeared where he'd been. Sunlight glinted from his round glasses, then he raised his hand to shade his eyes and shouted, "We have River enough for all of you, if you wish it!"

Sai shouted, "We want Orient, then we want to search your building!"

Specs looked at all the silent kids. No weapons were visible yet, but most of them wore their bike gear, protective boots, jackets, and helmets. "I will not say, *You and whose army!* But I assure you, we do not know where this Orient is to be found!"

Sai said, "Better find out fast! We're not going until we have him or we've been through every inch of your place!"

"I see." Specs scanned the crowd again. I moved out where he could see me. Even if he remembered the kid called Gone, he couldn't suspect Gone had let his hair grow since then. I heard nothing in his voice to suggest he saw anything more than a kid in a furry mask. "You're quite sure?"

"Positive!" Sai answered.

Specs nodded. A shotgun blast threw up chunks of dirt maybe thirty feet from Sai. I bit my lip as she dove for cover behind the rusted remains of a taxi.

Tick-Tick called, "You all right?"

Sai touched her chest. "Sure. If this is just fear and not a heart attack."

Milo, near Tick-Tick, said, "It was too fast—"

We could not see Specs, but we heard his voice. "That was a warning! Heed it! You will not get another!"

Tick-Tick said, "Let's return the favor. Stay back." She reached into a pouch, pulled out something small and spherical wrapped in wire and electrical tape, and threw it into the middle of the lawn that separated us from Specs's warehouse-turned-fortress.

Clods of dirt and grass sprayed the air as Tick-Tick's homemade bomb exploded. I felt a little ill. She had one left, which we thought we might use if we needed to blow open a door.

Sai shouted, "See, Specs? We've both got things that go boom! There's nothing you can do. Don't worry, we're not going to hurt you or your people. We only want our friends back."

It is hard to reason with people who have different things in their bloodstreams than you do. A third Rat stood up on the roof and raised a pistol, aiming it toward Sai, who was still crouched behind the rusted car.

Tick-Tick said, "We need to lower the technology level around here."

Milo closed his eyes and mumbled something. An explosion came from the roof that was almost as loud as Tick-Tick's had been. Someone began to scream. We all stayed where we were. We had taken first blood, and none of us liked it.

Sai swallowed once, nodded, and we ran to the front door. I reached it first, jumped up against it, and fell back onto the grass. Tick-Tick grabbed the handle, turned it, and swung the door wide. She held her second bomb in one hand, ready to throw it in.

Sai and Leander reached the building and pressed themselves against the outer wall. Leander carried the hunting bow; he peeked through a paint-spattered window, began to draw back an arrow, then grimaced and froze, perfectly still, the arrow half-drawn.

A small kid, maybe twelve years old, in a yellow T-shirt stood inside the door with a pistol in both hands, saying, "Oh-god-oh-god-oh-god-oh-god." His eyes were closed. Tears ran down his cheeks, and the barrel waggled, threatening Tick-Tick and everything in front of the kid, and maybe the kid's feet, too.

Tick-Tick said, "It's fine. Honestly. See? I'm setting down my weapon. See?" She slowly placed her bomb on a table in the hallway. "You do that, too, okay? We'll all be all right, then."

"Oh-god-oh-god-oh-god," the kid said, and the pistol continued to waggle.

"Please," said Tick-Tick. "If you put that down—"

The kid dropped the gun and turned, beginning to run. His pistol hit the floor and fired. Leander grunted, clutched his hip, and fell into the shrubbery by the window. His arrow skidded across the dirt, hurting no one.

I looked back into the house. The kid was partway down the hall. Tick-Tick started forward, as if to follow. Someone stepped into the far hallway, silhouetted against a grimy window. The running kid yelled, "Spe—"

Something exploded. The kid slumped to the floor. Specs held a sawed-off shotgun. Tick-Tick stooped, picking up the kid's pistol. Specs went through a door. Tick-Tick ran after him. The door closed. Tick-Tick kept running toward the stairs.

I needed to leave this place, but Tick-Tick was in there, and Orient was in there, and maybe Florida and Goldy and Mickey were in there, too. Tick-Tick disappeared up the stairs. I yelled, " 'Ih-'Ih!" and followed.

Specs had gone through a rusty sliding door. I put my ear against it; a dumbwaiter was smoothly ascending. It may have been the only thing in this house that had been maintained. In my mind, I saw Specs drawing on the pulley with both hands, his shotgun by his side, a smile of victory or disaster on his face.

I took the stairs two at a time. Above me, Tick-Tick slowed on the second floor, then ran up to the third. Skidding into a long hallway of boarded doors, I saw her boots and the hem of her jacket as she darted into a far room, opposite the open door of the dumbwaiter.

An explosion preceded the crash of broken glass. As I reached the doorway, Tick-Tick shrieked, "Lobo! All clear. Get your ass in here!" Her voice raced the scales and cracked, all elfin calm gone.

The room stank of sweat and gunpowder and blood. It had been a library sometime in the ancient past. It still held a lot of rotting and moldering furniture. A fireplace was inadequately sealed with plywood. One wall was splashed with reddish water. A broken jar lay beneath it.

Orient lay in Tick-Tick's arms. He looked like someone who'd been hit over the head with a tire iron, then left in a room without water for more than a day. His arm was splinted with rags and bits of wood, probably torn from some of the furniture. Tick-Tick looked worse than Orient, who lay there as though he hadn't quite decided yet whether to live or die.

Specs, sprawled on the floor, didn't have that choice.

I swallowed and stepped over Specs's body to give Tick-Tick a canteen and a clean handkerchief from my satchel—we'd been able to figure out some of what we'd need. She soaked the cloth, then held it to Orient's lips. He couldn't swallow at first, but when he was able, Tick-Tick said, "Know anything about Florida, Mickey, or Goldy?"

His eyelids twitched, as if they were scraping over sandpaper. He shook his head. I nodded and ran back into the hallway.

Sai and Milo were there. I could hear people running on the floors below us, opening doors. We did the same, moving down the hall, trying every handle. One door opened. Inside, we found eight or nine Rats huddling in a small room full of dirty mattresses.

One said, "Please, please, we didn't do anything, it was all Specs's idea, he—"

Sai said, "The black guy with gold hair, the armless woman, and the little elf. Where are they?"

Several of the Rats looked toward the back of the house. "They're fine—" one began as another said, "The last room. It doesn't leak or—"

Which was all I needed to hear. I have never run faster than I ran through the hall and toward the farthest door.

(I don't know how to describe the desperate sense of relief that I felt at that moment. I'd been confident that Florida was alive, though I hadn't known whether we could find her. I hadn't been so sure about Mickey and Goldy. I kept telling myself that only people who read too much bad fiction would expect the Rats to casually kill two human beings simply because keeping them as prisoners was inconvenient.

(But people caught up in extreme actions kill in moments of carelessness, anger, or fear. And now, while Specs's stronghold was under attack, the Rats were very likely to commit an act of carelessness, anger, or fear.)

I was the first one into the far room. It stank of decaying cardboard and rotted upholstery. Two windows let the sun knife into the gloom of an open room used for storage, mostly boxes and furniture. One of the items stored there must've been a cage for wild animals, or maybe it was a well-built stage prop. Whatever it had been, it had been turned into a cage for Mickey, Goldy, and Florida. There were blankets on the floor for them, and a wooden table with tin mugs and a jar of reddish water. By the Rats' standards, these prisoners were being treated very well.

The door to the cage was open; the three prisoners were filing out, Florida first, Mickey last. Goldy's hands were fastened behind his back, and his shirt was dirty and torn, but no more than Mickey's or Florida's clothing.

Two Wharf Rats were ordering them out of the cage. I recognized one. Doritos, a wiry black girl who might've been my best friend when I was Gone, held a twenty-two rifle. A tall white guy carried a spear made out of a broomstick and a Bowie knife.

Doritos, turning toward me, began to lift her rifle. I dove behind a pile of decaying sofas and chairs. Milo, two steps behind me, mumbled something. I thought, I should tell him to wait, that we should try to talk first, but how can I tell him anything before he finishes what he's begun?

As my fur tingled, I looked up to see the effect of his magic.

This is the picture I will carry with me always:

Goldy leans forward, his face distorted as he screams something, his elbows wide to his sides as if he thinks he can tear his bonds apart with only a little more effort than he has managed so far.

Mickey mirrors him. The empty sleeves of her dirty dress shirt have come unpinned. They trail behind her like streamers or scarves or some strange holiday garb.

The boy with the homemade spear holds it in front of him like a quarterstaff or a shield. He looks over his shoulder, perhaps to see if more intruders are coming that way, perhaps to see if there's any escape.

Doritos has her rifle butt to her shoulder and the barrel at a sixty-degree angle to the floor. Her lips are taut, as if she's about to cry or laugh or both.

Florida— Well, Florida is leaping toward Doritos. Around her waist, cinching her oversized T-shirt, is a thin beaded belt. From it hangs the empty sheath for the Bowie knife that makes the point of her guard's spear. Her hands are empty. Her fingers are spread like talons or a cat's claws as she grabs at Doritos's rifle. I cannot see her face.

And from Milo's hands, something shimmers through the air like heat above the highway on a summer's day.

I screamed, " 'Ow'!" as I started to sign, *Get down!* I didn't even have time to begin the gesture properly.

When Milo's spell struck her, Florida vanished, not with a bang or a whimper, but as if she had never existed.

Milo said, very quietly, "Oh, dear God."

Doritos stared at the place where Florida had been, then placed her rifle against a box and raised her hands over her head.

The other Rat threw his spear aside and raced into the back of the room. I don't know if he hid there or if he scrambled down a drain or a fire escape. No one went to find him.

Goldy looked from where Florida had been to where Milo stood crying. Goldy twisted from side to side, wrenching madly at whatever held his wrists together. "You—"

Mickey put her shoulder against his and said his name over and over again, quietly: "Goldy. Goldy. Goldy."

Sai said, "Shit. Oh, shit."

Milo said, "I didn't—I mean, I didn't—"

I walked into the middle of the room to meet Mickey and Goldy. Steel handcuffs held Goldy's arms. I gripped the cuffs and pulled, and I pulled, and I pulled, and a steel link broke. That strength was one of the gifts that Leda had given me when she made me Wolfboy and took my voice.

Mickey said, "Ron?"

I walked around the room quite slowly, looking back into the shadows, up into the rafters. Then I went again, a little more quickly, with my nose high, trying to smell everything that was in the room, everything that had been in the room.

"Ron," Mickey said, stepping in front of me.

I ran around her. Sai and Mickey and Goldy all stood in the middle of the room, watching me. I raced back and forth, only pausing to sniff deeply before running again.

Mickey said, "She's not here, Ron."

I picked up the Rat's spear, tore the Bowie knife free of the broomstick shaft, and sniffed the blade and handle. It smelled of wood and steel, adhesive tape, the hands of the boy who had fastened it to the broomstick. I dropped it and ran back to the far end of the building, sniffing, sniffing.

Goldy asked, "What happened?"

Milo said, "The spell, it's um, to—oh, hell, it's supposed to take ten years away from someone, to make them younger, and I thought I could make a Rat helpless that way without hurting anyone, only—"

"Florida didn't have ten years to take," said Mickey.

"I know," said Milo. "I'm not, I'm not—" He licked his lips and started backing away. "It said, *enemy's* life, meaning you can't hope to reverse the effect, and I didn't think she'd jump in the way, I never thought she'd—" He bumped into the door and gasped. "I've got to go home. I'm sorry. I've got to. I really am sorry. I am."

I wrenched open one of the painted-over windows to smell Bordertown. I smelled elves and humans and halfies and dogs and cats and squirrels and pigeons and hawks. I smelled bread baking and meat roasting and soup simmering and garbage rotting and wood burning. I smelled trees and grass and rainwater and Mad River water and mud and earth. I smelled the smells of things living and things dying. Maybe I smelled a smart part of life itself.

I didn't smell Florida.

I howled with all my heart and lungs and guts. Still howling, I turned and ran for the stairs. Goldy tackled me. "No, you don't!" he whispered in my ear. He held me until Mickey could come and press herself against us. We cried until we stopped.

CHAPTER ELEVEN
The Roses of Elfland

I don't know if Sai marched Doritos downstairs or if she let Doritos go. All I know is they went down before we did. Sai met us on the second floor with a goatskin bag of water. Goldy squirted some into Mickey's mouth, then some into his own.

"Better?"

She nodded. "Makes it easier to cry again when I need to."

He looked at her.

"Which isn't yet." She opened her mouth like a goldfish. "More."

Sai half said, half asked, "You guys only had River water with you, too."

Mickey said, "We didn't drink any."

Goldy squirted more clear water into his mouth, then said while Mickey drank, "You ask yourself if you'd rather become an addict or drink urine to put off the decision. Seems a tough choice until you have to make it."

Sai said, "What do we tell people about Florida?"

Mickey looked at Goldy and me. "That we haven't found her."

Goldy said, "And Milo?"

Mickey said, "He's suffering, like us. I don't think we could make it better or worse for him."

An ambulance showed up from the Free Clinic. Leander was loaded in and gone before I could approach him. The kid on the roof whose gun had exploded had lost several fingers; he went in the ambulance, too. The people from the clinic said we could keep Orient, as long as we got someone to look at him soon.

I followed a wad of electrical tape and a few coils of wire and a number of small mechanical pieces across the yard to where Tick-Tick was pouring something out of a small bottle. As I approached, she tossed the bottle aside, then said, "No matter how badly you need a cigarette, don't light it here for at least a minute."

She looked at the Bowie knife in my hands, then looked at my face. She handed me the canvas pouch in which she had carried her two bombs. I nodded my thanks, put the Bowie knife in it, and slung it over my shoulder.

Tick-Tick, Caramel, and a few others carried Orient off on a stretcher. They decided that'd be easier on him than stuffing him into Milo's Mustang and bouncing him through the streets. He looked like he'd decided to live but was reconsidering the decision. He gave me a weak smile with a weak thumbs-up, and I returned them as best I could. No one had told him about Florida.

They carried Orient's stretcher past a tree where two people sat. They both lifted their hands to wave at Orient, and I saw Milo hadn't gone home after all. Sparks was with him, holding his hand, saying nothing. Her head rested against his. I went to find something to do where I couldn't see them.

After a lot of arguing, we let the Rats go, except for the three that Caramel said had helped kill Tejorinin

Yorl. Specs had been the fourth, and the fifth was the one in the ambulance. I was glad Doritos wasn't one of them. I looked for her, but she was gone, probably already seeking another gang of Wharf Rats so she could stay near the River.

Laid out on a table in the Rats' house for the return of the clinic's ambulance were the bodies of Specs and the kid who had dropped his pistol instead of shooting Tick-Tick. I wrote a note and pinned it to Specs's shirt: HE WAS CALLED THE KING OF SPECTACLES. IF YOU CREMATE HIM, POUR HIS ASHES IN THE RIVER. HE'D LIKE THAT. For the little kid, I wrote, HE DIED AFTER SPARING AT LEAST ONE LIFE. TELL HIS FRIENDS AND FAMILY THAT, IF YOU FIND THEM.

Sai thanked everyone who had shown up, and the Gathering of the Gangs dispersed. Sai, Goldy, King O'Beer, Taz, Q. Paul, and Gorty marched the three Rats to the C Street Station while the rest of us followed.

Sai told the copper in charge that they'd only give the Rats to Sunny Rico. Rico came out after a couple of minutes, looked at the three Rats, and said, "For me? How thoughtful. What'd they do?"

Sai said, "Killed Yorl. Let Strider go."

Goldy said, "You get more than you see. A fourth is at the Free Clinic, and a fifth is dead in a Rat nest at Riverside and Morrison."

Rico looked at the three Rats. "Did you kill Yorl?"

One Rat said, "No way."

Another said, "Aren't you going to read us our rights?"

Rico said, "You've got the right to hope you get a smart lawyer or a stupid judge. You've got the right to be polite so people might treat you the same way. You've got the right to tell me the truth, so I won't be pissed that you think I'm simple enough to believe your lies. Want more rights?"

Caramel said, "I saw them do it."

One Rat said, "She's lying," as another said, "It wasn't our fault."

"Oh?" said Rico.

"Specs told us to do it. The elf attacked first."

"Who's Specs?"

Sai said, "The one who won't need to go to trial."

Rico said, "Or be able to tell us why he ordered this."

Sai said, "Add kidnapping to the list." She ticked off the names on her fingers: "Caramel, Orient, Goldy, Mickey, and Florida."

"Why?" Rico asked the Rat who'd confessed.

He said, "Specs told us to."

Rico shook her head and frowned. "So, if this story stands, we'll have who, but not why." She shrugged. "I should be grateful. That's more than we usually get."

Caramel told her story. When she mentioned the ring, Sai said, "It's somewhere safe."

Rico listened through it all, then said, "Look, this'll probably free your friend. You'll have to wait until tomorrow to hear what a judge says. As for the ring, if it's Linden's, there's nothing to prove Specs didn't steal it. Bring it to me tomorrow, and I'll pursue it when we've got some free time. Which means never, unless you can give me more than this."

We headed outside. Gorty, Taz, and Q. Paul left us then. Taz said, "Good luck finding the little elf. She's a good kid."

I nodded, hooked a thumb in the strap of the canvas satchel at my side, and lifted the other hand in farewell as the three Packers drove away.

Mickey told Goldy she wanted to check on the cats, asked me if I was okay, and walked off when I nodded. As she walked away, Goldy signed, *She needs some privacy. You?*

I signed, *I'm fine. Linden won't be.*

Sai, Goldy, and I walked without talking to Orient's apartment. A couple members of the Horn Dance had fetched Doc. She had cleaned and splinted and bandaged Orient, and was preparing to leave when we arrived.

"What do we owe?" Tick-Tick asked.

"Ah, forget it. Wasn't interesting enough to charge you for."

I fetched Doc's coat. Next time she put her hand in her pocket, she'd find seven four-leaf clovers.

We all went out and sat on the steps so we wouldn't disturb Orient. No one spoke. Tick-Tick's face was drawn and tired, almost gray. One pointed ear was bruised and slightly bloody. Sai squinted in the distance, her eyes very Oriental and very elfin at the same time. She wasn't watching anything that I could see. Goldy rubbed his hands over his metallic hair and stared at the sidewalk. It was just after noon of a beautiful day. We needed to celebrate, and we needed to mourn, and we couldn't do either until we had finished this.

Caramel stood nearby, looking like she didn't know whether to stay or leave. Sai called, "Hey, c'mon. Sit and rest. You could use it. We all could."

"Thanks." Caramel sat cross-legged beside me, glanced at Sai, and then at the rest of us. "What're you going to do?"

"We're going to talk too much," Goldy said. "As usual."

Tick-Tick nodded. "And maybe we'll figure it all out. What've we got?" Sai brought the ring from her pocket. "We have the ring," Tick-Tick said. "And a witness." She nodded at Caramel. "We've cleared Strider."

"It's not enough," Sai said.

"It frees him," Tick-Tick said.

"It's not enough," Sai repeated with a shake of her hair.

Goldy nodded. "We've lost Florida. Crystaviel

would've let the rest of us die. The Rats were just Rats, but she's the one who used them."

Sai said, "Strider's friend Leander will have a limp. If he doesn't lose his leg. If he lives."

"Even if we do nothing," Tick-Tick said, "Crystaviel will have to live with it. If she lives long enough, she will see that someday. And even if she never sees it, what she has done will color her life." I wondered if Tick-Tick was remembering Specs. When is someone too far gone for redemption? What do you do when you don't have time to ask that question?

I raised my hand, then started scribbling while they waited: WHY IS RING IMPORTANT? IF LINDEN IS CRYSTAVIEL—& I THINK SHE IS—WHY KILL PARTNER? IF SHE'S NOT C., WHY KILL SOMEONE WHO MEANS LITTLE TO HER? WHY WERE RATS AT DANCELAND FRI. NIGHT IN 1ST PLACE?

"Very good questions," Goldy said. "But do you have very good answers?"

WHY WAS YORL AT DANCELAND? *WHO* IS LINDEN? I underlined *WHO* at least three times.

Goldy said, "No, no, no, my friend. Good *answers*." No one laughed.

"I doubt she's in Rico's files," Tick-Tick said.

I agreed with a nod. Records in B-town are pretty thin.

WHERE IS LINDEN? I wrote last.

Before I could underline WHERE, Tick-Tick sighed. "We're going to have to wake poor Orient."

He woke slightly hysterical, scattering his bedcovers. Tick-Tick put her hand on his brow and he settled down.

"Sorry, kid," he whispered.

"It's all right. Lobo's got some questions."

Orient nodded sleepily. "You guys can't do anything without me." He looked pale enough to be an elf, but he sounded pleased.

I wrote, WHERE'S LINDEN, WILD HUNT'S SINGER?

He closed his eyes, which turned into a wince. After a second, he waved his hand as if feeling for a breeze, then snapped his finger toward the hotel area in midtown. "Thataway," he croaked.

WHERE'S CRYSTAVIEL?

He closed his eyes, then pointed in the same direction. "Ditto."

After that, back sitting in the street, we talked more. Everyone liked my theory; no one liked my plan. No one came up with a better one, so finally we scattered to the various bikes. Tick-Tick stayed with Orient because someone had to—and because she thought this was unnecessary, I think. Or maybe she didn't want to get in a position where she might have to hurt someone else. Caramel was willing to play the part I wanted Tick-Tick to take. The Theater of the Wolf set out for its first bit of improv.

We asked at a few places in midtown for the lead singer of Wild Hunt; somebody said she was staying at the Roses of Elfland. Sai and Goldy weren't happy about waiting in the street, but they agreed. They thought they were there in case the plan fell apart. They were there because I didn't trust them to keep to the script when faced with Linden.

The desk clerk at the Roses of Elfland was a professional; her face never showed us that she knew we couldn't afford to rent a broom closet there for a half-hour nap. She smiled and said, "May I help you?"

I nudged Caramel, who had been gawking at the expensive furniture decorating the lobby and the expensive clothes decorating its occupants. Caramel said, "Uh, what's Ms. Linden's room, please?"

"Do you have an appointment with her?"

"Well, uh, sort of."

"Oh?" There was nothing judgmental in that "oh."

There was almost something hopeful in it, as if the desk clerk wanted Caramel to say the thing that would free the clerk so she could help us.

"We, uh, have something for her."

"Oh?" This was the first "oh," repeated perfectly.

"She, uh, lost it."

The clerk nodded. "You may leave it with us, and we'll see she gets it."

"Yeah, right," Caramel said, then added quickly, "Uh, I mean, we need to see she gets it. Not that we don't trust you or anything, honest, but, uh, we need to see she gets it."

"Oh." This "oh" carried a polite amount of doubt, or perhaps merely confusion.

"Can you tell her we have something for her?"

"I'll see if she's in." The clerk stepped through a door beside the key cabinet. Caramel looked at me, her eyes wide, and I grinned and nodded to tell her she was doing fine. The clerk returned. "What is this you have?"

"It's, uh"—I nodded, and Caramel finished—"a ring. She really ought to look at it, 'cause we really think it's hers."

The clerk went back to the other room, then returned. "Ms. Linden will see you. Room Nine Fifty-one."

Caramel squeezed my hand hard but only let a small smile touch her lips as she straightened her back and said, "Thank you *ever* so much, my good woman."

We rode a very quiet elevator to the ninth floor, then Caramel and I knocked at 951. Linden answered, opening it enough that we could see sunlight and expensive furniture behind her. The room smelled of clove cigarettes, cut roses, and some tart perfume, hiding her true scent.

She wore a sea green dress with billowing sleeves. It was cut on one side to reveal golden stockings set with tiny diamonds. Her hair fell over her right shoulder like a moonlit avalanche of virgin snow. I tried to see if she was Crystaviel, and though I told myself I was sure, I wasn't.

"Yes?" Catching my gaze with her silver eyes, she said, "You helped pack up after the gig at Danceland. We appreciated that." She smiled kindly.

I resisted the urge to bow and say something gracious. Caramel and I looked odd in the clean hall of the Roses of Elfland. We hadn't changed: My jacket and jeans hadn't been improved by the morning's adventure, and Caramel's gray traveling clothes were coated with grease, mud, soot, and half a dozen things less easy to identify.

I almost laughed—our clothes were the least of our oddness. Caramel seemed very shy and very young before Linden, and I was hardly the boy next door. I nudged Caramel. She said, "Uh, we have something."

"So I understand. A ring?"

"Yes," said Caramel, growing more sure of herself. "Belongs to a Crystaviel. Is it yours?" She showed the silver and sapphire ring. It was almost identical to the three on Linden's right hand.

"No." Linden blinked at us. "But it looks just like mine. Your Crystaviel and I have remarkably similar taste." When neither of us said anything immediately, she smiled thinly and began to close the door. "Good day."

Okay, it was a stupid plan. I had an impression ball in my pocket, recording since we stepped off the elevator. Nothing we recorded would be proof, not in court, but I'd hoped we'd get something that would convince Rico to probe into Linden's past. That was shot now.

Then Caramel said, just before the door closed, "So you won't care if we take it to the coppers." Something about the way she said it reminded me that she'd watched Tejorinin Yorl die.

The door stopped swinging. Linden's face was

framed in it, a porcelain face haloed in sunlight. "Why should I?"

"No reason." Caramel stroked the ring between her thumb and forefinger. "What do you think a wizard could learn from this? Betcha one could find its owner, at least. Betcha we'd get a good reward."

Linden's lips pressed together, and she shook her head slightly. Silver strands of hair drifted freely. "What do you want?"

I grinned. I doubt I could've put my whole face into it. Baring the teeth was probably enough.

"Money? It is a nice ring." She reached for it, and Caramel stepped back.

I waggled a finger at her: *Tut, tut, tut.*

"So," she said. "What's the price of your silence?"

I nodded and looked at Caramel until she asked the obvious question: "Silence about what?"

Linden stood in the doorway and stared as if she was seeing something besides us. Then she swung the door hard to close it. I let it bounce against the palm of my hand.

Linden had begun to run back into her suite. As she whirled to face us, her face settled into something angry and strong, as if a glamour to disguise her was sliding away or she was an actor shifting from one role to another. None of her features changed, yet now she was unmistakably Crystaviel.

I opened my pouch and held it open before her.

Crystaviel stood still. I wondered what options she was weighing, what emotions she wanted to satisfy. She satisfied curiosity. After she looked, she said, "A knife?"

"Is it any knife?" asked Caramel.

"No," said Crystaviel, smiling tightly. "It is not *any* knife."

Caramel smiled, too. She crooked her finger, beckoning Crystaviel to continue.

Crystaviel said, "You have her? She is safe?"

I cocked my head to one side.

Crystaviel said, "I can take her across in the morning."

Caramel said, "Money?"

"I paid Specs!"

I shook my head quickly.

"—half," Crystaviel said, as if finishing the sentence.

"Specs is dead," said Caramel. "So's that deal."

Crystaviel closed her eyes and nodded. "What do you want for her?"

"For Florida?"

"Yes," said Crystaviel. "I've only got the funds I planned to pay Specs—"

"Or for being quiet about you hiring Specs to kill Tejorinin Yorl?"

"When I'm back in Faerie with the child, I can triple—"

Caramel and I drew the conversation out as long as we could, and then we left after setting a meeting place for the next morning.

In the elevator, Caramel gave a quick jab in the air with her fist and said, "Yes!" The operator glanced at both of us. I gave my best rabid wolf laugh, and the operator pretended we weren't there for the rest of the ride down.

Rico liked the impression ball. Lieutenant Linn preferred the ring—he coaxed all the magic out of it and found not just Crystaviel-as-owner but a little trick that made it seem that where the ring was, Crystaviel was, too. Just in case somebody being led into an alley should need a little magical reassurance that this was a safe place to go.

We put together two stories. This is the official one, the one that Rico filed:

In the Elflands, Crystaviel and Tejorinin Yorl had

been joined in whatever passes for marriage there. It was not a good union. Crystaviel ran away to Bordertown, changed her name, and became a musician.

Then Yorl inherited wealth, whatever that might be in Faerie. It came with a condition: For Yorl or Crystaviel to keep the inheritance, they had to be living together, or if one had died or left their union, the other must be living with their child.

Since they had no child, Yorl came to Bordertown to fulfill the first condition. Crystaviel decided to arrange for the second by killing Yorl and stealing an orphaned elfling to present as their child. When Yorl walked into Danceland, the hired Wharf Rats were already waiting for him.

The same Rats kidnapped the elf child and her human guardians. But before Crystaviel could arrange to take the child into Faerie, the humans' friends rescued them. In the rescue, the elf child fell into the Mad River and went under, never to be seen again.

To reinforce this story, Orient's going to edit together pieces of his diary and mine, add the necessary lies, and publish it in *Surplus Art*. It'll stop people from wondering about what happened in Specs's home so they can wonder about something new.

If the story falls apart in Faerie because someone notices that Yorl and Crystaviel were never the subjects of an eccentric will, Crystaviel will say Yorl told her a desperate lie in the hope of getting her to return with him. And that lie led to his death. It's the sort of moral tale that elves like.

As for Crystaviel's friends who know she was hunting for Faerie's heir, she will tell them that she could not find the child in Bordertown, which is nothing but the literal truth, and that the Yorl affair prevents her from returning, which is also quite literally true. Strider assures me that it is not easy to pass unnoticed between Bordertown and Faerie.

And why should Crystaviel support this story? Here's the true version:

When Yorl learned that Strider was in Bordertown, he swore that he'd kill Strider for the sake of his honor—I have no idea what had happened in Faerie, but judging from their conversation at Orient's apartment, Yorl thought Strider was more than a political opponent. Crystaviel tried to dissuade him while she searched for the Elflands' missing heir.

And at last she found Florida. When Florida had had her fifteen stitches at the Free Clinic, the docs took her into a magic-free room for a physical—standard practice in a place where magic is undependable. None of Florida's protectors had considered that in our concern for her. Someone saw the moles on the kid's shoulder.

Crystaviel's first move was to set up the confrontation at Danceland, where Strider would not suspect her and, if he recognized Yorl, would not think their meeting had anything to do with Florida. Yorl, confident of his ability with his dueling blade, expected to kill Strider. He never saw that Crystaviel won no matter who died. Whether Strider was killed or arrested for Yorl's death, he would be out of Crystaviel's way. So, when Goldy and Sai broke up the fight in Danceland and Strider didn't demand an immediate duel, Crystaviel sent Specs and his Rats after Yorl.

Both stories end with Crystaviel arrested for arranging the death of Tejorinin Yorl. Why would she prefer the first? Because in it, she is not ultimately responsible for the destruction of the Elflands' heir.

Why would we let her tell the first? Because Strider and Leander said it would give their side more time to plan what to do next in Faerie, now that Florida wasn't a factor in their struggle.

A week after Caramel and I visited the Roses of Elfland, we all went to the Wall to watch two elven Silver

Suits escort Crystaviel through the gate to Faerie. No matter what happened to her there, she wouldn't come through the gate again—not as Crystaviel, not as Linden. Rico told us she was officially Not Welcome in Bordertown.

We dressed in our best, of course. Orient was up and around, maybe a little too pleased with the effect his arm made in a black sling. Caramel stayed close to him; Tick-Tick thought Orient didn't need any more nursing, but Caramel was very protective of him still.

Crystaviel saw us. We meant her to. I saw her give a quick look to Orient, but he didn't move an eyebrow.

As Crystaviel went through, Strider called out something in Elvish.

"What was that?" Sai asked him.

"Jealous, love? Never you mind."

But I had learned enough Elvish to recognize the proverb. At least, I'd always thought it was a proverb. Now I'm not sure. Loosely, it's, Love wealth and glory more than life itself, and starve in splendor. It might be a curse. It might be part of Faerie's penal code.

Strider and Sai went to visit Leander in the hospital. They brought him a black walnut cane. They said Wiseguy was there with a brass-and-mahogany one.

I went to the banks of the Mad River and watched it roll from Faerie into the World. After a while, I threw a Bowie knife far out into the water. The splash it made was like a hand waving in the sunlight. I signed, *No, you have big fun.*

We all met back at Danceland. Goldy made coffee, and Orient found Dancer's lost receipt book. And I began to write this, the story of Florida and Crystaviel.

It's over now. Go home.

CHAPTER TWELVE
Fast Forward #2

I find there's something else to tell you. That and the fact that about a year passed uneventfully in Bordertown—uneventfully by B-town standards, anyway—are all you really need to know from this chapter. If you want, skip to the next.

If you'd like to know a little about that uneventful year, you're in the right place. Read on.

Leander and Wiseguy went to Faerie. Leander told Strider that maybe he could do more for their side at home. Wiseguy said she'd tell us all about the other side, "Elves be damned," then added, "If I can," as Tick-Tick said, "Intentions and deeds are often strangers. Good luck."

I don't know if Wiseguy's departure means halfies can get into Faerie, or only those who marry rich and powerful elves. At the gate, Leander saluted us with his cane (the gnarly one that Strider and Sai had given him), Wiseguy blew us a kiss, and their dark-skinned elven baby clapped his hands. I gave them a Shel Silverstein book so they could bring the kid up right.

Milo announced that he'd never do magic again. His home became a used car lot once more, or rather, it became a used bike lot, since he only managed to sell two of his cars.

Sparks began working at the Free Clinic while taking medical classes at the University Without Floors.

Mickey decided to sell Elsewhere and teach poetry and philosophy at the U. Goldy quit working at Danceland and began at the U. also, teaching reading and sign to little kids.

Gorty and Q. Paul died in a fight with some Trues. They say one died going back to help the other, but no one agrees who fell and who returned. Taz said she'd tell if anyone could give her a good reason why it mattered.

Taz and Caramel moved in together. Taz left the Pack and took Goldy's job at Danceland, and Caramel began waiting tables there. They seemed happy.

Strider and Sai kept their Danceland jobs, and Tick-Tick kept fixing things, and Orient kept finding things. Life rarely changes significantly for everyone.

I did two things worth mentioning.

I fixed up my homesweet. I moved the stacked office furniture downstairs, and I cleaned the windows, and I rigged a rope ladder so I could haul up large things lashed onto my back. Remembering Milo's arrangement in the car display, I turned what had probably been an office lounge into a kitchen, and I turned what must've been the president's office into a library. I kept thinking I'd invite someone over, but I never did.

And I spent more time in—passed more time in? gave more time to?—the Nevernever. I began to wonder if anyone had written about it yet, and I started to keep notebooks of what I saw. Sometimes I'd find plants that

I'd never seen before, or animals that the history books said were extinct.

Once I thought I saw a dragon. After comparing my sketch with paintings in dinosaur books at Elsewhere, I found I'd seen a primitive pterosaur—flying reptile—called *Rhamphorhynchus*. I watched for Rhamphy on every trip after that, but I never saw her again.

I spent enough time in the Borderlands that I quit trying to figure out exactly how much time passed in B-town. It didn't matter. Things changed. So did I.

That sounds like philosophy, but it wasn't. It was a way not to think. For at least a year, however you count time, it worked.

CHAPTER THIRTEEN

Dancing at the Dead Warlocks' Ball

The third act began one sunny spring afternoon while I was standing in line at the Magic Lantern. The marquee promised *The Seven Samurai* and *The Court Jester*, and I could use a few hours of forgetting my woes. A couple of Dragon's Tooth elves in shiny red leather were talking too loudly behind me. They would drop their parents' Faerie silver in front of the ticket taker and get in without a second's hassle. I'd probably be laughed at for my last, rather wilted, four-leaf clover.

Just before I got to the ticket window, something crashed and rattled in the street like a sink chucked from a fourth-floor window. There aren't any fourth floors near the Lantern, so I turned.

Someone wearing leather coveralls and a helmet decked with purple mop braids was somersaulting down the middle of Ho Street. A big plum-black Triumph Bonneville was spinning on its side, with its front forks badly twisted. The bike didn't have any wheels. I looked to see if the wheels were rolling away, then realized what that meant.

Someone snickered. Someone else said, " 'Nother Dead Warlock lives down to 'is name."

That was one of the Dragon's Tooth elves. He was taller than me, of course, but I stared. Some poor bastard may've died in the street, and this kid's making jokes so he won't have to care. He looked nervous, then said to his friend with forced cool, "C'mon, let's catch the show."

If the Dragon's Tooth kid hadn't said anything, I might've gone into the theater, too. I left the line and went into the street. The Dead Warlock was standing by her bike, shaking her head in disgust. What I'd taken for a helmet was purple-and-white hair that hung in matted strands about her face. The leather coveralls might've been any color once. Now they were a study in dust, mud, and grease, cinched at her waist with a studded black belt.

A couple of thoughts zoomed by: She shouldn't be standing up or moving around until a doc or a healer has looked her over. I shouldn't be out here. All I knew for situations like this was to keep her still and keep her warm. She clearly wasn't interested in either.

She seemed to be fine. Either she'd been thrown into a patch of magic where a protective spell saved her, or she had the kind of stupid luck that saves suicidal people and kills innocent bystanders.

She glanced at me and lifted her left eyebrow, which was perfectly white, then her right, which was the same purple as the right half of her hair. She was short for an elf, though she didn't look like a halfie. Cocking her fists on her hips, she said, "Well, furball, you gawkin' or helpin'?"

I shrugged and grabbed the Triumph's front fork. She'd need someone with tools or magic to get it perfect, but I straightened it to a reasonable degree.

She wasn't impressed. She said, "Help me drag this."
It wasn't an order or a request. She treated me like an
old friend who'd help out as a matter of course.

The line at the Lantern watched us without com-
menting. I was probably the reason they were silent.
(Most B-towners think Dead Warlocks are silly or
frightening, so they get a lot of harassment and not
much sympathy. I thought the Dead Warlocks were silly
and frightening. How do you explain people who ride
helmetless through B-town on bikes without wheels?
They're either magicians or able to afford one. But if
you're peeling wheelless and hit a patch where magic
fails, you're not frightening. You're hamburger.)

I didn't have to help move her bike. Magic would
have flowed back to the spot where it lay in a second or
an hour. The Dead Warlock could have sat and waited
till then. People would have passed by her and gawked
or sneered or laughed, as they pleased. . . .

I hoisted her bike and carried it about ten feet away.
The engine kicked in, a healthy rumble to impress or
annoy everyone within three blocks. I set the bike
down. Once vertical, it hovered about six inches above
the dusty street.

"Thanks," the Dead Warlock shouted, throwing one
leg over the bike.

I nodded.

"You don't talk much, Dutch."

I raised an eyebrow.

" 'S right, Dwight. People babble constantly, never
say a thing."

I hear that too many times from kids who want to
sound profound. She just sounded tired. I looked at her
again. If she'd been human, I'd've put her at seventeen,
tops. I lifted my right hand as if I held a cup by its handle, and I tipped it once toward my lips.

"Coffee?" Her gaze settled on me. Her silver eyes
were as opaque as mirrors or camera lenses. "Hot

damn, Sam." Her grin was almost a sneer. Her teeth were small and feral and yellow. "Coffee'd be nice."

I picked up a rock and scrawled TACO HELL on the pavement.

"I know it. Hop on, Juan."

I swung onto the back of the bike, and we headed out. The Dead Warlock smelled of wood smoke and oil and leather and old sweat, an ugly but erotic scent. If you've got a dog's nose, anyway. I could feel her ribs beneath her stiff leathers.

Her seedybox began to play Home Service's eerie cover of an ancient Roundhead hymn. I nodded to the rhythm. Once, as the bike raced along a downhill slope, the volume decreased, telling me we'd hit an eddy of low magic. Before I could jump, the Warlock downshifted and hit the throttle. The Triumph coughed like a sick submachine gun, but we rocketed.

I closed my eyes until the engine ran normally again. The Dead Warlock laughed delightedly. The moment she did, I knew who she was. I've never been so glad I couldn't speak. If she wondered why I let go of her waist, she never said anything.

Mingus was tending counter at Taco Hell. He said, "Yo, the Wolf!" and set out a mug of black coffee. "That's twenty-five and a half World dollars, six Faerie silvers, or one ounce of fresh four-leafs you owe us."

I cocked my thumb at the Dead Warlock.

Mingus grinned wider, set out the second mug with a bit of a bow, and said, "Twenty-six seventy-five, six and three coppers, or one and a twentieth, but, hey, who's counting?"

Mingus is three-fourths Ojibway, one-fourth elf, and five-fourths nice guy. When he was younger, he led the Thunderbirds, a mostly Amerindian gang that operates out of a couple of blocks called Little Earth.

As I turned to go, Mingus said, "You okay?"

I nodded quickly and carried the mugs to a corner

booth. The place was quiet in the afternoon. That's one of Bordertown's unwritten rules: Nothing comes alive until night. There were two Native American kids and an elf with dyed black braids, all in Thunderbird vests, at one table. Near them, four humans in Pack-black ignored two elves in Bloodred at a third table, who were ignoring the Packers. Like most of the places I like to go, Taco Hell's neutral territory. People got tired of fighting for the right to go into debt to Mingus for his Meltdown Burritos.

The Dead Warlock dumped cream and honey into her coffee until it was dessert. "Nice place, Ace."

Taco Hell used to be a car dealer's showroom. Mingus and the Thunderbirds dragged in furniture from a dozen different restaurants, then painted the boarded-up windows with a mural showing a running bird outwitting an inventive but unlucky dog in a wasteland that reminded me of the barren parts of the Nevernever.

We sipped our coffee. I spilled sugar on the table and wrote: NAME? Then I tapped on the table with a claw to get her attention.

"Huh?" She looked from her mug to me, then to the table. "Oh. I'm The Scent of Heather One Dewy Dawn in Autumn, of the House Where Two Queens Fell." Her bitter smile touched her face again and disappeared as quickly.

If I were elven, I would've understood immediately. Being human (having been human?), it took me a minute. Her clothes, her hair, and her manner said that she was of Soho. Soho elves rarely use their elven names, not even their elven names translated into English. I wondered whether to think of her as Dawn or Heather, then understood her joke. She had given me the name of someone she had been, not someone she was. She'd given me the name of someone she thought was dead.

A Dead Warlock. Right. If I hadn't recognized her, I

would've pitied her. I wondered if a real name hid somewhere in her, then wondered why I cared.

The answer came quickly. If she didn't think she was alive, I couldn't make her hurt.

"What about you, McGoo?"

I almost wrote LOBO, then decided to stick to what I'm usually called: WOLFBOY. I didn't want to romanticize my condition. Not for her.

She nodded and went back to her coffee. She played with her drink, slurping loudly, then swirling the surface with her spoon, then slurping again, every so often glancing out one of the few remaining windows. Kids passed by, some human, some elf, some not so easy to identify.

She said, "Many of you in town?"

I shrugged my confusion.

"Wolfboys. There many wolfboys in town?"

I lifted my index finger.

"Oh." She stared at me. "Thought I knew one once. Must've been the family dog." She laughed, much too loudly.

When she drained her mug, Mingus refilled it, giving me a look that said he didn't understand why I was hanging out with this sullen, dirty elf. I ignored him. If I'd wanted advice, I'd've taken the Warlock to Danceland and let Sai treat me as though I were only two years old.

The Dead Warlock glanced out the window, then drummed her forefingers on the table and whistled tunelessly, then sat perfectly still and fixed me with a stare. "So, whatcha do for fun, son? Chase cats?"

I could've answered half a dozen different things, but that's when the Plan came to me in all its soiled glory. I wrote: I HIT THE NEVERNEVER. I was Montresor offering Fortunato a taste from the cask of Amontillado.

She looked at me, and I was sure she saw through me. All she said was, "The wild woods? I hear it's bad.

Monsters and all. But the best dream'shrooms, if you call tell 'em from the poisonous ones."

I shrugged, smoothed the sugar, and wrote: NEVER BEEN?

"Nah." She had her nose back in the coffee mug.

WANT TO?

She looked down, frowned. "With you?"

I grinned, which isn't always reassuring.

"Hard to imagine there'd be anything worse than you out there, McHair." She smiled a little, like she'd meant it as a compliment.

You should know, I thought, and worried a tiny bit because she didn't seem to. I wrote: BIGGER THAN ME. NOT WORSE. I love a good line. I smoothed that out quickly, wrote, NAH. STORIES ARE JUST STORIES. I spilled more sugar. Mingus should've gotten after me for wasting the stuff. I'VE MADE 12 TRIPS. NO HASSLES.

"Why me?"

Her brain hadn't shut down entirely. Good. I'VE LEFT THINGS I COULDN'T CARRY.

"I'm the only person you can sucker into this?"

FOR 10% OF THE TAKE.

"Ten percent." Her eyes narrowed.

YOU'RE FEET AND HANDS. I KNOW THE WILD LANDS.

"Feet and hands and a bike, Ike. Don't dismiss me."

I started to smile, then squashed the impulse. 20%, I wrote.

"All right, Dwight," she said, getting bored again, and I began to wonder if I was crazy.

The Scent of Heather One Dewy Dawn in Autumn, of the House Where Two Queens Fell, was the elf I'd known as Leda, the elf who cursed me. I was sure I knew why she didn't recognize me. She thought she had turned me into a dog, not Teen Wolf—just another case of Magic Not Always Working Right in Bordertown. Or maybe my transformation wasn't important enough to remember. Maybe she didn't remember anything of what she'd done as a pampered Dragon's Tooth princess.

For a second, that made me wonder why I was sure I'd found her. My senses had changed; I no longer saw or heard or smelled things quite the way I had. The Dead Warlock was fifteen pounds lighter than Leda or the Dragon's Tooth princess, her hair was chopped short and dyed extravagantly, her clothes were grungy leather and coarse cotton without the slightest bit of the care that Leda or the princess had shown in what she wore—

But I remembered the laugh. In the Warlock's weary features, I saw Leda's death mask.

And when I saw Leda, I remembered Florida leaping for the rifle that threatened me. I remembered being unable to catch her eye to sign to her, being unable to say a single word to warn her, to save her.

"So, when do we go, Joe?"

MAÑANA. DAWN.

"Don't'cha wanna sleep before?"

I underlined the DAWN.

"Yeah, yeah. I dunno, Moe. The Nevernever. You don't worry about monsters? Or the wild elves?"

I looked at her and said nothing.

She laughed. "Listen to me! Worry like a Dragon's Tooth matron, eh? Hey, if we've got a day, let's find some real fun."

I looked at her.

"It's gonna be dull in the woods."

I doubted that.

"C'mon, I'll take you to a proper house party. Show you what Dead Warlocks do on a blitz, Fritz."

Humans on the downhill slide become River addicts. For elves, the Big Bloody is just water. What did a self-destructive elf do? What would be the effects on me as boy werewolf?

If I left her, I might never find her again. I wrote: FUN COULD BE GOOD.

* * *

We rode to a house in the heart of True Blood territory. Half a dozen wheelless bikes hovered outside where anyone with the guts could steal them, drive them away slow, ready to jump if they hit a spot of dead magic, then wheel, paint, and sell them. But what thief was that desperate?

The Dead Warlocks' house was a mess from the outside, so I figured the inside would be worse. It was. The only thing that distinguished it from the lowest Rat hideout was that the kids sprawled on the ancient mattresses were elves. The mix of social types was surprising. Some seemed to be further gone than Leda (I could not think of her as The Scent of Heather). Others were immaculate visitors, slumming for kicks. I recognized one.

His eyes opened wide when he saw me. "Can it be? Our own good Wolfboy in this sordid den of elven degradation?"

I gave him a thumbs-up and a grin. Ash Bieucannon may live near the heart of Soho, but he's the ultimate slummer. He wore a loose white silk shirt, a thin lizard-skin belt, baggy green cotton trousers, and rope sandals. A lock of silver hair hung in his eyes. One arm was around a halfie whose ruddy skin betrayed her human heritage; the other was around a slender, blue-haired elven boy. I couldn't tell if he was clinging to them from affection or for support. All three had slightly bloody bandages around their left wrists, as if they'd sworn a suicide pact, then changed their minds. Most of the inhabitants of the house wore similar bandages.

Ash said, "Hale wants to paint you. You should go. It'd make him happy."

I nodded. Hale's the lone human artist sharing work space with Ash and several elves at the Mock Avenue Studio. Hale had spotted my face in Danceland and mentioned something about me posing. If I stayed away from Danceland for a week, he might forget about it. If you're not vain, posing is like watching paint dry, but with the exciting parts removed.

"He hasn't long to live, you know."

I stopped. I didn't know Hale well, but I liked him.

"After all, he's"—Ash began to grin—"human." All three doubled up in laughter.

Leda jerked a finger at Ash. "This a friend of yours?"

I shrugged.

"What a douche."

"I?" Ash indicated himself with an extravagant sweep of his long, perfect fingers. "A douche? I am an artist, my dear lady . . ."

"Scumbag."

He nodded. "Excuse me. My dear Lady Scumbag. And if I must . . ." He paused and frowned. "I must . . ." He looked back at me. "Wolfboy! Did I say that Hale wanted to paint—"

I nodded. Leda sneered and shoved Ash's shoulder. He fell back among his companions, and they all began to giggle. Leda took my hand and drew me toward the back room.

A huge bald elf in Blood leathers draped with silver chains stepped in front of us. Her jacket was open, showing a body-builder's corded muscles. "What's this?"

"Get outta here, Sunshine. You know me."

"Not you. Him."

Leda spun on her heel and stared at me, then looked back at the behemoth. "He looks human to you?"

"This is elf turf."

"You want to shave his ears to see, McGee?"

I snarled. A couple in the corner suddenly noticed they weren't the whole of the world. Both of them gasped. Sunshine took one step back. Her fists closed, then opened slightly.

Leda looked at me. "Any reason you should leave, Steve?"

I shook my head.

"See?" she said to Sunshine. "Everything's copacetic."

"Copacetic." Sunshine grinned, savoring the word. "Ye-es. Truly copacetic." She nodded and, with a flourish of her hand, indicated that we might pass. Leda hadn't convinced her, and I hadn't frightened her. We'd kept up appearances, the most important thing to do when dealing with elves.

In the back room, an elf with a red Fu Manchu mustache sat with his sneakers on a desk. He wore a long, brightly colored tie-dyed cotton coat over something like green pajamas. His eyes were closed and an impression ball was in one hand. I recognized the label: Cats Laughing's third album. He opened his eyes, set aside the impression ball, put his sneakers on the floor, and smiled. "The Doctor is in."

His desk was bare, except for the impression ball, a scalpel, a tube of Gold-N-Rod, a bowl of white paste, and a roll of clean bandages. Leda unzipped a pocket that ran down the thigh of her coveralls and brought out a battered copy of *Love and Rockets #73*.

"A pre-Change comic book," she said, placing it in front of him. "It's good. Has nothing to do with the band that stole the name."

"I recognize it. Hardly mint condition."

"I can take it elsewhere."

He picked it up and set it on a shelf behind him that was cluttered with items of high trade value, like art deco lamps and video recordings in half a dozen formats. "No need, my dear." He gestured toward the scalpel and paste. "Be my guest."

She nodded at me. "Him, too."

The Doctor laughed. "The back cover is missing.

There's tape on the front. The staples are rusty. Some-one wrote on—"

I pulled out my wallet and shook out my last four-leaf clover.

"This?" The Doctor held it up between two fingers so it dangled, wilted and limp and sad. "This is to laugh." I shrugged.

"But since you're making your first visit, you may owe me." He tucked the four-leaf behind his ear.

"Right-o." Leda shoved back her sleeve, revealing a white wrist crisscrossed with ugly little scars. She placed the tip of the scalpel a third of the way up her forearm.

"Damn it, don't—"

The Doctor's words came too late. Leda slashed downward without expression and grunted, "Do it, Hewitt."

The Doctor, clucking disparagingly, smeared her cut with the white paste. She gasped, then grinned as it mixed with her blood. While the Doctor wiped her arm with Gold-N-Rod, he said, "Little shallow sideways slices, please. I *do not* want to lose a good customer."

Leda kept her eyes closed while the cut contracted under the Gold-N-Rod. I doubt she heard the Doctor. Her smile made me wonder what she did hear.

The Doctor bandaged her, then wiped his scalpel on a rag that smelled of alcohol. "Next patient, please."

I looked at the white paste until he said, "You don't know? It's *abed peca'aryn*." I tucked my chin and raised an eyebrow, not because I didn't recognize it but because I didn't recognize it in this form. It smelled like catnip, ginger, and something, well, elven. "Oh, you Bordertown youths have no education. Dragon's Milk, *capisc'*? A purer form. Trust me. You'll love it."

Hale'd drunk Dragon's Milk. He said it only made him ill. God only knew what it'd do to me. I held out my wrist. The Doctor said, "Hmm," clipped away a little fur, said, "Next time you come prepped or I charge double," then sliced. Before I felt the cut, he smeared cool paste on it. I had just enough time to wonder if this would affect me at all.

Someone tore off the top of my skull and threw my brain skyward.

Then Leda and I were in the front room, drinking something bitter with Ash Bieucannon and his friends. Ash said, " 'S won'erful, eh, Wolfboy? I always knew you were elven. Those eyes and those ears . . . and you're so serene." He began to giggle, so I roared, knowing that they'd all laugh more. Sure enough, they did.

In the Dead Warlocks' house, we listened to music and danced and played hide-from-the-monster (I was the monster) and find-the-monster (me, again) in the many dilapidated rooms. I remember being delighted that everyone liked me, and I remember how much I liked them all, even Leda.

That delight lasted until the end of find-the-monster, when I was alone in a dusty closet on the third floor. I began to snuffle, as if I was about to cry. To stop myself, I howled. Three elves threw open the door and dived on me, screaming, "Die, monster, die!" I threw them back. One hurt her head against the wall. She looked at the blood on her fingers and laughed. Leda and I must've left the house soon after that.

I was walking through Soho. It had begun to rain, a warm rain that flattened my fur and made it smell good. Something was in my hand. I looked: a Chinese menu. I thought of beef chow mein and wondered if I was on my way to or from Lee Ho Fouk's.

In the Dancing Ferret, I went to the bar and growled, " 'Eer! Wa' 'eer!" I don't know if they gave me beer, or if they gave me anything at all.

It was night. Sai was escorting me out of Danceland. "I didn't think you did this crap anymore." Her grip was firm, but her voice was sad. As she shook her head, lush black hair swung in strands across her plump halfie features, hiding and revealing her eyes like a strobe light's flicker.

I shook my head, too, trying to say I didn't think I did this anymore either. Strider was escorting Leda. He wore the same emerald Danceland T-shirt that Sai did; they were on duty. I remembered that I was wearing a gold one and felt ashamed that they were throwing me out. I had no idea why they were throwing me out, no awareness that there was a reason or that there should be one.

"Screw you, Blue," Leda told Strider. "We didn't do a thing."

"Yep. And you won't."

" 'Orry," I howled. " 'I'er, I 'orry."

He let go of Leda and came over to me. " 'S right, Wolf. We each get to do something stupid once or twice." He threw an arm around my shoulders. "Don't make a habit of it, hey?"

They turned to go back into Danceland. Sai paused at the door, then said, "Stop by for brunch in the next day or two, okay? *Huevos rancheros*, all you can eat."

" 'Ai," I yelled. "I 'ove 'ou, 'Ai!"

The rain must've quit while we were in Danceland. The stars were out, large and misty like will-o'-the-wisps. They sang. I leaped in the street, reaching for them. Though I fell every time, I didn't mind. Leda followed behind me, singing something elven with an amazingly pure voice.

One last disjointed memory of that night: I lay in the dark on an old foam mattress for which I'd traded a statue of a grinning black mouse in yellow shorts and red shoes. I was still dressed. A sound had woken me. I started to sit up, then realized that someone was sleeping with his or her head on my stomach. The someone had taken all the blankets. I was not alone. I smiled and went back to sleep.

CHAPTER FOURTEEN
Vengeance Is Mine

Another sound woke me early the next afternoon. I had a headache, just enough to keep me from appreciating the day, which was warm and bright through the thin paisley curtains I'd hung over the east windows. I heard the sound again. Someone was vomiting in my kitchen. How do you ignore that?

I stood, reeled slightly, caught my balance, and padded into the next room. Leda was in the center of the kitchen with an empty—well, previously empty—ice pail in front of her. She wiped her chin with my dish towel, threw that into the sink, and said, "How you feel?"

If I'd picked her up and spun like a shot-putter, I could probably have thrown her from the kitchen, through the central room, and out a window. If I'd roared and lunged at her, she would've jumped through a window by herself and run away with her heart pumping triple-time. Neither choice would have measured up to the Plan.

I just shook my head and went to the fridge. The ice pails in its bottom held cool water. The last of the milk smelled a little funny, but I chugged it.

"I don't suppose you have any peca?"

I don't suppose you'll shut up, I thought.

"Alcohol? Smoke? Anything?"

I shook my head again.

"Screw it. I don't need anything."

Don't deserve anything, I thought. I couldn't remember the night and was grateful when I saw we were both still wearing yesterday's clothes. There was half a bottle of grape juice left, so I handed that to her. She took it and smiled. "You're all right, Wolfboy. You know how long it's been since anyone's been nice to me?"

Shut up, I thought. I'm setting you up. I'm setting you up good.

She shook her head, fluffing the purple-and-white hair. "Forget I said anything. I'm fine." She sipped the grape juice, then put her hand on my arm. "I want you to know—"

I jerked my arm away and went into the central room. I knew all I needed to know.

"Head hurt?" she said, following me.

I nodded too fast, but she didn't seem to notice.

"I'll try to be quiet. You'll feel better in a bit." She returned to the kitchen while I lay on the mattress. I heard her come back but didn't open my eyes for several minutes. When I did, she held out the last of the bread and smoked sturgeon. As I accepted the food, she smiled again, a very small and almost sisterly smile. Yeah, I thought, I'm setting her up good.

I stuffed a change of clothes, a blanket, a frying pan, a tinderbox, a quart of water, a bag of flour, a bag of wild rice, some salt, and a tin of lard into a rucksack. When I asked if she had anything to fetch, she said she had everything she needed.

On leaving, she looked at the rope ladder and said, "I

climbed that last night?" I shrugged, meaning I might've carried her. She shook her head. "We're both loco, Lobo."

At Trader's Heaven, I looked longingly at coffee beans, then sacrificed a red baby blanket with an attractive yellow "S" design for two pounds of walnuts and raisins.

We took the West Road out of Bordertown. Leda kept yelling over the engine's roar about what a wild thing this was to do. I kept thinking the word she wanted was *stupid*. I felt better when we left the burbs behind. Bordertown has its own smell, something dirty and vital that I love. The woods have something old and pure that I forget in the city.

Leda kept the Triumph at eighty mph. Maybe she thought that if she hit a magicless current, her speed would carry us through. The accident in front of the Lantern wouldn't contradict that; she'd probably been doing twenty or so in the city. Or maybe she figured that eighty would ensure a quick death, if we lost our luck. Maybe she just liked speed.

While we rode, I tried to piece together the previous night. All I could remember were the bits I've already told. So I tried to develop the Plan, which was simple. I'd take her far into the Borderlands, then leave her to wander helplessly through the woods and the wastes, just as she had left me to wander through B-town as a dog or a freak. I wanted my face to fill her thoughts, for her to hate me as I hated her.

If she made it back to B-town, I'd consider us even, all debts paid in full. If she made it back to B-town, she wouldn't be the same person. The Borderlands change those who travel through them.

Leda yelled something in Elvish that I didn't catch. The engine quit. I let go of her, ready to leap, then realized that we were cruising fine. She laughed. "Sorry,

Wolf. Should've warned you. No need for the engine noise. Doesn't seem right out here."

I heard a crow laugh, seconding her statement, and a nearby stream, hidden in the brush, rushing down from the hills to parallel the West Road. She had her seedybox on low. When I pointed over her shoulder at it, she said, "Mozart. I've got some new stuff, if you'd rather." I shook my head. She turned her attention back to the road. It was nice, cruising along with the classical playing under the shading oaks and elms.

I began to appreciate the wheelless, too. Bordertown hasn't the resources to keep its streets in good shape, let alone its highways to nowhere. Leda's bike stayed close to the earth; when we passed over a pothole or jumped a fallen branch, the bike rocked or dipped like a boat meeting small waves.

Our speed whipped our clothes and our hair. Leaves and litter rustled as we passed. The sun was warm on my fur. I leaned against the pack strapped behind me and wished I'd brought grapes to eat. The ruins where I was headed were a three- to five-day hike from Bordertown, but we might make them in a few hours on the bike, with luck.

"We heading anyplace in particular?"

I nodded when she glanced back at me.

"Gonna tell me how to get there?"

I nodded again.

"Ever use being mute as an excuse not to communicate?"

I laughed, leaned forward, and traced on the back of her hand a *W*, then an *A*, an *I*, a *T*.

"Yeah," she said. "All day, Ray."

I don't know how other people get around in the Borderlands. I trust my impulses. If you stay on the West Road, you'll cruise through woods and hills until you're bored and turn back. Sometimes I think if you continue lòng enough, you'll return to Bordertown, but I've never felt like playing Kid Columbus to find out.

Many smaller roads and trails intersect the West Road. I watched them without letting myself become curious. I knew where I wanted to go, so I kept our destination in mind. I didn't let myself become obsessed with finding it. We could ride for days on the West Road, if we wanted to. We might even try to find its end. We had food and drink; we didn't need anything. The first thing, maybe the only thing, that I learned out here is you can't find a place in the Borderlands if you have to.

When I saw a gravel road angling toward the southern hills, something inside me said it might be fun to take. I tapped Leda's shoulder, and we cut off. Gravel rolled in our wake. After we'd turned a bend or two, the hills became more barren. Trees were smaller and browner and more twisted than before.

A dirt road intersected the gravel, and we turned left. Two trails, which I ignored, crossed the road. The dirt was dry. We kicked up dust that streamed behind us like a smoking exhaust. We took a short rest under something like a yucca tree, then rode on.

The third trail was somehow promising; I didn't suggest we leave it until late in the afternoon, when it brought us back to what looked like the West Road. I can't say how I knew it wasn't. This highway seemed newer, maybe, not quite as overgrown. I don't know why I was sure, but we were close to the ruins.

We stopped on the grassy shoulder of the highway. Leda looked at me. I shrugged and pointed right. Ten or fifteen miles later, we came to a road sign in remarkably good repair: MONAGHIE DRIVE. I tried not to feel smug.

We passed a few ruined buildings, then a clump of them, then we topped a hill and came to a rusty green sign full of bullet holes: Los(something)E(something)s.

Loses is a good name for these ruins. Civilization was interrupted in the World when Faerie returned, but only a few unstable places full of unstable people collapsed. Loses was one, a city that lost.

Leda said, "What's this?"

The valley before us was filled with the broken, abandoned buildings of Loses. The setting sun brought out red hints in the purple half of Leda's hair and made the pale half gleam like white gold.

I shrugged.

"Everything's dif—"

I put the tip of my finger near her lips.

She frowned, then smiled. "We can't talk about—"

I shook my head and touched the finger to her lips. I pulled it away quickly, embarrassed and annoyed with myself. I'd forgotten how soft another person's lips could be.

"Old magic," she whispered, pleased.

I nodded.

"Anyone live here?"

I nodded again.

"Wild elves?"

I shook my head once.

"Humans."

Nod.

"No lights. No fires. Can't be many."

Nod.

"Savages, then?" Her voice was cautious, a little scared. "Can we avoid 'em?"

Shrug.

"Well, thanks a lot, Spot. If you can get by here, I can, too. Where d'you want to camp?"

We stopped at a service station at the edge of Loses, a place I'd found on my second visit. It's back from the road and half-surrounded by the wild, disquieting woods that cover much of the Borderlands. Huge rustling machines and a pit suggest that Faerie's return halted a construction project there. Now the land was reverting to forest. I made a quick scouting to see if anyone was in the neighborhood and found no signs.

When I returned, Leda had gathered wood to build a fire. I boiled some wild rice, then strained the rice through a clean rag. I used the lid of the frying pan to mix flour, lard, salt, and water, then added raisins, walnuts, and the cooked wild rice, then used some lard to grease the frying pan, then dumped my batter into it, cleaned the lid quickly, and covered the pan, and baked wild-rice bannock over the fire. We ate hot chunks in our bare hands.

Leda said, "Hey, Wolf. This tastes better than peca!"

I took a stick and scratched in the dirt, THANKS. A HUMAN FRIEND TOLD ME WHAT PECA TASTES LIKE.

She laughed. "Hey, okay. It tastes better than peca tastes to elves."

I nodded and tried not to feel flattered.

After dinner, I scrubbed the frying pan with dirt. As I wiped it out, then repacked my rucksack, Leda said, "Listen, Wolf, if you'd done something that hurt someone—"

I stopped her by snatching a stick to write, EVERYONE HURTS SOMEONE SOMETIME.

She shook her head. "I mean, really hurt someone. So bad you can't fix it. So bad that saying you're sorry'd just be a joke."

I remembered an elven child grabbing at a rifle. YOU CD. ALWAYS KILL YR. SELF.

"Wouldn't fix a thing. It'd just get me out of it."

I scratched out the words KILL YR. SELF and wrote, APOLOGIZE & TAKE WHAT YOU GET.

She said, "Like that's easy. What if—"

I didn't need to help her find excuses. She stopped speaking to watch me write, YOU'RE AT THE BORDER. THE PAST IS PAST.

"But—"

I stood.

"Where you going?"

I pointed outward.

"For a walk?"

I nodded.

She hesitated, then said, "Yell if you want me."

I nodded again and went.

I had no real purpose, other than a desire to be away from her. I strolled for an hour or so, but it didn't help. I thought about leaving her on the outskirts of Loses. There was nothing in the rucksack that I couldn't replace. I could even go back to the camp, take the sack, and leave while she watched me. While she begged me to explain why I was doing this. While she cried, then swore at me. She wouldn't know how hard returning to Bordertown would be. She wouldn't really appreciate what I'd done until she set out alone on her bike and learned how completely lost she was.

Two things argued against that:

One. She was a magician. I was already carrying one of her curses; I didn't need another. I'd rather be Wolfboy than Ratboy, Roachboy, or Great-spreading-pool-of-mucus-boy.

Two. It was too soon. I wanted to get her into the heart of the ruins, surrounded by monuments to failure and dead dreams. I could leave her there when she didn't expect it, and she'd never have a chance to try her magic on me.

I stood by a live oak and looked out over the dark valley. I thought about Leda, and I thought about Russian nesting dolls sitting side by side, ready to be dropped inside each other.

Here's the first. This Leda leads a gang of elves, humans, and halfies called the Strange Pupae, who've given a place to stay to a kid who's new in B-town. Runaway Ron has a crush on her.

Drop that Leda into the next. This Leda drinks Drag-

on's Milk and laughs while her lieutenants fight over
the future of Castle Pup, their home. Drop Runaway
Ron into Just Ron, who pities her.

Drop those Ledas into a third. This Leda is a Dragon's Tooth Hill princess. Drop Just Ron into a Wharf
Rat called Gone, who only feels contempt for her. He
dares to make fun of her, and she turns him into a monster.

Drop that Leda into the fourth and final shell, a Dead
Warlock who does not remember that she created a
mute monster. Drop Gone into Wolfboy, who hates her.

I listened to the night, and I smelled it for messages.
It told me nothing but what I knew: I could take my revenge whenever I wished. It would not restore me. It
would not bring back Florida. But it would be sweeter
than Sai's baklava.

I hit the tree trunk hard with the heel of my fist. It
didn't hurt enough, but I turned and went back to camp.
When I came near, I heard something sad playing on
the seedybox, then smelled our dying fire, then smelled
Leda. She was leaning against her bike, facing the fire
and hugging herself. The rucksack was near her, not
quite where I'd left it. The top flap was open.

I stepped into the light. Leda gasped slightly, then
said, "Wolf. I was beginning to think you weren't
coming—" She saw where I looked and said, "Oh. I
thought maybe you had a beer or something in there. I
don't feel so good. Some peca would be nice."

I held my hands open before me and despised her.

"You don't mind, do you? I figured if you had something that'd make me feel a little better . . ." Her voice
trailed off as I shook my head. "Yeah. Oh, well." I
stared at her until she looked away. "I think . . . I think
maybe I'd better get some sleep."

She zipped her coveralls up to her throat, lay down
near the fire, thrust her hands into her pockets, and
closed her eyes. After a minute or two, she rolled over,

facing into the dark woods. She shivered slightly but said nothing. I don't know how quickly she fell asleep.

I squatted by the fire and listened to the night. It told me nothing. I went to my rucksack and donned my black denim jacket. After standing there for a long minute, staring into the rucksack, I took out my blanket, spread it over Leda, and slept on the opposite side of the fire.

I woke to a sound that was becoming too familiar. Someone was vomiting. It was still dark, though it was late in the night—our fire was out. It took a second or two to tell that this was Leda again, not some late-night visitors with delicate digestions. I might've sworn at her, if I could've spoken. Instead, I sat up, angry, annoyed, not yet thinking clearly.

She lay on her side, propped up on one elbow. After a second attack of heaving brought up almost nothing, she said, "Wolf? Sorry. I . . . I'm feelin' ill, Bill."

I put my hand on her forehead. Her brow was slick with sweat. I growled softly in what I hoped was a comforting tone.

"Help me up. I gotta go . . . in . . ."

I put my arm around her waist to steady her, and we walked away from our campsite. I started to leave to give her some privacy, but she reeled, then caught herself before I caught her. She said reluctantly, almost amused, "Stick around, okay?" So I held her shoulders, then helped her clean herself and walked her back to the fire. "You're a good nurse," she said, and then, more quietly, "I don't want to be a nuisance."

I shook my head to say she wasn't, though I didn't know if she could see that in the dark. I settled her on some grass and tucked the blanket around her, then blew on the ashes of our fire and found that a few red embers remained. A couple of dry leaves began to burn when I placed them on the coal, so I added twigs and slowly rebuilt the fire. I threw dirt over the place where she'd vomited. Then I tried to go back to sleep. Her sickness hit her again about fifteen minutes later.

Her fever grew worse. So did the diarrhea and vomiting. I gave her cold bannock for breakfast the next morning, but her body rejected that right after she ate. I made a tea with bark stripped from a willow I'd noticed when fetching water for dinner. The tea seemed to help her pain. Averting my eyes, I took her coveralls and dressed her in my extra shirt and jeans. I washed the coveralls in a shallow stream, rinsing and wringing and beating them on a rock until I was exhausted, then hung them on a limb to dry. They were silver-gray.

That afternoon, she laughed and said, "I didn't think I'd miss the peca quite so much. Wouldn't've come with you if I'd known. Ought to start a new gang. Magical Addicts. A gang for gutless Dead Warlocks. Whattaya think?"

Later that night, shortly before she became delirious, she said, "I don't know why you stay with me," and she patted my hand.

Even later, she begged me to take her back to Bordertown, to do something, anything, to get her some peca, or she would die. Had I thought she could survive the trip, I might've taken her. I could have postponed revenge. How could she suffer if I let her die?

Finally she cursed me as an evil dog bastard and called me elven names that I didn't recognize. Her strength came and went. Once she flailed at my chest and face with her fists until she collapsed, and I carried her back to her bed.

Her lucid moments became increasingly rare. During one, she whispered, "Wolfboy?"

I said, "Err?"

"If I don't make it, the bike's yours."

"Rro."

"To activate its spellbox, say, 'Hiyosilver.' 'WhoaIsaywhoa' shuts it down."

"Rrff."

"One thing I'd appreciate. Run up the Tooth to Thirty-seven Avalon. Knock on the door and tell 'em the foundling's dead. If a balding elf in a suit answers, you can spit on him." She coughed, then added, "Or rip his lungs out, Jim." She'd been quiet long enough that I thought she was asleep when she whispered, "Wolfie? Forget that last bit, okay? Tell Dad he did the best he could."

I didn't sleep during those three days, or if I did, it was never for more than ten or fifteen minutes at a time. I hunted for herbs that might help her, but I didn't dare go far from the camp. I gave her water and tea. I baked some plain bannock and crumbled some into the willow-bark tea. Maybe it helped her. Mostly I sat beside her and held her hand.

Her fever broke on the fourth morning. That's when the wild elves came.

CHAPTER FIFTEEN
Wild Times with the Wild Elves

I woke near noon. Since I'd slept for three or four hours without interruption, I touched Leda's forehead to see if she'd been quiet because she was getting better or getting worse. Her temperature felt almost normal. She was still very pale, bringing her elven pallor too close to corpse-white, but her features were peaceful, her breathing easy. She opened her eyes, smiled at me, and went back to sleep immediately. I realized I'd smiled, too. I hoped she'd seen that as a vicious grin.

Carrying the frying pan and water jug to the stream, I asked myself over and over again why I hadn't abandoned her already. The answer was more important than the world around me, or maybe I simply hadn't had enough sleep.

Whatever the reason, I almost bumped into the wild elf as I came through a clump of bushes. He stood in the middle of the narrow trail, waiting downwind of me, his body striped in camouflage by the shadows of the forest. I froze, more surprised than frightened.

He was obviously descended from the True Blood. He had the height, the pale skin, the pointed ears, the silver eyes, the star-white hair. He wore a commando knife hung from a thong over one shoulder, a string of plastic trinkets tied around his forehead, and nothing else. His hair was waist length, loose around his slender body. An eagle had been daubed in red on his hairless chest, and a spider in yellow on his smooth cheek.

We stared at each other. I couldn't think of a sound that might seem soothing, and I couldn't make myself purr, wag my butt, and bash into his knees with my forehead.

He lifted one hand to tap his chest. "Weyaka'an."

I lifted the water bottle toward my chest and imitated him. Maybe this was a gesture of greeting. When he remained still, I set down the water bottle and frying pan to scrawl WOLFBOY in the dirt. The wild elf stared at it, then frowned. "Your name? Or your species?"

NAME, I wrote. SPECIES, TOO, MAYBE. YOU FROM BORDERTOWN?

"Bordertown?" He squinted, then grinned. "Ah, the humans' city! No." He came closer, stopping about a foot from me, too intimately near for my comfort. He frowned, then moved his hands in the air like a mime tracing a shell around my body. I didn't know what he intended. I growled a warning while remaining perfectly still.

"There's a spell on you."

I nodded.

"This isn't your true form."

I shook my head.

"Come. We will help."

I wondered why he should want to help me, but I only pointed toward my camp.

"The young woman?"

I nodded, then was suddenly suspicious. If he knew of her, he'd spied on us. Had he seen smoke from our fire? I'd been less cautious than usual. How long had he watched us? Had he waited to approach us until she'd begun to recover? Why had he waited for me on the trail, rather than approaching us both in—

I turned, abandoning the water bottle and frying pan, and raced away. Behind me, Weyaka'an called, "Wait, Wolfboy!" I heard him follow, as quickly and as quietly as me.

Except for our fire, the camp was deserted. "Wolf—" Weyaka'an began. I whirled and leaped for his throat. He ducked aside. "Wait! Others are taking her to Aula'ai. We shall help her. Be comforted."

My fur tingled, and I growled another warning.

"She is important to you. We know. The city poisons have gone from her. We can make her what she was. You, too. Trust us."

He spoke the last words almost as a command. Perhaps they were one, because I did trust him. I let my arms fall to my side.

Someone behind me said in Elvish, "He is docile?" It was a woman's voice, young, husky, imperious. She spoke with what Strider calls a True Blood's snot-nosed accent.

Weyaka'an nodded. "At last."

"Good." I heard the woman approaching, but I felt no need to turn to look at her. When she stepped in front of me, I saw she was of the same type as Weyaka'an, perhaps of the same family. She wasn't beautiful by Bordertown standards, being too thin and too tall, with her neck and her nose too long, yet I could've watched her for hours. Her hair was held in a silver ring on the crown of her head. Its ends fell to her buttocks. She wore sandals of woven hemp, and nothing else. Her only decoration was a black bird, perhaps a raven, painted across her right cheekbone.

She walked around me, squinting at me as Weyaka'an had when we met. Her eyes were the moon hue of her hair. "A curse."

"Yes, Lady."

"Laid by whom?"

He shrugged. "An elf."

"An elf." The woman nodded. "Thank you. If I ask whence he came, will you say, 'From the lands of short-lived Man?' If I ask what we might do next, will you—"

"I cannot tell," he said softly.

"You told him we could restore him? That should make him wag when we are near."

"Human gratitude is a fragile thing."

The woman cocked an eyebrow at him. "The sky is blue, the grass green, your subservience insincere, and my love—for you and all my husbands—true."

He smiled with something I thought shy embarrassment, and spread his hands before him. "Shall we change him now?"

She nodded. Her next words were in another elven tongue, similar in sound to what they'd spoken earlier, but nothing like the Elvish that I'd learned from Strider and Tick-Tick. She barked several words, then he did, then she, then he. I couldn't tell if he was repeating her sentiment and rephrasing it, or completing her thoughts, or adding something else to the ritual. It happened too quickly to follow. I paid no attention to what they did because I began to hurt worse than I had when I was first Changed.

I screamed and fell to the ground. The wild elves smiled as I passed out.

I woke on soft grass in the shade of a sequoia and knew I was no longer near the ruins. I must've been brought into the oldest part of the woods of the Border-lands. The knowledge didn't alarm me. It didn't even interest me. The elven woman was at my side, stroking my brow with a cool, damp cloth. She smiled and touched her sternum. "Eilva'ar. Eilva'ar."

"Wolfboy," I said. Then I realized what I'd done. Eilva'ar stared at my expression, covered her mouth, and giggled.

I was wearing the same clothes I'd worn earlier, but they were looser on me. I felt the air on my bare face and neck and hands and ankles. I wanted to laugh. I stood, then turned around and around, looking at myself and grinning.

Eilva'ar and I were at the edge of a glade surrounded by sequoias. Small groups of naked elves sat or lay about under each tree. They looked over at me with expressions of fond concern, like Eilva'ar had when I woke. That made me laugh more and more. I felt much as I had when the Doctor smeared peca paste into my open wrist.

"I'm not Wolfboy. I'm—" I remembered Ronald Reagan Vasquez, who I'd been when I ran away, and Just Ron and Gone, who I'd been when I was human in Bordertown. None of them were the person I'd become.

"Fool," Eilva'ar said in Elvish, with the same innocent smile. She tapped my chest. "Fool."

She thought I didn't understand Elvish, but I wasn't insulted. "Fool," I agreed. The name seemed affectionate, like Sai's "Bowser-brains" when she wanted to sound annoyed with me and wasn't.

Several trees away, a group of young elves began to sing. Their voices were perfect, their range greater than any human's. The bass was a tall female who could mimic thunder. The soprano was a boy who sang as high as hummingbirds or bumblebees.

Near us, men and women were weaving tapestries rich with stylized deer and eagles. Farther away, older elves sat conversing, occasionally puffing from a shared pipe or sipping from tiny wooden cups. The smell of bread made me notice another group tending a claybrick oven. In the glade, children and adults played a game with a leather ball that involved four waist-high wooden goalposts. There seemed to be two or three teams, yet everyone laughed when anyone scored. Beyond the ballplayers, at the far side of the glade, a tall male addressed a group of skinny children with shaggy hair and high, batlike ears.

As I studied the elves, I realized that I was looking for someone. In English, I said, "Eilva'ar? Where's Leda? Ah, Scent of Heather?"

"Scent of heather?" She gestured and whispered something; the air was suddenly sweet with the smell of mown heather.

"No." I laughed, delighted by the magic. "The elf who was with me."

"Ah. I don't know. Weyaka'an is over there, Fool." She pointed at the lecturer, then glanced at me and smiled. "Perhaps he can help you." I returned her smile and circled the ballplayers to interrupt Weyaka'an.

He sat cross-legged before his class with his back to the largest sequoia. The children scrambled up and ran away giggling as I approached. I stared after one, a girl with tangled white hair who was no taller than my waist, and wondered why I was looking.

Weyaka'an bowed slightly to me. "Didn't I say we could help?"

"Yeah. I mean, yes. Thanks." He studied me as if something might be wrong, which I didn't understand. I said, "Where's Scent of Heather? The elf I was with?"

"With healers. She's still very weak."

I felt a cool tingle on the fur on my back, or rather, where my fur would've been. "We'll, ah, have to go soon, I'm afraid."

"Oh? We are sorry to learn this, friend."

I shrugged and smiled my sadness.

"There is something you should know. Your curse . . ."

"Yes?"

"We can lift it while you remain among us, but if you leave, it will return. Perhaps so strongly that no one will be able to lift it again, not even for a brief while. I am sorry." Weyaka'an sighed. "You are welcome to stay here until you decide what you will do. We have had humans among us before. We enjoy your presence."

I blinked, then thought, Why not stay? You're not a monster anymore. They like you. They'll care for you. Live here forever among the wise savages. Don't worry. Be happy.

"Are you, perhaps, a musician?" Weyaka'an asked.

"No."

A flicker of disappointment crossed his face. I wondered if he'd ask if I was a clown, then knew he didn't need to.

"A poet?"

Before I could speak, I heard a commotion of elven voices. Several naked women fluttered around an elf in a high-collared red dress who stalked through the ballplayers' game as though it were not there. The central woman's hair, as long and as white as any of the others', had been bound in strands of rubies and diamonds.

Her mouth moved fiercely, with more animation than seemed appropriate for anyone wearing those clothes. I heard Leda yell, "Wolfboy! Yo! Wolf-face! Get your shaggy butt out here!" It took a moment to connect the elf in red with Leda's voice.

"Leda?" I said numbly, then corrected myself. "Scent of Heather?"

"Ah." Weyaka'an squinted across the glade. "She is feeling, um, better, I see."

Leda broke free of the crowd, ran toward me, then stopped abruptly. "Wolfboy?"

"Yes." I grinned. "They fixed me."

"Yeah." She didn't seem impressed, which saddened me. "Let's shake this scene, okay, Gene?"

Her attendants hovered uncertainly some twenty feet away. The ballplayers had stopped their game to watch. Eilva'ar strode toward us from the tree where she'd tended me. An old male elf hurried to keep up with her. His hair was as sparse and as fine as spiderwebs.

At my side, Weyaka'an stroked his jaw and studied me. I told Leda, "What's the hurry? It's nice here. They've helped us."

"Helped?" She spit, and the wild elves looked shocked.

"Besides, if I return, I'll turn back into Wolfboy."

She tucked her chin and glared at me. "Say what?"

"I'll turn back into Wolfboy."

"You'll . . . ?" She spun to face Eilva'ar. "What've you done? What the hell have you done!"

"You are not pleased?" Eilva'ar asked in Elvish.

"I didn't ask any favors," Leda said, still in English.

"Had you, we might not have granted them." Eilva'ar kept to Elvish. "You each have what you desire. He is human and happy. You have your magic back."

"In truth?" Leda asked in Elvish, her accent that of Dragon's Tooth Hill. She gestured upward. A rainbow sprang into existence between her hands. "Or is this more of your—" The rainbow faded into multicolored lights that fell onto the grass like mist.

"No!" The old elf spoke for the first time. "We are of the Blood. We would not use our own for entertainment! Not without consent!"

Weyaka'an said, "Father, she's of the city. She cannot know us."

Eilva'ar put her hand on the old elf's shoulder. "Rest, Aula'ai. All is well."

The old man frowned, then hobbled away. "The Game was better when I was young," he muttered, loud enough that we all could hear.

Eilva'ar laughed. "He does not realize that the world has changed."

Leda said, "So? Do you?"

Weyaka'an nodded. "Of course. That is why we keep ourselves from it."

"Except to take the occasional human for a pet," Leda said in Elvish. She put her hands on her hips and switched to English. "Well, this one you can't keep, Bo Peep. C'mon, Art, time to depart."

I shook my head, giving up on understanding what all of this meant. "I'll lose everything again."

"You don't have a thing to lose! Can't you tell what they're doing?"

I gnawed my lip, and finally said, "Yes. Aren't you grateful?"

"Course I am, dickbrain. To you, not them!"

"Then let me stay."

She whirled to face the elven woman. "Release him!"

Eilva'ar smiled. "He is the price for the return of your magic."

"Great. Take it away again."

"Oh?" Eilva'ar leaned her head to one side. "It is not so easy."

"Your damn game?"

"The Game," Eilva'ar said. The watching elves nodded, pleased.

"We didn't agree to your game."

"You came to our lands," Weyaka'an said. "You have received our gifts."

Eilva'ar said, "Are you strong enough?"

Leda said, "Could you delay this, at least?"

"Ask, would we?"

"I'm strong enough." Leda looked at them all, then said slowly, deliberately, "The old one was right. You don't know how to play anymore. Your game is a sham."

"Ah." Eilva'ar smiled. "The challenge." The others nodded in unison. "And now, the terms."

"You have no right . . ." Leda began, then said, "Forget it. What terms?"

"These. If you convince the mortal to renounce our gift, we shall restore you both to what you were, and you may leave us. If you fail, you keep our gifts. He stays as our Fool. You leave or stay as you please."

"Oooh," said several of the younger elves. One, the small girl, clapped her hands.

"Bitch," said Leda.

"It is the Game," Eilva'ar explained contentedly. "Play if you wish to keep him. Go if you prefer."

Leda touched her tongue to her upper lip, then nodded. "Wolfboy. Concentrate. Can't you tell what they've done?"

"Yes. They've made me human. It's nice."

"Oh, screw it." She started to say something in the odd Elvish speech, the one they used to shape spells.

"No!" Weyaka'an said. "You may not use magic to undo our gift to him. It is our only condition."

Eilva'ar said sweetly, "You will make us take your powers back, should you persist. Do not turn this into a test of force, for that you could never win."

"You suck. What about illusion, then? Surely that's fair."

Eilva'ar glanced at Weyaka'an and back at Leda. "It would have a certain elegance, should you succeed. And a piquancy, should you fail."

"All right." Leda snapped her hands and shouted. I was Wolfboy then, and the others were dressed in elaborate silks and leathers, not like savages but like Elflands elves.

"No!" I howled, and filled my mind with, *Illusion, she said it was illusion, so this is a lie, a damned lie for whatever damned reason, she doesn't want me to be free again, it's illusion! Pure illusion!*

I was human once more. The wild elves smiled,

watching us in their paint and trinkets. A few applauded.

Leda scowled, then shouted again. Stars whirled about me. There was nothing to stand on, only more stars below, the only lights in a darkness through which I fell, ever faster. I felt ill. Both parts of my mind, the watching part and the acting part, said, *This isn't true! Reject it!*

The glade returned, flickering oddly, as if two images of the world were fighting for dominance. I couldn't make out details until I saw what I knew was true: my human form, the kind wild elves, Leda in her rich elf's dress.

"Yes," Eilva'ar said. "As I predicted." The watchers laughed when she added, "Have you any other tricks for us?"

"Forgive me, Wolfboy," Leda whispered. She slapped me, hard and fast.

I touched my cheek. "Why?" I was hurt by the fact that she'd hit me, not by the blow. Though she seemed to have put her strength in the slap, for all the effect it had, I might as well still have been the Wolf.

"Renounce them, Wolfboy! They want to keep you as a damn pet!"

"It'll be fun here. I won't be a freak."

She hit me in the stomach with her fist. For a flicker of an instant, I saw myself covered with reddish fur, Leda in her silver-gray coveralls, and the other elves in silk and leather. That faded.

"Wake up, Wolfboy!" She hit me again, and I saw she was crying. "Oh, gods, wake up, please!" The wild elves laughed and clapped their hands. "It's not worth it, Wolf. You get speech, that's all. They couldn't make you human. There's a curse so tangled around you that no one could undo it. Even if those bastards could help, it wouldn't be worth this."

"Go away. If you have to lie to me, just go away."

She stared, then raised her hand to slap me again. I caught her wrist. In a low, grating voice, I said, "I. Want. To. Stay."

"Oh, God," Leda whispered.

"So. You admit defeat?" Eilva'ar pointed away, where the plum-black Triumph bobbed near a tree. "Your floating disturbance is there, if you wish to leave us now."

Leda snapped her head toward Eilva'ar. "You're so pathetic. Hiding in the woods, afraid of what's happening in Faerie and the World and Bordertown. Your stupid Game is out of date, Kate. Pretending to be savages so humans won't know about you when they already live among us in Bordertown, when Faerie and the World trade regularly—"

Weyaka'an sneered. "It is degeneracy."

"It's progress. Look at you! You can't even get the details of your Game right. Why should you pretend for Wolfboy's sake that Weyaka'an's the leader? Because humans were ruled by men when we dealt with them before, back when they were little more than the savages you're pretending to be? It's stupid!"

"Perhaps." Eilva'ar plainly did not care. "The Game still entertains us. Your human may amuse us for forty years or more, eh? And then our antiquated ways will win his replacement, I suspect." She pointed again. "Your vehicle awaits you."

"Did I say I was quitting?"

"There is no need. You have clearly lost."

Leda glanced at me. I nodded, seconding Eilva'ar. Leda closed her eyes briefly, swallowed, then stepped close to me. She lifted her hand. When I flinched, she said, "I won't hit you again."

I let her touch my cheek. She said, "I'm sorry I hit you. I thought I could startle you into seeing the truth. I was wrong. I'm sorry." She took me by both wrists and tugged. We sat on the grass, cross-legged before each other. She continued to hold my hands. The wild elves watched intently, but Leda ignored them.

"I don't know what to say. You've been good to me. I can't repay you by leaving you here."

"I'm happy."

She shook her head, a quick, pained movement. "Please. Don't say anything." I smiled; I liked sitting there with her holding my hands. After a moment, she spoke. "Wolfboy, I—" She shook her head and started again. "When I was going through withdrawal, what bothered me most was that you didn't know anything about me, yet you took care of me. I got over being embarrassed about being helpless, but I can't get over your helping me. I'm not a good person."

I opened my mouth to speak. She touched my lips to seal them. "I'm not. Maybe the folks who adopted me were too strict, or maybe they weren't strict enough, I don't know. I didn't think my parents loved me, but now I'm not sure that's true. Or that it matters. I was a brat. Okay, Jose?"

She stared at me until I nodded to please her.

"I got worse. Lots of running around, so the parents got more strict, so I ran around more. And I did stupid things. Maybe the worst was abusing my magic. I used it for pranks, making people's pants disappear, turning a teacher's necklace into a cobra. The teacher almost died when it bit her. I ran away, and things were better for a while, but when things went bad, I went home again. And I went back to my old habits."

She bit her lips. " 'Bout two years ago, my father wanted to send me to Faerie. I went on a party instead. He had some wizards strip me of my magic. I guess he thought it was the only thing left to do. So I took my bike and ran away again, knowing this time I didn't have a home to return to."

It was an interesting story because it was important to Leda, but I had trouble remembering its beginning. She squeezed my hands. "I didn't care about anything, Wolf. You know how the last couple of years were, what I did to get by. You saw what I was when you met me."

I nodded. I hadn't liked her, for some reason. I liked her now, though, so why did that matter?

"Yet you took care of me." She exhaled abruptly, a harsh laugh, so I laughed too. "I thought you were really stupid." That was hilarious, so I laughed harder. "Why would anyone take care of someone like me?" I opened my mouth to laugh even louder, and she said, "What made it horrible is I figured something out."

That wasn't a punchline, so I waited. She winced, then said, "*I* turned you into Wolfboy. I didn't see it right away. Not until I was getting sick and . . ."

I nodded to reassure her. The punchline was coming, but I was getting worried because I'd forgotten the setup for the joke.

"You knew me, then. And it didn't matter to you. I couldn't figure that out. 'Cause I'm—" She shook her head again, then pulled on my hands so I'd stop watching a dragonfly that had landed on her knee. Its blue-green wings sparkled in the sun.

"When I was a kid, I thought I acted wild 'cause I didn't have real parents, just adopted ones, as if being a parent was something you were instead of something you did. And I acted wild 'cause the world wasn't like in stories. No perfect people doing nice things all the time.

"Then you came on like the knight in shaggy armor, y'know? In spite of everything." As she said that, I felt for a second as if I'd eaten something rotten.

"That's when I realized people had been taking care of me all along. Even when—no, especially when—I ran away, when I was on my own and it didn't matter what I did, everyone took care of me. The people who gave me food or spare change or a place to sleep. The people who got out of my way when I went racing through the streets. None of them perfect and nice all the time, but all taking care of me, whether they realized it or not."

She looked at her hands, then turned her face up to meet mine. The dragonfly had flown away, to where I couldn't see it without turning away from her, which would make her sad. "I care, okay? That's why I want to get you out of here. Because I owe everybody something. Because I—" Her upper lip got an odd crease in it as she worked her mouth in frustration, and I wondered if I should tell her about it. She finally said, "I owe *you* everything."

She studied my face. I decided not to say anything about the crease, because it was gone. She touched the back of my hands to her eyes, blotting her tears with the fur—no, the skin there. She kissed each hand once above the knuckles, then released them. I watched her stand.

Eilva'ar asked, "You admit defeat?"

Leda looked down and shrugged.

"Go, then," Eilva'ar said.

Leda bent over, put her arms around me, and kissed me lightly on the lips while I sat perfectly still. She whispered, "I love you, Wolfboy." Then she turned and ran toward the bike. All the dragonflies had gone away. Maybe she had scared them. Was she going to find more?

"It is victory." Eilva'ar glanced at me and beckoned. "Rise, Fool."

I lifted my head enough to meet the wild elf's eyes. Something damp trickled along either side of my nose.

I looked at Leda approaching her bike, then back at the wild elves' camp. Two scenes rested uneasily on top of each other, each blurring the other. In one, Eilva'ar, Weyaka'an, and the rest stood, distant and imperious, dressed in elaborate brocades and silks like rich Elflanders on a picnic. The trees around us were live oaks, not sequoias. Beyond them, something built of crystal and silver stood like a palace or an airship.

That scene disappeared like a vision in a popped soap bubble. Eilva'ar, a naked wild elf once more, beckoned impatiently with one finger. "Now, Fool."

Leda gunned her engine. I looked. Her hands moved stiffly, as if she was doing some magic that she hadn't tried in years.

Watching the shapes she carved in the air, I thought, What a strange elf, to say in farewell, *No*, you *have big fun*.

I said, "Eilva'ar?"

She nodded, waiting to see how I would begin the rest of my life as her clown. "Yes, Fool?"

"Kiss my furry ass, Cass!" I spun on my heel, screaming, "Hey!" at Leda's back. "Wait up!"

She glanced over her shoulder. She wore her faded coveralls, and her hair was as short and wild as ever, though the elves had managed to wash the purple dye from it, and I thought I'd never seen anyone so beautiful.

Shouting, "Wolfboy!" she raced the Triumph toward me. I leaped onto its back. It dipped under my weight, bouncing once on the ground before it leveled itself.

Leda grinned. Her engine's roar obliterated the cries from Eilva'ar's camp.

CHAPTER SIXTEEN
Homeward Bound

Leda cut the Triumph's roar as soon as we left the wild elves' sight. Sometimes you want defiance, sometimes, discretion. Or maybe Leda just wanted to talk. After a minute or two of riding in silence, she said, " 'Ass, Cass?' I dunno, Wolf. If that's what rhymetime reduces you to, maybe I'll give it up."

I tried to answer and could only growl.

She said, "Oh. Sorry."

I looked back. We were leaving the forest. No one was following that I could see, hear, or smell. If the large silvery thing was a vehicle, it probably couldn't maneuver among the trees.

My nose was close to Leda's neck. If I hadn't known to hunt for it, I would never have been able to find, somewhere under the smell of the woods and the bike and her soap and all the glands that had kicked in since puberty, Florida's scent. I didn't need to ask to see the birthmarks on her shoulder.

Plucking paper and a pencil stub from my pockets, I

scrawled a note, using my knee for a desk. The wind tried to snatch the page, so I shielded it with one hand. On the wheelless bike, there was no vibration to make it hard to write. The only challenge was finding the right words. I wrote, DON'T BE SORRY. I CHOSE. IF I COULD DO IT AGAIN 1,000X, I'D CHOOSE THE SAME. & BE GRATEFUL. I passed that up to her.

She smiled over her shoulder. "Woofboy."

I passed another note. WHY DIDN'T YOU JUST TELL ME?

We probably covered two miles of open plains before she spoke. "Tell my first best friend that the kid he'd befriended had turned him into something he hated? Guess."

I wrote, WHEN DID YOU RECOGNIZE ME?

"Like I said in front of the would-be wildies. Not until you were nursing me through the worst parts. I couldn't believe it then, not till later, when I woke up among the would-bes. Still doesn't make sense." She laughed. "You're not nearly as big as the Wolfboy I remember, but you're at least as pretty."

I didn't want to write the next one. I BROUGHT YOU HERE TO ABANDON YOU. I KNEW YOU WERE LEDA, WHO CURSED ME.

She laughed. "Yeah, you sure made me suffer."

I MEANT TO.

She nodded. "Okay. Why?"

'CAUSE YOU WERE RESPONSIBLE FOR FLORIDA—She glanced back over her shoulder at my notepad. I crumpled that sheet and threw it away. 'CAUSE IF YOU HADN'T CURSED ME, I WOULD'VE BEEN ABLE—

When she saw the second paper wad fly, she said, "Hey, Critter, don't litter. Oops. Already backsliding."

I wrote, I'M GLAD YOU'RE BACK.

She said, "Big ditto."

We rolled on. The sun wasn't part of the wild elves' magic, and when you've got a bike, you've always got wind. I grinned as the country turned from plains to new forest. Eventually, I wrote, So, WHAT HAPPENED?

She laughed. "I was going to ask you. It was eleven or twelve years ago for me, and I was just a kid then."

I wrote, REMEMBER MILO'S SPELL?

She shook her head. "Milo cast a spell? I remember being locked up with Mickey and Goldy. One of the guards had a gun and she was going to shoot—" She looked back at me, then ahead at the road. "Oh. She was going to shoot you. I was trying to jump her, to stop her, I guess. I can't remember if I had a plan. I just had to stop her."

She spoke as if she saw something dimly in the distance and describing it drew out its details. "I landed on the floor. I thought the girl had dodged me, and I couldn't see well or breathe well, 'cause I'd kicked up a lot of dust, a lot more dust than I remembered being on the floor. So I spun around, trying to catch the girl's gun while I was blind and coughing, and—"

She nodded decisively. "The room was empty. The light through the window was brighter than it'd been. It hurt my eyes. The cage they'd locked us in had been pushed up against a wall and packed full of cardboard boxes. The floor was covered with dirt and guano. Some rats—nonhuman ones—ran to hide as I looked around. They and I were the only living things in the room. I couldn't—" She shrugged. "I guess I felt like Alice Through the Looking Glass, only I didn't think of that then. And I was a lot more scared than Alice. What was Milo's spell supposed to do?"

I wrote, I'M GETTING A THEORY. TELL MORE, PLEASE.

"A theory." She laughed. "That's reassuring. Okay. I ran—" She lifted her head, swerved around an ancient pileup of cars, wrecked at the time of the Change, and said, "Outside. I wasn't yelling, 'cause I was afraid to, but I was listening, and I'm pretty sure there wasn't anyone in the building."

I nodded.

"Outside was scarier. Bordertown had changed, too. I couldn't quite see how, then, but I knew it. Some of the buildings were in better shape than I remembered, some were worse, some were the wrong colors. The ones that were the right colors were the wrong hue. Even the plants had changed. Trees and bushes were the wrong size, or they were growing in places where there hadn't been any. I hunted for someone who could explain what'd happened, but Elsewhere was just an empty storefront, and Danceland was a boarded-up bus station."

I winced, which she couldn't see. She seemed pleased to be remembering this so well.

"The most frightening find was Castle Pup, where I'd been safe the first time I'd been homeless in B-town. I remembered watching it burn, yet now it stood where it had always been. It may've had fewer broken windows than I remembered, and more rubbish in its doorway, but it was the same building. I went in. The entry was dark, but it was always dark, remember? I heard noise inside, like people talking. So I climbed the front stairs, calling the names of people we knew there."

I winced again. She didn't need to say that mine had been one of the names.

She laughed. "I don't know if I expected to be met by you and the old gang or by your ghosts. I think I'd decided I was in a dream world by then. What met me were a bunch of Packers who chased me off, yelling about what they did to elves who didn't keep to their own turf. I escaped 'em easily. In some ways, it was nice to face a familiar problem. Does that help your theory?"

I couldn't make myself laugh with her. I nodded and handed her my note. MY THEORY, BY WOLFBOY. MILO DIDN'T WANT TO HURT ANY OF THE RATS. HE THOUGHT "TO REVERSE TEN YEARS" WOULD MAKE

THE SUBJECT OF HIS SPELL 10 YEARS YOUNGER. WHEN HE HIT YOU INSTEAD OF A WHARF RAT, WE BELIEVED YOU'D BEEN REGRESSED PAST BIRTH, TO SOMETHING LESS THAN AN EGG AND A SPERM CELL. NOW I THINK HIS SPELL WORKED PERFECTLY—HE JUST MISINTER-PRETED IT. IT MOVED HIS SUBJECT TEN YEARS BACK IN TIME.

"Hmm."

I turned my finger in a circle in front of her, our old signal to keep talking.

"Well, that was the effect. I had nothing to compare it with. It felt like I'd gone into the future, 'cause you were all just memories, or maybe like you were all imaginary friends who'd gone away. It's hard to re-member how I thought about it, 'cause after a while, I forgot most of what'd happened. Maybe that was part of Milo's spell. Maybe it was the only way to cope with something that didn't make sense."

I finger-spelled in front of her, W-H-A-T-H-A-P-P-E-N-E-D-? and pointed at her to add, *to you*?

"Oh, I was lucky, if you think about what might've happened. I climbed Dragon's Tooth, looking for Lean-der and Wiseguy. Instead, I found someone who took me to someone else who took me someplace where they gave me food and a bed. And after a little while, a childless elven couple adopted me. Maybe that wasn't all luck—I was clearly of the True Blood of Faerie, not some halfie or human."

We rode on, and Loses appeared on the horizon. Leda said quietly, "Don't assume the new folks were elf big-ots. Now I think they were good people. They tried to be, anyway." She laughed. "Good people *and* elf bigots. That's why they were so damn hard to live with. Where to?"

I pointed, and guided her into Loses as she told the rest of the story.

"I told the new parents my name was *Flor'da*, which

they contracted pretty quickly to *Lorda*, then *Lada*, and finally *Leda*. Which was more comprehensible than the other choices. When they adopted me, they gave me my elven name. The Scent of Heather, yaddada yaddada."

I wrote, ONE OF THE WAYS WE POSSESS PEOPLE AND THINGS IS BY NAMING THEM.

She nodded. "Maybe. You also give names to show you've accepted someone as part of your group. I dunno. No easy answers, Wolf." We left the broken freeway and cruised into one of the better-preserved business districts of Loses.

She said, "Except for hating my life, it wasn't bad. When I couldn't stand it anymore, I ran away to Soho and called myself Leda, since that was what the folks said I'd called myself when I was little. I found friends there—Wiseguy and Sai—and we decided to make a safe place where elves, humans, and halfies could live in peace."

I pointed at a bookstore, and she pulled over. "Trading stock?"

I nodded and signed, *Since we're here.*

We went inside. The bookstore's roof had held up and the scavengers who'd been through Loses hadn't been interested in books or magazines. I told myself that on the next trip, Mickey and Goldy and I would borrow a horse and wagon and empty this place.

I signed, *You talk while I look for goodies.*

She nodded, dusted off a glass countertop, and sat cross-legged on it. "We found this empty building that seemed perfect for what we wanted. When Wiseguy called it Castle Pup after our group, the Strange Pupae, I giggled and couldn't stop. Scared Wiseguy and Sai bad. But it was like, *di-da-di-da*, Twilight Zone *Déjà Vu* Review time. When I finally stopped giggling and we went upstairs, I remembered the place had scared me when I was little, but I couldn't remember why." She pointed. "Hey, that's *Treasure Island*; you got to take that. And the Jules Verne next to it."

I sighed and added them to the pile.

"So Castle Pup was a major hit. We found heaps of people who shared the dream. I felt I'd known most of 'em all in a previous life, and that was nice. It should've been perfect, but it wasn't. I was constantly aware that it wasn't what it could've been, if that makes sense. And when a kid called Florida started sleeping in the backyard—" She shrugged. "I'd already started drinking peca. I just found a lot more excuses to drink it. The appeal of drugs is you don't mind not understanding what's happening around you, I guess. In some ways, I was relieved when Castle Pup finally went ka-pow."

She didn't need to tell the rest. She'd told it in the glade while Eilva'ar's people watched. She shook her head. "A tale told by an idiot, full of sound and fury, signifying—" She shrugged.

I pointed at the title of an ancient magazine in the display case under her: *Life*.

In the back room of a motorcycle shop we found wheels that fit the Triumph. The ride to Bordertown was a little bit bumpier and a whole lot safer.

I could tell you many good things about that trip, but I'll leave it at this: At one point, Leda whispered, "Look," and pointed at the sky. From horizon to horizon, passenger pigeons flew toward the World.

Eilva'ar's people seemed content to let our escape be the end of their Game. When I remember that last minute as we raced away from their camp, I sometimes wonder if the sounds we heard were cries of joy, rather than rage. Maybe their Game encompasses more things than I can know. If they meant for it to end as it did, I'm grateful. But I'm not going back to ask.

In Bordertown, we rode directly to Milo Chevrolet's

lot. The NO that had been painted above the crossed-out ALL of ALL OFFERS CONSIDERED had been crossed out in turn. Someone had written beside it, OK—*ALL*. The bikes were gone, and I didn't remember a Cord in his automobile collection.

I knocked. When Milo answered, I pointed at the signs in his windows: MILO CHEVROLET, CONSULTING MAGICIAN and WE MAKE HOUSE CALLS.

He shrugged. "Life goes on." Then he smiled. "Never surrender, eh?"

I nodded and handed him a note. Leda began to laugh as he read, I'D LIKE TO INTRODUCE YOU TO SOMEONE.

Someone said you write a book by starting at the beginning and ending at the end. Since this is my book, I say, Screw that, Matt.

The end of the story is okay: Strider, Sai, and Leda go through the gate, returning to Faerie, where they'll try to change the Elflands, and those of us left on this side may never know if they succeed—my guess, for what it's worth, is they do. The departure wasn't sad. Okay, it was sad, but it wasn't only sad. I'm not sure who did the largest, *No*, you *have* BIG *fun*! Call it a tie.

I'd rather end this at the party at my place.

Milo showed up first, to help me unlock the doors on the ground floor so Mickey could get in. She played the host, which pretty much consisted of yelling at everyone to quit banging on the door and use the rope ladder.

Goldy made pancakes, which didn't mean anything to me until he set a plateful and a glass of chocolate milk in front of Leda. She didn't touch either immediately. Then she said, "You old goldhead," and began to cut the pancakes into cubes.

I let Leda's adoptive parents use the front door. They were a very nice businesswoman who sold jewels into or maybe out of the Elflands and a quiet gardener or maybe a landscaper who told some funny jokes about bankers and politicians. They stayed through dinner, and smiled a lot, then left early. Leda kissed them and promised she'd see them again before she left.

After dinner, Ms. Wu and Milo sat in the library, deep in conversation, so I went in to see if it was anything a non-magician could follow. They both looked up, and Milo said, "Hey, Wolf. Ms. Wu thinks it'll be hard to restore Leda's magic. I say if woodland posers can do it, it'll be a snap for the two of us."

Ms. Wu laughed. "I did not say it would be difficult. But—" She shrugged. "Well, this isn't a place where an abundance of confidence will hurt."

Milo glanced at me, then at Ms. Wu. "You want to tell him?"

She rolled her eyes. "I suppose I shall have to, now."

"I can, if you want. But you've known him longer—"

I held both hands in front of me in supplication: *Enough, already! Please*, somebody *tell me.*

Ms. Wu nodded. "If you wish, we can make you human again."

I felt my smile disappear.

"Should've been obvious," Milo said. "No. It was obvious. We simply didn't see it."

"You didn't?" Ms. Wu asked.

Milo frowned. "All right, all right. *I* didn't see it. But you couldn't do anything about it."

"True." She looked at me. "I say 'if you wish' because that's literally true. The curse resists lifting because, in your heart, you like being Wolfboy."

"See?" Milo said, "So if you'll just stand over there, we'll—"

Ms. Wu spoke for Milo's sake as I touched a finger to my lips and signed, *Shh. Someone might hear.*

The opening notes of Wild Hunt's last album stopped our conversation. We all looked up then, and glanced at each other.

After a moment, we each nodded or shrugged, and whoever had started the song did not stop it. Goldy and

Mickey began to dance, their heads together, his hands on her hips. Strider took Sai's hand and said, "Care to learn a step that's done in Faerie?" and she said, "Why? They'll all be swiping *our* moves." Jeff and King O'Beer began a circle dance with Taz and Caramel. Tick-Tick grabbed Milo's hand, and Orient grabbed Ms. Wu's. Leda saw me look at her, or I saw her look at me, and I took her in my arms and didn't trip either of us. She said, "I'll miss you, Wolf," and I nodded once and spun her.

When the next song, a louder and faster number, began, Sparks tapped Leda's shoulder. "Mind if I cut in?"

Leda looked at me and at her, and smiled. I had told her a good deal on our drive from Loses to Bordertown. She gave me a quick kiss on my nose and walked away.

Sparks glanced at the floor, then at me. She wore a forest-green dress that may have been made in the 1930s. A table lamp behind her brought out a red sheen in her dark brown hair and made her parrot earring sparkle. She smelled of peppermint. When she held out her arms, we both smiled.

The song enclosed us, so even when she spoke loudly, she spoke privately. She said, "I left Milo."

I nodded.

"He told you?"

I nodded again.

She glanced at Leda and Strider, who laughed with Sai as they tried to fit the steps of one world to the music of another.

Sparks smiled at me. "They move well together."

I wanted to say, "We all do." It was better to dance.